THE DEVIL'S CODE

ALSO BY JOHN SANDFORD

THE DEVIL'S CODE

JOHN SANDFORD

G. P. PUTNAM'S SONS   NEW YORK

This is a work of fiction. Names, characters, places, and
incidents either are the product of the author's imagination
or are used fictitiously, and any resemblance to actual
persons, living or dead, business establishments, events,
or locales is entirely coincidental.

G. P. Putnam's Sons
Publishers Since 1838
a member of
Penguin Putnam Inc.
375 Hudson Street
New York, NY 10014

Library of Congress Cataloging-in-Publication Data

Sandford, John, date.
The Devil's Code / John Sandford.
p.   cm.
ISBN 0-399-14650-4
1. Conspiracies—Fiction.   I. Title.
PS3569.A516 D48   2000   00-44559
813'.54—dc21

Printed in the United States of America
1   3   5   7   9   10   8   6   4   2

This book is printed on acid-free paper. ∞

BOOK DESIGN BY AMANDA DEWEY

For Pat and Ray Johns

THE DEVIL'S CODE

ST. JOHN CORBEIL

A beautiful fall night in Glen Burnie, a Thursday, autumn leaves kicking along the streets. A bicycle with a flickering headlamp, a dog running alongside, a sense of quiet. A good night for a cashmere sportcoat or small black pearls at an intimate restaurant down in the District; maybe white Notre Dame–style tapers and a rich controversial senator eating trout with a pretty woman not his wife. Like that.

Terrence Lighter would have none of it.

Not tonight, anyway. Tonight, he was on his own, walking back from a bookstore with a copy of *SmartMoney* in his hand and a pornographic videotape in his jacket pocket. He whistled as he walked. His wife, April, was back in Michigan visiting her mother, and he had a twelve-pack of beer in the refrigerator and a bag of blue-corn nachos on the kitchen counter. And the tape.

The way he saw it was this: he'd get back to the house, pop a beer, stick the tape in the VCR, spend a little time with himself, and then switch over to Thursday Night Football. At halftime, he'd call April about the garden fertilizer. He could never remember the numbers, 12-6-4 or 6-2-3 or whatever. Then he'd catch the second half of the game, and after the final gun, he'd be ready for the tape again.

An unhappy thought crossed his mind. Dallas: What they hell were they doing out in Dallas, with those recon photos? Where'd they dig those up? How'd that geek get his hands on them? Something to be settled next week. He hadn't heard back from Dallas, and if he hadn't heard by Monday afternoon, he'd memo the deputy director just to cover his ass.

That was for next week. Tonight he had the tape, the beer, and the nachos. Not a bad night for a fifty-three-year-old, high-ranking bureaucrat with a sexually distant wife. Not bad at all . . .

Lighter was a block and a half from his home when a man stepped out of a lilac bush beside a darkened house. He was dressed all in black, and Lighter didn't see him until the last minute. The man said nothing at all, but his arm was swinging up.

Lighter's last living thought was a question. "Gun?"

A silenced 9mm. The man fired once into Lighter's head and the impact twisted the bureaucrat to his right. He took one dead step onto the grass swale and was down. The man fired another shot into the back of the dead man's skull, then felt beneath his coat for a wallet. Found it. Felt the videotape and took that, too.

He left the body where it had fallen and ran, athletically, lightly, across the lawn, past the lilac, to the back lot line, and along the edge of a flower garden to the street. He ran a hundred fifty yards, quiet in his running shoes, invisible in his black jogging suit. He'd worked out the route during the afternoon, spotting fences and dogs and stone walls. A second man was waiting in the car on a quiet corner. The shooter ran up to the corner, slowed, then walked around it. If anyone had been coming up the street, they wouldn't have seen him running . . .

As they rolled away, the second man asked, "Everything all right?"

"Went perfect." The shooter dug through the dead man's wallet. "We even got four hundred bucks and a fuck flick."

They were out again the next night.

This time, the target was an aging '70s rambler in the working-class duplex lands southwest of Dallas. A two-year-old Porsche Boxster was parked in the circular driveway in front of the house. Lights shone from a back window, and a lamp with a yellow shade was visible through a crack in the drapes of the big front window. The thin odor of bratwurst was in the air—a back-yard barbecue, maybe, at a house further down the block. Kids were playing in the streets, a block or two over, their screams and shouts small and contained by the distance, like static on an old vinyl disk.

The two men cut across a lawn as dry as shredded wheat and stepped up on the concrete slab that served as a porch. The taller of the two touched the pistol that hung from his shoulder holster. He tried the front door: locked.

He looked at the shorter man, who shrugged, leaned forward, and pushed the doorbell.

———

John James Morrison was the same age as the men outside his door, but thinner, taller, without the easy coordination; a gawky, bespectacled Ichabod Crane with a fine white smile and a strange ability to draw affection from women. He lived on cinnamon-flavored candies called Hot Tamales and Diet Coke, with pepperoni pizza for protein. He sometimes shook with the rush of sugar and caffeine, and he liked it.

The men outside his door stressed exercise and drug therapy, mixed Creatine with androstenedione and Vitamins E, C, B, and A. The closest Morrison got to exercise was a habitual one-footed twirl in his thousand-dollar Herman Miller Aeron office chair, which he took with him on his cross-country consulting trips.

Morrison and the chair rolled through a shambles of perforated wide-carriage printer paper and Diet Coke cans in the smaller of the rambler's two bedrooms. A rancid, three-day-old Domino's box, stinking of pepperoni and soured cheese, was jammed into an over-flowing trash can next to the desk. He'd do something about the trash later. Right now, he didn't have the time.

Morrison peered into the flat blue-white glow of the computer screen, struggling with the numbers, checking and rechecking code. An Optimus transportable stereo sat on the floor in the cor-ner, with a stack of CDs on top of the right speaker. Morrison pushed himself out of his chair and bent over the CDs, looked for something he wouldn't have to think about. He came up with a Harry Connick Jr. disk, and dropped it in the changer. *Love Is Here to Stay* burbled from the speakers and Morrison took a turn around in the chair. Did a little dance step. Maybe another hit of caffeine . . .

T he doorbell rang.

Eleven o'clock at night, and Morrison had no good friends in Dallas, nobody to come calling late. He took another two steps, to the office door, and looked sideways across the front room, through a crack in the front drapes. He could see the front porch. One or two men, their bulk visible in the lamplight. He couldn't see their faces, but he recognized the bulk.

"Oh, shit." He stepped back into the office, clicked on a computer file, and dragged it to a box labeled *Shredder.* He clicked *Shred,* waited until the confirmation box came up, clicked *Yes, I'm sure.* The shredder was set to the highest level: if the file was completely shredded, it couldn't be recovered. But that would take time . . .

He had to make some. He killed the monitors, but let the computer run. He picked up his laptop, turned off the lights in the office, and pulled the door most of the way closed, leaving a crack of an inch or two so they could see the room was dark. Maybe they wouldn't go in right away, and the shredder would have more time to grind. The laptop he carried into the kitchen, turning it on as he walked. He propped it open on the kitchen counter, and pulled a stool in front of it.

The doorbell rang again and he hurried out the door and called, "Just a minute." He looked back in the computer room, just a glance, and could see the light blinking on the hard drive. He was shredding only one gigabyte of the twenty that he had. Still, it would take time . . .

He was out of it. The man outside was pounding on the door.

He headed back through the house, snapped on the living room overhead lights to let them know he was coming, looked out through the drapes—another ten seconds gone—and unlocked the front door. "Had to get my pants on," he said to the two men on the stoop. "What's up?"

T hey brought Morrison into the building through the back, up a freight elevator, through a heavily alarmed lock-out room at the top, and into the main security area. Corbeil was waiting.

St. John Corbeil was a hard man; in his early forties, his square-cut face seamed with stress and sun and wind. His blue eyes were small, intelligent, and deeply set beneath his brow ridge; his nose and lips narrow, hawklike. He wore a tight, military haircut, with just a hint of a fifties flattop.

"Mr. Morrison," he said. "I have a tape I want you to listen to."

Morrison was nervous, but not yet frightened. There'd been a couple of threats back at the house, but not of violence. If he didn't come with them, they'd said, he would be dismissed on the spot, and AmMath would sue him for violating company security policies, industrial espionage, and theft of trade secrets. He wouldn't work for a serious company again, they told him.

The threats resonated. If they fired him, and sued him, nobody would hire him again. Trust was all-important, when a company gave a man root in its computer system. When you were that deep in the computers, everything was laid bare. Everything. On the other hand, if he could talk with them, maybe he could deal. He might lose this job, but they wouldn't be suing him. They wouldn't go public.

So he went with them. He and the escort drove in his car—"So we don't have to drag your ass all the way back here," the security guy said—while the second security agent said he'd be following. He hadn't yet shown up.

So Morrison stood, nervously, shoulders slumped, like a peasant dragged before the king, as Corbeil pushed an audiotape into a tape recorder. He recognized the voice: Terrence Lighter. "John, what the hell are you guys doing out there? This geek shows up on my doorstep . . ."

Shit: they had him.

He decided to tough it out. "I came across what I thought was anomalous work—nothing to do with Clipper, but it was obviously top secret and the way it was being handled . . . it shouldn't have been handled that way," Morrison told Corbeil. He was standing like a petitioner, while Corbeil sat in a terminal chair. "When I was working at the Jet Propulsion Laboratory, I was told that if I ever found an anomaly like that, I should report it at least two levels up, so that it couldn't be hidden and so that security problems could be fixed."

"So you went to Lighter?"

"I didn't think I had a choice. And you should remember that I *did* talk to Lighter," Morrison said. "Now, I think, we should give the FBI a ring. See what they say."

"You silly cunt." Corbeil slipped a cell phone from a suit pocket, punched a button, waited a few seconds, then asked, "Anything?" Apparently not. He said, "Okay. Drop the disks. We're gonna go ahead on this end."

Corbeil's security agent, who'd been waiting patiently near the door, looked at his watch and said, "If we're gonna do it, we better get it done. Goodie's gonna be starting up here in the next fifteen minutes and I gotta run around the building and get in place."

Corbeil gave Morrison a long look, and Morrison said, "What?"

Corbeil shook his head, got up, stepped over to the security agent, and said, "Let me."

The agent slipped out his .40 Smith and handed it to Corbeil, who turned and pointed it at Morrison.

"You better tell us what you did with the data or you're gonna get your ass hurt real bad," he said quietly.

"Don't point the gun at me; don't point the gun . . ." Morrison said.

Corbeil could feel the blood surging into his heart. He'd always liked this part. He'd shot the Iraqi colonels and a few other ragheads and deer and antelope and elk and javelina and moose and three kinds of bear and groundhogs and prairie dogs and more birds than he could count; and it all felt pretty good.

He shot Morrison twice in the chest. Morrison didn't gape in surprise, stagger, slap a hand to his wounds, or open his eyes wide in amazement. He simply fell down.

"Christ, my ears are ringing," Corbeil said to the security agent. He didn't mention the sudden erection. "Wasn't much," he said. "Nothing like Iraq."

But his hand was trembling when he passed over the gun. The agent had seen it before, hunting on the ranch.

"Let's get the other shot done," the agent said.

"Yes." They got the .38 from a desk drawer, wrapped Morrison's dead hand around it, and fired it once into a stack of newspapers.

"So you better get going," Corbeil said. "I'll dump the newspapers."

"I'll be to Goodie's right. That's your left," the agent said.

"I know that," Corbeil said impatiently.

"Well, Jesus, don't forget it," the agent said.

"I won't forget it," Corbeil snapped.

"Sorry. But remember. Remember. I'll be to your left. And you gotta reload now, and take the used shell with you . . ."

"I'll remember it all, William. This is my life as much as it is yours."

"Okay." The agent's eyes drifted toward the crumbled form of Morrison. "What a schmuck."

"We had no choice; it was a million-to-one that he'd find that stuff," Corbeil said. He glanced at his watch: "You better move."

Larry Goodie hitched up his gun belt, sighed, and headed for the elevators. As he did, the alarm buzzed on the employees' door and he turned to see William Hart checking through with his key card.

"Asshole," Goodie said to himself. He continued toward the elevators, but slower now. Only one elevator ran at night, and Hart would probably want a ride to the top. As Hart came through, Goodie pushed the elevator button and found a smile for the security man.

"How's it going, Larry?" Hart asked.

"Slow night," Goodie said.

"That's how it's supposed to be, isn't it?" Hart asked.

"S'pose," Goodie said.

"When was the last time you had a fast night?"

Goodie knew he was being hazed and he didn't like it. The guys from TrendDirect were fine. The people with AmMath, the people from "Upstairs," were assholes. "Most of 'em are a little slow," he admitted. "Had some trouble with the card reader that one time, everybody coming and going . . ."

The elevator bell *dinged* at the tenth floor and they both got off. Goodie turned left, and Hart turned right, toward his office. Then Hart touched Goodie's sleeve and said, "Larry, was that lock like that?"

Goodie followed Hart's gaze: something wrong with the lock

on Gerald R. Kind's office. He stepped closer, and looked. Somebody had used a pry-bar on the door. "No, I don't believe it was. I was up here an hour ago," Goodie said. He turned and looked down the hall. The lights in the security area were out. The security area was normally lit twenty-four hours a day.

"We better check," Hart said, dropping his voice.

Hart eased open the office door, and Goodie saw that another door, on the other side, stood open. "Quiet," Hart whispered. He led the way through the door, and out the other side, into a corridor that led to the secure area. The door at the end of the hall was open, and the secure area beyond it was dark.

"Look at that screen," Hart whispered, as they slipped down the hall. A computer screen had a peculiar glow to it, as if it had just been shut down. "I think there's somebody in there."

"I'll get the lights," Goodie whispered back. His heart was thumping; nothing like this had ever happened.

"Better arm yourself," Hart said. Hart slipped an automatic pistol out of a belt holster, and Goodie gulped and fumbled out his own revolver. He'd never actually drawn it before.

"Ready?" Hart asked.

"Maybe we ought to call the cops," Goodie whispered.

"Just get the lights," Hart whispered. He barely breathed the words at the other man. "Just reach through, the switch is right inside."

Goodie got to the door frame, reached inside with one hand, and somebody screamed at him: "NO!"

Goodie jerked around and saw a ghostly oval, a face, and then *WHAM!* The flash blinded him and he felt as though he'd been hit in the ribs with a ball bat. He went down backwards, and saw the flashes from Hart's weapon straight over his head, *WHAM WHAM WHAM WHAM . . .*

Goodie didn't count the shots, but his whole world seemed to consist of noise; then the back of his head hit the carpet and his mouth opened and he groaned, and his body was on fire. He lay there, not stirring, until Hart's face appeared in his line of vision: "Hold on, Larry, goddamnit, hold on, I'm calling an ambulance . . . Hold on . . ."

2

The Canadian winter arrived on Friday morning.

Bleak Thomas and I had been fishing late-season northern pike along the English River, sunny days and cold, crisp nights, the bugs knocked down by the frost, pushing our luck down a lingering Ontario autumn.

The bad weather came in overnight. We'd gotten up to a hazy sunshine, but by nine o'clock, a dark wedge of cloud was piling in from the northwest. We could smell the cold. It wasn't a scent, exactly, but had something to do with the sense of smell: you turn your face to it, and your nose twitches, and you think *winter.*

The bad weather was no surprise. We'd seen it on satellite pictures, forming up as a low-pressure system in the Arctic, before we left the float-plane base five days earlier—but waiting for the plane on the last morning, looking at our watches as we listened for the noisy single-engine Cessna 185, with nickel-sized snowflakes drifting in from the northwest . . . maybe we began to wonder what would happen if the plane had gone down. And if there'd been a mix-up, and the people at the base thought we'd gone down with it.

Winter was long in northwest Ontario, and Bleak Thomas probably wouldn't taste that good. Bleak might have been thinking along the same lines, with a change of menu. When the Cessna turned the corner at the end of the lake, like a silver wink, and the roar of the aircraft engine rolled across the water, Bleak said, "Only an hour late."

"Really? I thought he was a little early." I yawned and stretched.

"Sure," Bleak said. "That's why you chewed your fingernails down to your armpits."

The pilot was in a hurry. He taxied up to the rickety dock, pushed along by a gust of snow. Bleak and I threw our gear onboard, and we were gone, bouncing across the whitecaps and into the air. The pilot didn't bother to check that the boats had been rolled or that the fire was dead in the potbellied stove; he took our word for it. Ten minutes after takeoff, we broke out of the snow and he said, "Good. I always land better when I can find the lake." Then, to me, "You got some woman calling about every ten minutes."

"Yeah? Did she say what her name was?" I was thinking *LuEllen* because she was the only woman I knew who might want to get in touch in a hurry. But the pilot said, "Lane Ward."

I shook my head. "Don't know her."

"Well, she knows you and she's hot to talk," the pilot said. We were half-shouting over the noisy clatter of the engine. "She didn't say what about. She says she's traveling and doesn't have a call-back number."

He didn't have much to say after that. We all concentrated on the lakes and canyons flicking by eight hundred feet below. In three weeks, the pilot would need skis to land. A few miles out of the base, as the pilot slipped the plane sideways to line up with the long axis of the lake, Bleak leaned forward from the backseat and said, "We were getting a little worried about you, back there."

"Had a little trouble with the plane, getting off this morning," the pilot said. "I was warming her up and the prop come off." We both looked out at the prop and then over at the pilot. He just barely grinned and said, "That joke was old when Pontius was a pilot."

The pilot's wife's name was Moony. She was a leftover hippie with a toothy grin, paisley shifts, and a little weed growing in the window box. After thirty years of cooking for fly-in fishermen, she still couldn't put together a decent meal. Clients would take her flapjacks down to the lake and skip them off the water like rocks. When they sank, the fish wouldn't touch them.

Moony offered to throw together a quick lunch, but we hastily declined, jumped in the rented station wagon and drove down to Kenora. Six hours later, we were walking up the stairs at the local-carrier ramp at Minneapolis–St. Paul International.

I been on worse trips, I guess," Bleak said.

His way of saying he'd had a good time. Bleak was a furniture maker, who got a thousand dollars for a chair and fifteen thousand for one of his hand-carved, ten-place craftsman-style walnut dining sets. He gave most of the money away, through the Lutheran Social Services. Bleak believed that craftsmen who got rich got soft, a sentiment I didn't share. Not that he was a religious fanatic: he was on his fifth wife, and all five of them had been excellent women. And as we walked up the stairs into the terminal, he spotted a dark-haired woman standing at the top and said, quietly, "Look at the ass on this one, Kidd."

"Jesus, Bleak, you can't talk like that in Minnesota," I muttered; and looked.

"Intended purely as a compliment," Thomas said, under his breath.

The woman turned, and was looking us over as we climbed the steps, taking in the duffels and gear bags and rod tubes. She checked Bleak for a minute, the way a lot of women check Bleak—he had long black hair and was bronzed like an Indian guide—then her eyes drifted back to me. As we crossed the top of the steps, she asked, "Are you Kidd?"

"I am," I said.

"I'm Lane Ward." She looked like her father might have been Mexican. She had the black hair and matching eyes, and the round face; but she was pale, like an Irishwoman. She stuck out her hand, and I shook it, and picked up the faintest scent: something light, flowery, French. "I'm Jack Morrison's sister."

"Jack," I said. "How is he?"

"He's dead," she said. "He was shot to death a week ago today."

That stopped me. I looked at Bleak and he said, "Yow."

The parking garage at Minneapolis–St. Paul International Airport is under permanent reconstruction, a running joke perpetrated by the Metropolitan Airports Commission. Since parking is impossible, we'd all taken taxis in. Bleak would take a cab down south of the cities to his workshop, and Lane and I got a cab to my place in St. Paul.

"How'd you know I was Kidd—that Bleak wasn't me?" I asked, as we waited for a cab to come up.

"You looked more like a criminal," she said.

"Thanks. But I'm an artist."

"Oh, bullshit. I know about Anshiser," she said. "I know what you and Jack did."

That she knew about Anshiser was disturbing. Anshiser had been a rough operation which, in the end, had taken down a major aircraft corporation. If I'd known Jack would tell her about it, I wouldn't have worked with Jack. But then, that might not be realistic. All kinds of people knew a little bit about what I did. They just didn't know each other so they could compare notes. "You think I look like a criminal?"

"You look tougher than your friend, with your . . . nose."

Hell, I've always thought I was a good-looking guy. Forty-something, six feet and a bit, hardly any white in my hair, and I still have all of it. The nose, I admit, had been broken a couple of times and never gotten quite straight. I thought it lent my face a certain charm. "It's part of my charm," I said, wounded, as the cab came up. I held the back door for her.

"Jack said you can be charming . . . if you wanted to be. He said you didn't want to be, that often." She got in the cab, and I slid in beside her.

"What happened to Jack?" I asked.

"Let's wait until we get over to your place," she said, her eyes going to the back of the driver's head.

Though winter was on the way, for the moment it was still in Ontario. St. Paul's trees were shedding their leaves, but the temperature was in the sixties as we crossed the Mississippi and headed down West Seventh Street into St. Paul. Lane was quiet, checking out the local color: most notably, a cigar-chewing guy humping along, slowly, on an ancient Honda Dream. He was wearing knee shorts and black dress socks. "Sophisticated place, for a Midwestern capital city," she said.

"Yeah. We're blessed with individualism," I said.

We spent the rest of the ride in idle chitchat; and I sort of took her in, physically. She was pretty, with a good figure, but a figure that came from a careful diet, rather than exercise; a magazine-model's figure, not an athlete's.

She had an undergraduate degree from Berkeley in philosophy and mathematics, and a couple of graduate degrees in computer science from Stanford. She now lived in Palo Alto and divided her time between an Internet start-up and teaching at Stanford. The start-up, called e-Accountant, would provide billing, collection, accounting, and tax services to Web sites too small to efficiently do it on their own. She expected to get modestly rich from it. She was no longer married to the guy named Ward.

"He always said he wanted children, but he always wanted one more thing first," she said. "A car or a boat or a house or a vacation place. I told him that I couldn't wait any longer, and if he didn't want to start on a kid, I was going to pull the plug. Even then, he couldn't decide."

"So you pulled the plug."

"Uh-huh."

"Any candidates for the eventual fatherhood?" I asked.

"Yes. A very nice man at Stanford, an anthropologist. He's working on his own divorce."

"Ah. Were you involved in *his* problem?"

"No. He doesn't even know he's a candidate for the new position," she said. "Although he should be getting that idea pretty soon, now. He'll be an excellent father, I think."

"Good for him," I said.

The cab driver's eyes came up in the rearview mirror, and I caught him smiling. Pretty women are easily amusing.

I'm not sure how glad your heart should be when you arrive home in a taxicab with the grieving sister of a friend who'd just been shot to death, but when the cab dropped us, I *was* happy. Always happy to head up north, always happy to get back. The water gives you ideas, and if you're up there long enough, you develop an irresistible urge to work, to get the ideas on paper. Bleak was the same way; leave him in a cabin long enough, and he'll start improving the furniture with his pocket knife.

And things were going on around home. We had to walk up five flights of stairs because the elevator was jammed full of Alice Beck's stoneware and porcelain pieces, which she was moving out for a show. Alice yelled down the atrium, "Sorry, Kidd, we'll be out in ten minutes." We traipsed on up the stairs, me with the duffel and rod tubes, Lane carrying the tackle bag.

We stopped on the third floor for a moment, so Lane could look at some of Alice's vases. She liked them, and Alice invited us to the opening, two days away.

Lane shook her head. "I'd love to, but we've got a funeral to go to," she said, and we continued on up. At the next flight, she looked down and said, quietly, "Beautiful stuff," and I nodded and said, "People say she's as good as Lucie Rie, but I'm afraid she's gonna burn the building down some day. She's got a Marathon gas kiln in her back room. I can hear it roaring away at night, that whooshing sound, like the cremation of Sam McGee."

"Is that legal?"

"The cremation of Sam McGee?"

"No, stupid: the kiln."

"I doubt it," I said.

"Have you complained?"

"Nah. I helped her carry it up."

H ome; and the Cat was in.

He was sitting on the back of the couch, looking out at the Mississippi, a red tiger-stripe with a head the size of a General Electric steam iron. He didn't bother to hop down when I came in. In fact, he pretended not to notice. An old lady artist downstairs, a painter, kept him fed for me while I was gone, and he had his own flap so he didn't need a cat pan except in deepest winter.

"Hey, Cat," I said. He looked away—but he'd come creeping around about bedtime, looking for a scratch.

"He looks like you," Lane said.

"Who?"

"The cat."

"Thanks." I supposed that could be a flattering comment; on the other hand, the Cat was pretty beat up. One ear had been damn near chewed off, and sometimes, on cold mornings, he'd limp a little, and look up at me and meow, like he was asking for a couple of aspirin. I dumped the duffel, stepped into the kitchen, and said to Lane, "Tell me about Jack," and asked, "Want some coffee?"

She agreed to the coffee. "I think he was murdered," she said, as we waited for the water to heat in the microwave. "He was supposedly shot to death after he broke into a secure area of a company called AmMath in Dallas. He was shot twice in the chest and died immediately. Another man was wounded."

"But not killed?"

"Not killed."

"So he could tell you what they were doing . . ." The microwave beeped and I took the cups out.

"No, no, no . . . The man who was wounded was supposedly shot by *Jack*," she said. "They say that Jack had a gun and opened fire when he was caught. There were two guards or security men, whatever you call them, and supposedly, Jack shot one, and the second guard shot Jack."

"*Jack?*" You had to know him.

"Exactly," she said. "There's no way that Jack would shoot at somebody. He wouldn't shoot at somebody to save his own life, much less to keep from getting caught in a burglary, or whatever he was supposedly doing. Unless . . ." She looked sideways at me, and her eyes sort of hooked on.

"Yeah?"

"Unless, working with you, you taught him to take a gun along. A technique, or something."

I shook my head: "Never. I never take a gun. The only thing you can do with a gun is shoot somebody. I'm not gonna shoot somebody over the schematics for a microchip."

"That's what he told me," she said. "That nothing you did involved violence."

Nothing that Jack knew about involved violence, I thought. But violence had been done, a time or two or three, as much as I tried to avoid it, and regretted it. Or, to be honest, as much as I regretted some of it. I'd met a sonofabitch down the Mississippi one time, who, if he came back from the dead, I'd cheerfully run through a stump chipper.

"What was Jack doing?" I stirred instant coffee crystals into the hot water and handed her a cup. She had a way of looking at you directly, and standing an inch too close, that might have bent the attention of a lesser man.

"Nobody will say exactly. All they will say is that he entered a high-security area in AmMath—they're the people doing Clipper II—and that he opened fire when they walked in on him," she said.

C lipper II was an Orwellian nightmare come true, a practical im-possibility, or a huge joke at the taxpayers' expense—take your pick. It was designed in response to a fear of the U.S. government that unbreakable codes would make intercept-intelligence impracti-cal. And really, they had a point, but their solution was so draconian that it was doomed to failure from the start.

The Clipper II chip—like the original Clipper chip before it—was a chip designed to handle strong encryption. If it was made mandatory (which the government wanted), everyone would have to use it. And the encryption was guaranteed secure. Absolutely un-breakable.

Except that the chip contained a set of keys just for the govern-ment, *just in case.* If they needed to, they could look up the key for a particular chip, get a wiretap permit, and decrypt any messages that were sent using the chip. They would thereby bring to justice (they said) all kinds of Mafiosos, drug dealers, money launderers, and other lowlifes.

Hackers, of course, hated the idea. They were already using en-cryption so strong that nobody, including the government, could break it. The idea of going back to less secure encryption, so that the government could spy on whoever it wanted, drove them crazy. No hacker on earth really believed that the government would carefully seek wiretap permits before doing the tap. It'd be tap first, ask later, just like it is now with phone taps.

The good part of the whole controversy was that everybody seriously concerned with encryption knew it was too late for the Clipper II. It had been too late for the Clipper I a decade earlier. Strong encryption was out of the bag, and it would be impossible to push it back in.

Lane had taken a sip of coffee, winced, and asked something, but thinking about Clipper II, I missed it. "Huh?"

She repeated the question. "Do people kill for software?"

"Not me. But Windows is software, and it made the creator a hundred billion dollars. In parts of some cities, you could get a killing done for twelve dollars ninety-five. So some software could get some killing done," I said. We both thought about that for a minute. Then, "If it really happened like you say it did—hang on, let me finish—if Jack shot somebody, it wasn't for the software, necessarily. It was to keep from getting caught and maybe sent to prison. Prison in Texas."

"But you know and I know," she continued, "that Jack didn't shoot anybody. Since *somebody* shot the guard, there had to be somebody else in the room when Jack was shot, even though the company says nobody else was there but the guard and another security man."

"Maybe one security guy shot the other to make it look like Jack shot first . . ."

I said it in a not-quite-joking way, but she took it seriously: "No, I thought about that. But the guard who was shot was hurt bad. The bullet went right through his lung. He's an old guy and he almost died on the way to the hospital."

"So the whole thing holds together."

"Almost too well," she said. "There aren't any seams at all. They searched Jack's house and found some supposedly secret files on a Jaz disk hidden in a shoe. Very convenient. That really nailed it down. The only thing that doesn't work is the shooting. Jack hated guns. They scared him. He wouldn't even pick one up."

She was getting hot: I slowed her down with a straight factual question. "What was he doing in Dallas?"

"A contract job," she said. "He'd been there three months and had maybe another three to go. AmMath had a couple of old supercomputers, Crays, that they'd bought from the weather service, and they were having trouble keeping them talking. Jack had done some work on them years ago, and they hired him to straighten out the operating software."

I said, "Huh," because I couldn't think of anything wiser.

"Ask me why I came to see you," she said.

"All right. Why'd you come to see me?"

"First, to ask if you were in Dallas? Ever? With Jack?"

"No." I shook my head: "Jack and I haven't worked together for two years."

"You're sure?"

"Yeah, I'm sure. He rewrote some software for me." So I'd be able to plug into a Toyota design computer anytime I needed to. "Two years ago . . . November."

"Then what's this mean?" She dug in her purse and handed me a printout of an e-mail letter. "Look at the last couple of lines."

I scanned all of it. Most was just brother-sister talk about their father's estate—their parents were both dead now, their father dying nine months back.

The last two lines of Jack's letter said, "I'm into something a little weird here. I don't want to worry you, but if anything unusual should happen, get in touch with Kidd, okay? Just say *Bobby* and *3ratsass3*."

3

If you look in the shaving mirror in the morning and ask what you've become, and the answer is "Artist & Professional Criminal," then you may have taken a bad turn down life's dark alley. While other people were wistfully contemplating the grassy fork in "The Road Not Taken," I'd lurched down a gutter full of broken wine bottles, and kicked asses and people telling me to go fuck myself. Nobody to blame, really.

Well, maybe the Army. The Army had left me a roster of dead friends, a vicious dislike for bureaucratic organization, and a few unusual skills. And hell, it was interesting. At least I'm not stuck in a garret somewhere, with a pointy little beard and a special rap for victim women, trying to peddle my paintings to assholes in shiny Italian suits. At least I'm not that.

What I am, is an artist. A painter. I make decent money from it. But even though I was working harder than ever, my production—artists actually talk about things like production—had been falling over the years. I'd always been a little fussy about what I sold, and I'd gotten fussier as I'd gotten older, so even as my prices went up, my income actually declined a little. The year before, I'd sold six paintings. I'd gotten a little more than $300,000, but let me tell you about the taxes . . .

Or maybe not. I sound a little too Republican when I get started on taxes.

In any case, I still worked at my night job. I stole things. Computer code, schematics for new chips or new computers, designs for new cars. I suppose I could have stolen jewelry or cash, but I wasn't interested in jewelry or cash—and besides, that kind of thievery didn't pay as well as my kind.

I knew that for sure, because my best friend is a woman named LuEllen, who was exactly that kind of thief: she stole cash and jewelry and coin collections and even stamps—or anything else that was portable and could easily and invisibly be turned into cash. LuEllen and I had known each other since I caught her trying to break into another guy's apartment in my building. That was several years ago. Ever since, we'd been friends and sometimes more than friends.

Even with that history, I had no idea what LuEllen's real last name was, or where exactly she lived. She was comfortable with my ignorance.

I'm not exactly embarrassed by the night job, though I've often thought I'd give it up if I could make nine paintings a year instead of six. Then again, I might not. If I were French, and philosophical, I might even argue that "professional criminal" wasn't that far from "freedom fighter."

But there was always that skeptical face in the mirror, the face that asked whether freedom fighting should generate large amounts of expendable income. I could say—"Hey, even freedom fighters gotta eat." But what do you do when the face in the mirror asks, "Yeah, but should freedom fighters get condos in New Orleans and painting trips to Siena and fishing jaunts to Ontario and season tickets for the Wolves?"

Being neither French nor philosophical—rather, a believer in the Great God WYSIWYG, that What You See Is What You Get— I had no ready answer for the question, except . . .

You gotta shave faster.

I did not immediately believe, or believe in, Lane Ward; believe that I was getting what I was seeing. "Let me get out on the Net for a couple of minutes," I said.

"Check me out?" Ward asked.

"See if I've got mail," I said, politely.

" '3ratsass3' sounds like a password," she said. "So who's Bobby?" She had large, dark eyes. I'd first thought maybe Mexican, with an Irish complexion. Now I was thinking Oriental, one of the robust-yet-delicate Japanese ladies of the Hiroshige woodcuts. Something about the eyebrows. I would like to draw her, from a quarter angle off her face, to get the brow ridge, the cheekbone, and the ear. I didn't say that.

"Bobby runs an information service," I said. An information service for people like me, I might have added—but I didn't add it. " '3ratsass3' is probably the password on one of Bobby's mailboxes."

"So let's see what's in it." She looked around. "Where's your computer?"

"In the back."

I 've been in the apartment for a while. I own it, part of a deal the city of St. Paul had going years ago, to bring people back downtown. I've got a tiny kitchen with a small breakfast nook off to one side; a compact living room with a river view; a workroom with maybe three thousand books, two hundred various bits and pieces of software, and, most of the time, three or four operating computers; a studio with a wall of windows facing northeast; and a bedroom. On the way back to the workroom, Lane paused in the door of the studio, looked up at the wall of windows, the big beat-up easel and all the crap that goes with painting, and asked, "What's this?"

"I'm a painter," I said. "That's what I really do. The computer stuff is a sideline."

"You really *are* an artist?"

"Yeah."

"Jack never told me," she said. She peered at me for a second, as if doing a reevaluation.

"Jack didn't know me that way," I said. "We mostly knew each other on the Net. I only met him twice face to face."

"He came here?"

"No, no, I saw him once when he was between planes, out at the airport, and once when I had some business out in Redmond."

"Redmond," she said, and, "Huh." She stepped over to a painting I'd propped against a wall. I'd finished it a few weeks before the fishing trip, a line of stone buildings dropping down a hill in the flat yellow light of a Minnesota September. The light is thin, then, but yellow-creamy—almost like the light you get in central Italy on hot summer evenings, although in St. Paul, it only lasts three weeks.

After a few seconds of peering at the painting, Lane cocked her head and did a little shuffle step to get a better look. "Only two di-

28

mensions and all that light," she said, "but it looks so like . . . it might be." I shrugged, and she said, "Jeez. I really like it."

I never know what to say, so I said, "The workroom's down this way."

An old cow-box Pentium was set up on a table at the far end of the workroom. A shoulder-high stack of Dell chassis were sitting on the floor, with a couple of big cardboard boxes. She looked at the chassis and asked, "What're you doing here?"

"Some people in Chicago want to build an America's Cup boat," I said. "They need a supercomputer to design the hull, but they can't afford it, so I'm making one, with a friend."

"Yeah? Neat." She wasn't particularly impressed, as though she'd done the same thing a time or two herself. "What's the setup?"

"We're gonna chain sixty-four Dell Pentium IIIs with an Ethernet array running through these stacked hubs"—I whacked a stack of cardboard boxes with the palm of my hand—"as a single distributed OS. We got the operating system off a freeware site . . ."

"Love the freeware," she said.

". . . and my friend—she's really doing the numbers—will come over and write whatever connections she needs, and . . . go to work."

"Cool." She looked around again, taking in the books. "Where's your Net hookup?"

I took her down to the cow-box machine. Some previous owner, or more likely the wife or girlfriend of a previous owner, had written "Fuck you, fat boy," on the beige front panel of the monitor, in pink indelible ink. "Top of the line, huh?" she asked.

"What can I tell you?" You don't need a workstation to read your e-mail. When we were up, I said, "Why don't you, uh, go look at the Dells?"

"Why?"

"Because I'm gonna dial a number I don't want you to see, and follow a procedure I also don't want you to see."

"Really?" she asked. "So it's out in the dark? Okay. I forgot."

"What?"

She smiled, for the first time, a smile bordering on greatness: "That you're a crook."

She wandered down to the end of the room, and I dialed Bobby's 800 number, a number I'm sure that AT&T doesn't know about, since ten digits follow the 800. I then waited through ten seconds of electronic silence; in the eleventh second, the modem burped and a "?" appeared on the screen. I typed eight digits, got another "?" and typed "k" and got a further "?" I typed "MALE," which was either a deliberate misspelling in the interests of security, or a joke. When the final "?" appeared, I typed "3RATSASS3."

A letter popped up.

Oh, fuck: Unless I'm reading this myself, I could be in deep shit.

Kidd: Get down to Dallas and find me—I might be in jail.

This is the deal: I contracted with AmMath to overhaul their system software, which job I got because I have a DOD clearance from when I was at JPL. It's all supposed to be secret, but everybody knows that they're working on software for the Clipper II—it's been in the newspapers. So I figure that's no big deal, because Clipper II is dead in the House and even deader in the Senate and everybody except the intelligence goofs in Washington knows it's too late anyway. But around here, they're acting like it's a new atomic bomb,

AND THESE PEOPLE AIN'T GOOFS. IN FACT, THEY SCARE ME A LITTLE BIT.

THE OTHER DAY I WAS MANIPULATING A BUNCH OF STUFF IN A FILE CALLED OMS JUST TO SEE IF THE SYSTEM WAS RIGHT. I GOT TO READING SOME OF IT, AND FUCK ME WITH A PHONE POLE IF IT HAS ANYTHING TO DO WITH CLIPPER. I WAS STILL READING THROUGH IT WHEN A SECURITY GUY CAME DOWN FROM CORPORATE AND ASKED ME WHAT I WAS DOING. I TOLD HIM, ACCESS TESTS, AND TOLD HIM I WASN'T REALLY READING ANYTHING, AND HE TELLS ME TO STAY OFF THAT LINK UNLESS I GIVE PRIOR NOTICE. I SAY OK. THEY MUST'VE HAD A TRIPWIRE ON IT.

SO ANYWAY, I'M GOING BACK TONIGHT WITH A BUNCH OF JAZ DISKS, I'M GONNA DISCONNECT THE TRIP WIRE AND DUMP THE OMS FILE. (OMS I FOUND OUT STANDS FOR OLD MAN OF THE SEA, BUT I DIDN'T SEE ANYTHING IN IT ABOUT HEMINGWAY.) ANYWAY, JUST IN CASE, I'LL STASH COPIES IN THE SAFEST POSSIBLE PLACE.

IF YOU'RE READING THIS, I'M PROBABLY IN A JAM. THE GUY TO WATCH IS A SECURITY ASSHOLE NAMED WILLIAM HART. THERE ARE RUMORS THAT HE USED TO BE SOME KIND OF MILITARY SECURITY GUY OR SOMETHING, AND HE GOT KICKED OUT. ONE OF THE SECRETARIES TOLD ME THAT HE'D DONE TIME IN PRISON BEFORE HE CAME TO AM-MATH, SO YOU WANT TO STAY AWAY FROM HIM.

SO, THAT'S IT. I HOPE TO HELL I'M READING THIS, AND NOT YOU. IF IT'S YOU, COME GET ME. SAY HELLO TO LUELLEN FOR ME . . . DON'T TAKE ANY WOODEN PUSSY.

JACK

That did not sound good. I looked at if for a couple of minutes, then buzzed Bobby: Bobby's always available. After I buzzed him, I got the "?" again, and went back with a "k." He was on immediately.

KIDD, WHERE YOU BEEN?

FISHING.

BEEN TRYING TO FIND YOU: SAW AIRLINE TO KENORA AND THEN LOST YOU.

OUT OF TOUCH. WHAT'S HAPPENING?

YOU READ ABOUT FIREWALL?

I KNOW NOTHING. JUST BACK NOW.

GO OUT ON NET, LOOK AT PAPERS, NEW YORK TIMES, WALL STREET JOURNAL, WASHINGTON POST. WE NEED TO FIND FIREWALL AND GIVE THEM TO COPS. BUT FIREWALL NAMES ARE NOT GOOD. YOU ARE NOT FIREWALL. STANFORD IS NOT. ONE2OXFORD IS NOT. CARLG IS NOT.

I DON'T KNOW WHAT YOU'RE TALKING ABOUT.

READ PAPERS AND GET BACK. YOUR NAME IS ON LIST.

DO YOU KNOW STANFORD IS DEAD?

Stanford was Jack's working name. There was a pause; something you didn't get with Bobby.

DEAD? ARE YOU SURE? WHEN AND WHERE?

LAST FRIDAY IN DALLAS. SUPPOSEDLY SHOT TO DEATH DURING BREAK-IN AT SOFTWARE COMPANY CALLED AMMATH.

DID NOT KNOW. WILL CHECK IMMEDIATELY. STANFORD IS ON FIREWALL LIST.

DO YOU KNOW LANE WARD?

NO. I'VE HEARD NAME. COMPUTERS AT BERKELEY.

I NEED BROTHERS AND SISTERS FOR LANE WARD AND ALSO PHOTO FOR WARD. SOONEST.

WILL DUMP TO YOUR BOX ONE HOUR. YOU MUST GO OUT ON NET!!! READ FIREWALL. I WILL CHECK ON STANFORD.

OK ... WILL CALL BACK.

Dial tone and out.

I read down the screen once more, wiped out everything but the letter, printed it, and then said, "Hey."

Lane drifted back. "What?" she asked.

"A letter from your brother."

"Aw, jeez."

I pulled it out of the printer and handed it to her. She took a minute reading it, a little vertical line between her eyes. Then she read it again and a tear trickled down one cheek. Finally, she looked up.

"Why would he do that?"

"Curiosity. Jack was a computer guy. If you tell a computer guy not to look in a file, he'll look in the file."

"Especially if he thinks of himself as some kind of cool James Bond guy," she said. Like it was my fault.

"Do you know anything about a group called Firewall?" I asked.

She gave me a long look and then asked, "Are you working for the government?"

That took a while to sort out. I told her about Bobby's strange anxiety and she suggested that I do what Bobby wanted: that I look up Firewall in the papers and on the Net. I went back out, with Lane looking over my shoulder.

E ight days earlier, as I'd been sitting on my living room floor sorting out pike lures, a National Security Agency bureaucrat named Lighter had been murdered walking near his home in Maryland. Jack was killed the next night, twelve hours before I flew out to Kenora.

According to the online papers, the Lighter killing was at first thought to be a random mugging, although the detectives working the murder had been disturbed by some of its aspects. There was no sign that Lighter had fought his assailants, or tried to run. He'd simply been gunned down. Lighter's wife told police that he'd been mugged once before, when they lived in Washington, and that he had calmly handed over his wallet while he tried to reassure the muggers that he was not a threat. In other words, there was no reason to kill him to get his money. And he'd been shot down on a quiet suburban street, where mugging, much less murder, was almost unknown.

A couple of days later, rumors began to surface on the Net that he'd been killed by a radical hacker group calling itself Firewall. Firewall claimed to be taking "preemptive revenge" for the Clipper II, although the Clipper II was widely believed to be a dead issue. And some names had surfaced . . . CarlG, Dave, Bobby, FirstOctober, RasputinIV, k, LotusElan, One2Oxford, Stanford, Whitey.

"Oh, shit," I said.

"What?"

To cover myself: "Do you know your brother's working name?"

"You mean, *Yellowjacket*? That's his gamer name."

"I never heard that. He'd always been Stanford." I tapped the list on the screen. "They've got him listed as a member of this Firewall."

She looked. "Stanford is Jack? Huh . . ." She turned away, slowly, thinking.

"What?"

"You don't talk with the government," she said. A statement, with a question inside.

"No. Of course not."

"I have," she said, slowly. "They asked me not to tell anyone. I talked to them on Tuesday. I was interviewed for two hours by the FBI. About Firewall. Where Jack had been traveling and who his friends are. I didn't know any of that, except some friends we have in common. Jack would travel about once a year, to Europe, but that was about it. The last time he was out of the country was six months ago."

". "You didn't mention me?"

"No, of course not. I know better than that," she said.

"What do you know about Firewall?"

"Nothing. I'd never heard of it. Jack would have told me, if he was involved. But those little Net conspiracies . . . you know what they are. They're socially retarded geeks who think they're living a comic book. Jack wouldn't have anything to do with them. Neither would I."

"Executing a guy because he's working on Clipper II . . . that doesn't sound like socially retarded geeks," I said.

"Oh, no?" she asked. "Then who else could it be? Murdering somebody over a chip—not even a real chip? And who else would care, besides geeks?"

"The Mafia?"

"Oh, bullshit." She rolled her eyes.

"It's too . . . physical."

She put her hands on her hips: "Look at yourself, for Christ's sakes, Kidd. You're some kind of aging jock-nerd-engineer-fisherman-artist with a broken nose. What if it's somebody just like you, with a taste for blood?"

No answer to that. The question was urgent, if the feds and spy people and God knew who else were tearing up the countryside, because Bobby was on the list. And so was I. I was "k."

Lane kept going back to Jack's letter.

"Where's the safest possible place?" she asked.

"Somewhere I could get at them, I guess." I had an idea, but wasn't about to show it. Not until I knew her better. "Maybe he shipped them somewhere. I've got a bunch of mailboxes, scattered around. I've even got one at AOL."

"Check them."

I went back online, checked them, and came up empty. Lane was reading Jack's letter again. She snapped it with a fingertip and said, "One thing that bothers me about the letter is the line about not taking any wooden pussy."

"Wooden what?" I'd barely noticed the line.

"Pussy. The thing that bothers me is, I don't think Jack talked like that. Are we sure this is from Jack?"

I had to laugh, because it sounded exactly *like* Jack; and exactly the kind of thing that Jack would never say around, say, a sister, or any other woman. "Yeah, he did talk that way, sometimes," I said. Then: "Is it possible that you really didn't know Jack as well as you thought you did? That he might have a life that you didn't know about. Maybe involving guns?"

"No," she said positively. "I mean, I'm sure he did things I don't know about, that he'd hide from me. He got along very well with a certain kind of ditzy chick. Maybe he'd say *pussy*—he just didn't say it to me. But with the guns, we're talking basic, rock-bottom personality. He didn't shoot anybody."

"Okay." Then I noticed something a little odd. "You say he was killed on Friday?"

"Yes. Friday night." She caught the puzzled look as I read the letter again. "Why?"

"Because the letter was time-stamped on Sunday—the Sunday before he was killed. He said he was going in then . . ."

"What have I been telling you? There's something seriously wrong with the whole thing."

We talked about the possibilities; and in the back of my head, there was that "k" floating around out there. The feds were looking for k . . .

So are you going back to Dallas with me?" she asked, eventually. "You're going back?"

"I've got to. I've got to sign papers and everything, when they're done with him." Another tear popped out and I turned away: I don't deal well with weeping women. I tend to babble. "So are you going? I made a reservation for you. I could really use somebody to lean on . . ."

"Yeah, yeah, okay," I said. "But don't cry, huh? Please?"

She'd made a reservation for that same night, on the last plane out. I took a moment to go downstairs to tell Alice to watch after the cat, and then I went back out on the Net and read everything I could find on Firewall: there was a ton of stuff, but mostly bullshit. Then I went to my box at Bobby's, and found a picture and a note. The picture was of Lane Ward, looking nice in a professorial business suit, a wall of books in the background. The note said, *Her only brother was JM.*

Finally, I called the Wee Blue Inn in Duluth, on a voice line, and got Weenie, the owner-bartender. He's a toothpick-chewing fat man with a steel-gray butch; an apron that he laundered every month, whether it needed it or not; and who always smells like greasy hamburgers and barbequed onion rings. I said, "This is the guy from St. Paul. I need to talk to LuEllen."

"She's off right now," he said. "I can take a message."

LuEllen was always off. Weenie theoretically paid her $28,000 a year as a waitress, and she paid taxes on the $28,000 plus $6,000 in tips. In reality, Weenie stuck the tax-free $28,000 in his pocket and sent LuEllen the W-2 form. Weenie was her answering service. The W-2 form explained to the government how she paid for her house, wherever that was.

"Tell her that Stanford was killed," I said. "The funeral's set for Santa Cruz next Wednesday. I'm going to Dallas, but I'll be in Santa Cruz for the funeral."

"I'll tell her," Weenie said. "That's Stanford, like in the university."

On the way out the door, on the way to the airport, I stopped, Lane already in the hall, went back to the workroom and got a small wooden box made in Poland. I stuck it in my jacket pocket. Just in case.

A t the airport, I picked up the major papers, and as soon as we were off the ground, began looking for Firewall stories. They all carried at least one, but nothing on the front page. Firewall appeared to be suffering media death.

While I read, Lane kicked back and slept. She was not a large woman and could snuggle into the seat like a squirrel on a pillow. I stared at the seat in front of me for a while, and when she was asleep, took the wooden box out of my pocket. Inside, I kept a Ryder-Waite tarot deck wrapped in a silk cloth.

I'm not superstitious. More than that: I refuse superstition. Ghosts and goblins and astrology and numerology and phrenology and all the New Age bullshit of mother goddesses and wicca; the world would be a happier place if it'd die quietly.

Tarot is different. Tarot is—can be—a kind of gaming system that forces you out of a particular mind-set. Let's say you're trying to ... oh, say, steal something. Your mind-set says X is a danger and Y is a danger, but the tarot says, "Think about Z." So you start thinking about things outside of the mind-set, and when you finally do the entry, you've considered a whole spread of possibilities that otherwise would have gone unsuspected.

Nothing magic about it; and it will definitely save your ass.

So I did one quick spread, of my own invention, working toward a key card. The card came up.

The Devil. Interesting . . .

I sat looking at the evil fuck for a few seconds, sighed, stood up, got my bag out of the overhead bin, and stowed the tarot deck. Thought about it for a second, then dug out the little eight-cake Winsor & Newton watercolor tin and my sketchbook. I got a glass of water from the stewardess and started doing quick watercolor sketches of Lane, the cabin, and the two business guys across the aisle.

The closest business guy looked like a salesman—balding, pudgy, triple-chinned, exhausted. He sat head-down and dozing, his red, yellow, and black necktie splashing down his chest and stomach like a waterfall. The guy behind him was just as exhausted, but was too thin, his skull plainly carving the shape of his head. I got three good ones of the two of them, the thin man like death's shadow behind the fat one. I struggled to get the red necktie right, working the planes as it twisted down his shirt.

A stewardess stopped to watch for a few minutes, then disappeared into the front of the plane. A couple of minutes later, the copilot came back, watched for a while, said he did a little watercolor himself, and asked me if I'd ever seen the cockpit of a D9S at night. I hadn't, and he showed me the way.

I did a half-dozen sketches of the crew at work, and left them behind: they all seemed pleased, and so was I. In the twenty years after I got out of college, I don't think I went a day without drawing or painting something, except during a couple of hospital visits; even then, when I could start moving, the first thing I did was ask for a pencil.

In all those years, the work got tighter and tighter and tighter, until I felt like I hardly had the muscle to pick up a pencil or a pen or a brush: I could wear myself out in an hour, just moving a brush around. Then I broke through. The brush got lighter, and the work became fluid. The actual breakthrough came during a rough visit to Washington, D.C. I'd left behind the Washington nightmares—hadn't had one for a couple of years, now—but the fluidity seemed to hang around . . .

I got back to my seat, restowed the Winsor & Newton tin and the sketchbook, and buckled up for the landing. When the wheels came down, Lane started, stirred, woke up and yawned, covering her mouth with a balled fist, pushed up the window shade, and looked out at the lights of Dallas and then, as we turned, of Fort Worth.

"My mouth tastes like something died inside it," she said, her voice a little husky. A good voice to wake up to. She looked me over: "What'd you do? Sit there and stare at the seat back?"

"Not exactly," I said.

Going out the door, the stewardess squeezed my arm and said, "Thanks so much, you're really good." Lane looked like she might drop dead of curiosity as we walked up the ramp, but then she finally asked, "What was that all about?"

I said, "Oh. You know . . ."

"Be a jerk," she said. But she was smiling.

We stayed overnight at a Marriott. Early the next morning, she was pounding on my door, and at nine o'clock, we were headed down to Dallas police headquarters. Lane wanted me to go inside with her, but I don't talk to cops when I can avoid it. She went in alone, a little pissed. Twenty minutes later, she was back, and told me about it as we drove back to the hotel.

The cops had been pretty straightforward about it, she said. "I got into their faces a little bit, but they wouldn't budge. This guy I talked to said Jack was into something *tricky*. That's the word he used. *Tricky*."

"And that's what they've got? That's all? That he was doing something tricky?"

"No." She was reluctant to talk; I had to pry it out of her. "They say they traced the gun he supposedly used. It was stolen in San Jose six years ago."

"Uh-oh," I said.

"Yeah. I kept saying Jack would never use a gun, and they kept saying, then how come the gun came from San Jose?" She was looking up at me with her dark eyes, pleading with me to understand that what the cops had said was all bullshit. "They said, 'AmMath framed him using a gun that was stolen six years ago in San Jose? How did they do that?'"

"Good question," I said.

"Jack would not shoot anybody," Lane insisted.

"You can't always tell what somebody will do when he's cornered, and he thinks that his life may be ruined. Or that he might go to prison," I said. "Or maybe he thought the guard was about to shoot him, and it was self-defense."

She didn't want to hear about it, and after we'd snarled at each other for a few minutes, I let it go. "So that's it—they got a gun."

"There were a couple more things," she said, reluctantly. Then, "Watch it!"

I hit the brakes; a blue Toyota pickup chopped us off just as we headed up a freeway on-ramp. He never knew I was there. I shook my head, and said, "Asshole," and then, "Listen, Lane, you gotta tell me everything they said. I don't want to have to drag it out of you. I'm supposed to be on your side."

"It's all bullshit. You should've come in, then you could have heard it for yourself."

"What're the other things?"

The cop had explained that there were three doors into the secure area—two of them alarmed. The third door came out of a short hallway connected to the system administrator's office, and the main entrance of his office was well down the hall from the secure area. But if you knew which doors were wired with alarms, you could force the door into the system administrator's office, which had the corridor leading directly into the secure area. That one locked from the system administrator's side, so it would not have to be forced. An outsider trying to intrude into the secure area would not know any of that, and would be stuck with trying to find a way around the alarms . . .

"What else?"

"It turns out that the guard wasn't responding to anything. He was making his regular rounds. Another guy, this security guy, was on his way to his office, and they went up together in the elevator, and the guard noticed that the door to the office suite had some damage around the door knob. So they went in . . ." She stopped, shaking her head.

"So what they're saying is, it wasn't like there was a sudden shooting and then a bunch of explanations. It was just a guard's routine trip through the building."

"It still could have been set up," she said, stubbornly.

"Yeah, but, boy . . ." Didn't sound good.

I concentrated on driving for a couple of minutes, getting us out of a pod of Texans headed up the freeway in what seemed to be a test of Chaos Theory: you sensed an order in their driving, but you couldn't say exactly what it was. I could see the Toyota pickup at the head of the pack, like the lead dolphin.

After the shooting, Lane said, the police went to a house Jack had rented, with a second security man from AmMath, and found a bunch of computer disks—"Two of them were in a pair of shoes in the closet, which doesn't sound like Jack at all"—and a lot of other unauthorized stuff from AmMath, including manuals and confidential information about the Clipper II. AmMath wanted to take it, but the cops wouldn't give it to them: instead, they called in the FBI.

"They've still got it?"

"Yes. The FBI."

"And that's all."

"Well. They say the back entrance and the secure area at Am-Math are covered with cameras. A call came into the building computer at TrendDirect—that's the building owner—and the security cameras were interfered with. The scanning range for the one in the back was changed so that it didn't scan a door at the end of the building; and the camera that watches the secure area was turned off."

"The guards didn't see that? Weren't the cameras monitored?"

"I asked that," she said. "The camera in back constantly scans back and forth, and the only change was to cut out part of the range. The other camera is one of about ten around the premises, with a constant cycle, three seconds at each station, and they cut out one station. They never noticed the changes."

We sat and thought about that for a moment; then Lane sighed and said, "They said we can probably get his computers back. Not the hard drives, but the rest of them. And the monitors, and his personal stuff."

"What about Jack? I mean, the body."

"I've got to go to the medical examiner's office and sign for him. They've released it . . . him."

"Huh. So maybe we should stop by his house and take a look around," I said. Over time, I'd crept up on the blue Toyota. He edged over to make it onto an exit, and I chopped him off, nearly sending him into the retaining wall. At the bottom of the ramp, I went right and he went left, but I could see his middle finger wagging out the window.

"For what?" Lane was unaware of the drama.

"Those Jaz disks. He said he'd put them in the safest possible place."

"You know what that means? I thought it was just a . . . phrase," she said.

"Maybe. But we could look around."

"The house is sealed."

"Yeah," I said. "With a piece of tape."

14

The rest of the afternoon was taken up with the melancholy routines of violent death: claiming the body, signing for a bag full of personal effects that the cops didn't want—besides the routine junk, Jack had $140 in his wallet, unless somebody had clipped it along the way, and Lane's high school graduation photo, which made her cry again. She also signed a contract with a local funeral home to handle shipment of the body by air freight. The coffin cost $1,799, and came with a guarantee that neither of us was interested in reading.

When Lane was in Dallas the first time, to identify the body, she'd gone to look at Jack's rented house, although she hadn't been allowed inside. We cruised it late in the afternoon, a two-bedroom, L-shaped cement-block rambler painted an awful shade of electric pink. The exact shade, I thought, of a lawn flamingo. A short circular driveway took up most of the front yard. There was no carport or garage. We could see only one door, right in the middle of the house, under an aluminum awning. We continued around the block, and from the other side, could see a small screened porch jutting into the backyard.

And there was a fireplace chimney. Not much of one, but there was one.

"He always rented the cheapest livable place," Lane said. "He'd fly back to California on weekends."

"Didn't like Texas?"

"Not a California kind of place," she said.

"Some people would count that as a blessing. Most Texans, for example."

She let the comment go by, as we cruised the house again.

"How do we get in?"

"I don't know. We'll have to see what lights are on, with the neighbors. If we can get in the back porch, we'll have some cover."

"Okay," she said. Simple faith.

We did the block once more, and I looked for kids' swing sets and bikes, basketball hoops, and dogs. LuEllen had trained me: if there are kids around, the parents in a family tend to be at home in the evening, and awake and alert. Basketball hoops often means teenagers, and teenagers come and go at weird, inconvenient times. Dogs are the worst. Dogs bark: that's how they earn their money, and in this neighborhood, they'd probably be listened to.

The house on the south side of Jack's had a hurricane fence around the backyard, which could mean either kids or dogs. The one on the north side, a noxious-green one, was as simple and plain as Jack's, with no sign of life. The house directly behind Jack's had an above-ground swimming pool in the backyard, which probably meant kids.

If there were kids running around, or splashing in the pool, we'd have to forget it. If not, the biggest problem might be the streetlight across the street and down one house.

"What do you think?" Lane asked.

"We probably ought to sky-dive onto the roof and cut our way into the house with a keyhole saw . . ."

"Kidd . . ."

"We ought to sneak around the back between the green house and Jack's place, if the green house doesn't show any lights, then cut our way into the screen porch and see what the situation is there. Usually, there's a way in."

"If we break in, they'll know it was us."

I shook my head: "No, they won't. We're leaving for San Francisco at eleven o'clock tonight. If they don't get around to the house for a few days . . . well, who knows what might have happened? And really, who cares? They've already searched the place."

We found a Wal-Mart and bought burglary tools—might as well have the best—spent some time eating Tex-Mex, dropped the rental car with the airport Avis, and checked in with the airline. When we were set to fly, we rented another car from Hertz, using a perfectly good Wisconsin driver's license and Amex gold card issued to my old pal and fishing buddy Harry Olson, of Hayward, Wisconsin. Harry didn't exist, but he had money in the bank, a great credit rating, and a perfect driving record.

The fake ID convinced Lane that we really *were* going to break into her brother's house: she'd been relaxed all afternoon, but now she was tightening up. "The question we have to ask ourselves," she said, "is whether this is worth the trouble we could get into."

"We won't know unless we find the Jaz disks. Like you've been telling me, there are some odd things about this killing. If Jack was killed because of something with my name on it, I want to know what that something is. Without the cops getting it first."

"Hmm."

"You don't have to go in," I said. "All you have to do is show up with the car when I'm ready to leave."

"If you're going in, I'm going in."

That would help; we could cut the search time in half. So I didn't say *no,* though I had the feeling that if I *had* said no, and insisted on it, she might have given in.

"We won't go in if the situation looks bad. If the neighborhood's lit up, or we see people on the street."

"Okay. That's sensible."

W hen we got back to the house, the neighborhood wasn't all lit up, and there were no people on the street. The green house on the north side of Jack's house was dark. There was no car in the drive, or in front of it.

We cruised it once and I stopped a block away. "You remember everything?" I said. "We're joggers . . ."

"I remember, I remember," she said. "If we're gonna do it . . ."

"Let's go."

We jogged down the street, loose sweatpants and T-shirts. I was carrying a small olive-drab towel wrapped around our Wal-Mart tools. If we ran into cops, I was hoping I could pitch the towel into a bush before we had to talk with them.

That was the plan. Or, as Lane put it, "That's the plan?"

The night was warm and you could still feel the day's unnatural heat radiating from the blacktop. We stopped two houses away from Jack's, as though we were catching a breather. Moved to the sidewalk. The streetlight was only about half-bright, and the shadows it cast seemed even darker than the other unlit spots.

"Anything?" I asked.

"No." She giggled nervously. "God, I'm going nuts."

"Be cool." We sauntered on down the sidewalk, looking, looking. At the green house, we turned up the driveway, walked halfway around the loop, then cut across the lawn, and in five seconds, we were between the two houses, in the shadows. If caught and questioned at that moment, Lane was finding a bush to pee behind. We waited for a minute, two minutes, three—about a century and a half, in all—and nothing happened. No lights went on, we saw no movement. No dogs.

The house behind Jack's, with the pool, showed a backyard light, and lights in the windows, but there was a croton hedge along the back fence, and it cast a shadow over us.

No sauntering, casual bullshit here. We duckwalked to the back porch, found the screen door locked, and the crack in the lock covered with a length of yellow plastic tape and a notice. I carefully peeled them off. The door wanted to rattle when I touched it: it was flimsy, meant to keep out nothing stronger than a blue-bottle fly. I unwrapped the towel, pulled out a short steel pry-bar, pried the door back enough that we could force the lock-tongue across the strike plate.

We eased the door open and slipped inside, crawling now. Listened again. Nothing at all: or almost nothing. Cars on a major street, three blocks away. A crazed bird somewhere, chirping into the dark. An air conditioner with a bad compressor. "Hope the rest is this easy," Lane whispered.

"Shh." We pulled on thin vinyl cleaning gloves and I stood up to look at the porch. The porch had been framed with two-by-fours, and around the top, where the two-by-fours met the screen panels, there was an inch-wide ledge. If I was naïve enough to try to hide a house key, that's where I would have hidden it.

Hoping that reports of black widows and brown recluse spiders were exaggerated, I ran my fingers down the length of the two-by-fours until, in the second panel from the end of the porch, I knocked a key off. It tinkled onto the concrete floor and we stopped breathing for a moment; then I got down on a knee and groped around until I found it. The key still worked: it was a little corroded, but I polished it on my sweatpants, slipped it in and out of the door lock a few times, and we were in.

The interior of the house was almost dark, with some illumination leaking in from the front, from the streetlight, and through the back windows. The place smelled like carpet cleaner. We groped our way to a hall, and I switched on one of our flashlights—I'd taped the lens to get a single needle-thin beam of light.

"Remember," I said, "Never turn the flashlight up. Always keep it down. If you don't bounce it off a window, nobody'll see us."

"Yeah, yeah, yeah," she said. She headed for the bedroom-office, while I went to the living room. I knew exactly where I was going. Jack had met LuEllen in Redmond, and we'd had a couple of beers together at a motel bar. The conversation had drifted to burglary, which wasn't unusual, given the circumstances of our being in Redmond in the first place.

LuEllen had told Jack about a guy who lived in Grosse Point Farms, Michigan, and had a lockbox built into the floor of his fireplace. The fireplace was one of those remote-control gas things, and all the heat went straight up—and the fireproof box under the fireplace was not only invisible, it was absolutely, completely counterintuitive: who'd put valuables where there was a fire?

LuEllen had said, "He thought it was the safest possible place. And it would have been, I'd never have found it in a million years, if his wife hadn't told me about it."

Jack had laughed about that: *the safest possible place.* Was the line in the letter just an easy cliché? Maybe.

A few minutes later, I was ready to give up. This was an old, crappy concrete-with-steel firebox, one of the instant fireplaces installed by the millions in low-end ramblers. There was a flue, which could be opened, but I could neither see nor feel anything inside it. When I got down on my hands and knees for an inch-by-inch inspection with the flashlight, there was no sign of a crack, a seam, a false plate.

Lane came out just as I was backing away. "What are you doing?" she whispered.

"I thought he might have hidden it around the fireplace," I said.

"Why?"

I explained, quickly, and she said, "That should have worked." But it hadn't. "There is a crawl space up above, under the eaves," she said. "There's a hatch in the bathroom."

"The feds probably already looked," I said.

"We should take a peek, anyway."

The hatch was right in the middle of the bathroom ceiling. I stood on the toilet and pushed it up, and could just barely feel around the edges of the opening. All I could feel was insulation.

"Anything?" Lane asked.

"Can't reach far enough in," I grunted, stretching up as far as I could.

"Make me a step and boost me up," she said.

I hopped off the toilet, interlaced my fingers. She stepped into it, and I lifted her belly-high into the hole. She pushed herself the rest of the way up, and whispered down, "Give me a couple of minutes. There's a walk-board up here, but there's all this insulation."

I stepped out of the bathroom and tried to think. Might the fireplace have some kind of hatch in the back, to shovel out cinders? I'd seen those on other . . .

I stepped back into the bathroom. "I'll be right back," I said to Lane, keeping my voice low. "I want to look in the utility room."

"Okay."

I found my way back to the utility room, passed on the washer, dryer, and water heater, and went to the furnace. The furnace was one of those baby things you find in the south, no bigger than a twenty-gallon can, with a grill on the front and an access hatch on the back. The access hatch was crammed with switches and valves, with no space for anything else, so I pulled off the grill. Nothing. There was a dark space above the grill opening, small pipes twisting around some furnace apparatus I didn't know about. I couldn't see anything, and just reached inside . . . and felt something hard, square, and loose. I rattled it, and a taped bundle of Jaz-disk boxes almost fell on my feet.

I pushed the grill back in place and headed for the bathroom: and that involved moving slowly along the front-room wall. Now that my eyes had adjusted, I could see a little better in the gloom, especially with the front room curtains half open. As I moved along the front-room wall, my eye caught a movement in the yard. I froze, uncertain that I'd seen it. Then I saw it again, a man's shoulder on the sidewalk, apparently walking up to the house.

I continued back to the bedroom, almost tripped over the tool towel, picked it up, and hissed up at the hatch: "Lane."

"What?" A white patch, her face, hovered over the hatch.

"Somebody coming," I said. "I'm gonna hand you the towel."

As I said it, I heard a scratching at the front door. Somebody was peeling the police tape off the front, and taking care to be quiet about it. I stood on the toilet, handed her the tool towel. "Take the disks," I said.

"You found them!"

"Move back; I'm coming up."

I had to stand on my tiptoes to get my hands around the joists at the edge of the hatch. I heard the key in the lock, got a grip, and did a pull-up and then a push-up through the hatch. The door opened outside, and Lane whispered, "Now what?" and I whispered, "Shut up. Shine your light on the hatch."

She turned her light on the hatch board. I picked it up, and carefully settled it back into its slot. As long as nobody was doing a thorough search . . .

W hoever was down below us was as quiet as we'd been. After a few minutes, Lane said, "Are you sure they're down there?"

I nodded: "I heard a key in the lock."

A minute later: "I don't hear anybody," she said.

"Quiet."

I was standing on a joist. A long plank ran down to the end of the house, to a head-sized vent that looked out over the front yard. Half hunched against the low overhead, I eased down the board and peered through the vent. A sports utility vehicle—maybe a 4Runner or a Pathfinder, I could only see the front end of it—was parked in front of the green house, a spot that had been empty when we came in. There was no other movement on the street, although I could see a television through a window across the street. Then I heard the door open below me, softly, and a man stepped out onto the curved driveway. He looked back and said, "Hurry, goddamnit."

As he turned to talk, I caught an image of his face, eye-blink quick. A second man pushed the door shut, and they hurried toward the SUV. The second guy was carrying what looked like . . .

"A gas can," I said aloud. "Ah, shit." I turned back toward Lane.

"Get out, get out," I said, "Get the hatch up, get the hatch up, get . . ."

"What, what . . . ?"

She was looking toward me, still whispering, as I scrambled frantically down the plank, and she was not lifting the hatch.

"Get the goddamn hatch . . ." I was almost on top of her before she lifted it up, still uncertain.

"Drop through," I said, urgently. "Hurry—they're going to burn the place."

She got it: no question. She put her feet over the edge, held on with her hands for a second, dangled, and then dropped into the bathroom.

"Disks," I said. I handed the bundle down, then dropped into the bathroom myself. I stepped into the hallway, and the air was thick with gasoline fumes and something else. "Out the back."

"What?" She'd taken a step toward the front room, to see what was happening. I took a step after her, caught her arm. Just beyond her, a burning rag hung from a string that must have been taped or thumb-tacked to the ceiling. The "something else" odor was burning cotton. As I caught her arm, the string, already burning, parted, and the rag dropped to the floor.

The gas went with a *whump,* like a giant pilot light—or napalm, for that matter—and I jerked her back, and her sweatshirt was burning and I beat at it with my hands as I dragged her through the firelight to the back door.

She was screaming and beat at her shirt with her free hand. I twisted her and got the bottom of the back of the shirt and ripped it up over her head and off, and she groaned and said, "I'm burned," and I led her out the door and around the house and said, "Run, run, run," and we ran through the backyards of the green house and the next house over, and then around onto the sidewalk and down the street.

In one minute, we were at the car. In three minutes, we were a mile away.

"How bad?" I asked.

"My arms, my hands, my face," she said. "I don't think it's too bad."

"Gotta find a good light," I said.

We found a good light at a hot-bed motel a couple of miles from the airport. I checked in with the Harry Olson ID. The clerk was locked behind a thick bulletproof glass window, and I said, "We'll want to check out early; we got a real early flight." He grunted, said, "Drop the key in the box," pointed at a locked box hung on the side of the motel, and went back to a gun magazine whose lead story was, "Exposed! Handgun Control Inc.'s 5-Year Plan to Disarm America: Read It and Weep."

Inside, we got the good light. Lane had been burned on the backs of her hands, her forearms, and under her chin. Her eyebrows were singed, and the dark hair over her forehead had taken on some new curls. The burns were pink, rather than white or black. The worst were on her arms; the biggest burn, under her chin, was the size of her palm.

"What do you think?" she asked, holding her hands away from her body, palms up. She was hurting.

"You probably ought to have a doctor look at it," I said.

"Then the police will know."

". . . but if you can stand it, we could catch our flight, and you could go to the doctor—or to an emergency room—out on the West Coast. We could tell them that you burned yourself with charcoal lighter at a barbecue, but didn't think it was bad until it started hurting overnight."

"It hurts now," she said.

"Which is good," I said. "Really bad burns don't hurt right away: the nerve endings are destroyed."

She actually smiled, which suddenly made me like her a lot, and said, "If the burns aren't too bad . . ."

"I really don't think they are, but they'll hurt," I said.

"Then I can stand it. Better than going to jail," she said.

". . . and I'm not a doctor."

"Do you think the airline people will notice?" she asked.

I shook my head: "No. You don't look bad at all. Keep your jacket over your arms, let me handle the tickets."

"Then let's go."

I checked my watch: "We've got some time yet. I'm gonna find a pharmacy, see if I can get some sunburn painkiller, or whatever I can get. That could help."

"Good . . . I held on to the disks." She turned her head up to smile at me again, and winced. "I guess I don't want to move my head too fast," she said.

"I'll go get the stuff."

"Don't tarry," she said, the woman with the big dark eyes.

ST. JOHN CORBEIL

S t. John Corbeil was sitting in a leather armchair, reading, light from the floor lamp glinting from the steel rims of his military spectacles. As he read—Orwell's *Homage to Catalonia*—he threaded and rethreaded a diamond necklace between his stubby fingers, as though it were a string of worry beads.

He liked the cool sensuality of the necklace, and the money it represented. He'd had it made to his specifications by Harry Winston of New York. One hundred diamonds, excellent cut, clarity, and color in each, and each a single carat in size. The Winston people had thought that curious—he'd seen the curiosity, unspoken, in their eyes—because a hundred-diamond necklace doesn't carry the flash of say, a big central stone or two, surrounded by a constellation of smaller diamonds.

Corbeil had good reasons: one-carat diamonds were easy to move, easy to sell, and anonymous. The necklace was a bank account. If you popped the diamonds out of their settings, you could put $300,000 in the toes of your shoes . . .

Another good reason was the sensuality of the stones. Corbeil's face might have been chopped from a block of oak, but he was a sensual man. He liked the feel of a woman, the sound of a zipper coming down on the back of a woman's dress, the smell of Chanel. He liked fast cars driven fast, French cooking and California wine, Italian suits and English shoes and diamonds. He hadn't been able to afford the very best in women, wine, and song until AmMath. Now he had them, and he would be damned if he would give them up . . .

The doorbell rang; he'd been expecting it. He put the book down, slipped the necklace into a shirt pocket, crossed to the intercom, and pushed the button. "Yes?"

"Hart and Benson." William Hart's voice. Four men were involved in various parts of the operation. Corbeil himself, as coordinator; Hart and Benson, as security and technicians; and Tom Woods, a computer-encryption expert who loved only money more than codes. Woods was not aware of the Morrison, Lighter, or Ward difficulties, other than that Morrison had been killed in a break-in. He was a nervous man.

"Come in." Corbeil pressed the door-release button, buzzing them in.

D one," Hart said.

Corbeil nodded. "So. There's no reason to think that anything remains here in Texas."

"Not as far as we know."

Corbeil turned away, fished the diamond necklace out of his pocket, and began unconsciously pouring it from hand to hand, as though it were a slinky. "There remains the possibility that he sent his sister something."

"He could have sent something to anybody; but we can't find any really close friends. No girlfriends, right now. The sister's the obvious candidate. I mean, we're still backgrounding him, but if there's somebody else, it's not obvious," Hart said.

"I wish we'd had time to interrogate him," Corbeil said. "But the pressure to get him out of the way . . . well, we couldn't both interrogate him and have a credible disappearance, could we?"

Hart shrugged. The other man, Benson, stood silently, listening. A follower. Hart asked, "So now what? Shut down the ranch for a while?"

"That won't be necessary," Corbeil said. "We can do it by pushing a button. No point in pushing it before we have to. There's a lot of money out there right now."

"I'll tell you, Mr. Corbeil, this whole incident scared the shit out of me. I'm still scared and Les is just as nervous as I am." Hart glanced at the silent man, looking for support, and got a nod.

"That's why we've been so careful setting it up," Corbeil said. "They'd need evidence to put us in jail, and there's no physical evidence of anything. If I tell Tom Woods to push the destruct button, everything is gone. Not even *we* could get it back."

"That's well and good, but there's still Lane Ward," Hart said. "If she does have something, or if Morrison set up some kind of dead-man's drop . . ."

"So we need to go out and look at her house."

"That's dangerous," Hart objected.

"You didn't have any trouble getting into Morrison's place out there. Or here, either."

"That was different. He was supposed to be out of town, and *we* knew he was dead, so nobody would be coming around to visit. With Ward, we don't know the neighborhood, we don't even know what we'd be looking for. It might be on a disk, on a hard drive, it might be stashed online somewhere. It might not exist."

"But if it does, and if it were sent on to the FBI, we'd be in desperate trouble," Corbeil said. "It's worth the risk. If the worst happened, and you were caught, we might explain it as a security matter. Something that we were terribly worried about: something that you did on your own to keep the nation's secrets from falling into unfriendly hands. If you did go to jail for a while—what would you get for an unsuccessful burglary, six months?—if that did happen, there would be a magnificent bonus at the end of the time."

"How much?" Hart asked bluntly.

"Say, two million a year, prorated for lesser amounts of time," Corbeil said.

Hart looked at Benson, then turned back to Corbeil. "So we look at her house. Actually, there's an opportunity coming up."

Corbeil's eyebrows went up, and when Hart explained, Corbeil smiled with pleasure. "I so like working with you, William," he said.

Benson spoke up for the first time. "You know what I don't like, Mr. Corbeil? I think we're really okay with this Morrison character, and his sister. I don't think he sent anything. We caught on too quick, and he was relying on Lighter to take care of the problem. But what I see . . ."

Corbeil was made impatient by the preface: "Yes?"

"I'm worried about Woods. Ever since Morrison was killed, he's been walking around with this doggy face. I think he knows something happened. They used to hang out a little."

Corbeil nodded, and said, "All right, Les. That's a legitimate concern. You know Tom Woods is a friend of mine, an old confidant who came over with me from the factory. And a mathematical genius, to boot."

"I know that, sir, but . . ."

Corbeil raised one hand: "If he becomes a problem, I will take care of it. I promise. But we already have two deaths that are too closely connected. A third one, if it becomes necessary to remove Lane Ward, would almost certainly draw attention. If Tom Woods had died in the interim . . . Well."

Hart said, "Unless Tom was the architect of it all."

Corbeil said, "You took the thought right out of my head, William. We can perhaps begin to prepare some documents. . . . So: you travel to San Francisco."

Hart nodded. "Tomorrow. We'll call back. After we see what we've got, we can make a call on the Ward chick. Take her out or leave her."

Corbeil said, "Mmm," and smiled.

The plane touched down in San Francisco a little after three in the morning, taking a turn out to sea, then landing across the stem of highway lights between the ocean and the bay. When we touched down, a tight wire in my spine suddenly relaxed. Whatever happened now, we could fake it. In Dallas, where the cops could look at us, where they could *see* the burns, we were in trouble.

A purely selfish reaction: because Lane hurt. I'd found some Solarcaine in a drugstore, and she'd smeared it on the burns, and she'd taken a half-dozen ibuprofen, though we weren't sure they'd help much. That was about the best we could do before we left for the airport.

At the check-in counter, Lane hung back, the shy Little Woman in a long-sleeved blouse, head down, while I handled the tickets. On the plane, she sat on the aisle, and got up twice to go to the bathroom, to lather on more of the Solarcaine.

"You okay?" I asked after the second trip.

"I'll make it," she said through her teeth.

"The ibuprofen . . ."

"Didn't help much," she said. "I hope I don't scar."

"It doesn't look that bad," I said. "I . . ."

She held up the bottom side of her arm, and showed me a half-dozen blisters the size of quarters.

"I'm afraid to lance them, 'cause of infection," she said.

"Ah, Jesus . . ."

Halfway through the flight, I half-stood and looked around. The woman in the seat in front of Lane was asleep, her mouth hanging open. There was nobody behind us, and the guy across the aisle had spread across two seats, and had his head propped uncomfortably against a window shade.

"You know," I said quietly, "The police know we left Dallas this evening and the house burned down before we left. They're gonna want to talk to you."

"Oh, boy. You're right."

"You're gonna have to lie a little," I said.

"I'm gonna have to lie a *lot*," she said.

"You can pull it off if you think about it," I said. "You've gotta be surprised and you've gotta be pissed. It's *their* fault—the cops' fault—that the place burned down. You *told* them that something was going on, that your brother had been murdered. You gotta yell at them."

"Not yell. But I'll be mad. I *am* mad," she said. "Somebody *did* murder him."

"You gotta *insist* that you go back to Dallas, and you have to demand to look at the hard drives on the computers. That might keep them from having a local cop come around to talk to you. There's no reason for them to suspect that you were burned in the fire, there's no reason for them to think that they have to see you right away. And you do have to stay here for the funeral."

"So it depends on how long it takes the burns to heal," she said.

"Yes. But you can't stall them: you just have to be busy. You have to leave them with the impression that you're pissed off and you're gonna be back in their faces as soon as you have the time."

She thought about it for a minute, then said, "I can do that."

"Cops aren't dummies. Not most of them, anyway."

"Maybe he won't be the same guy I talked to last time. I mean, I talked to a different cop the first time. . . . That'd make it easier."

"Whoever it is, you've got to be careful, and you've got to be real. Cops got built-in bullshit detectors," I said.

At San Francisco, we picked up her car from a satellite lot and drove south to Palo Alto, went straight to her house, dumped the luggage: "Emergency room," I said.

"I've got a doctor I see . . ."

"Emergency room is *right now,* and it's anonymous, and it may stop the pain," I said.

She didn't argue.

We even managed to get a little sleep that night.

At ten o'clock in the morning, after five hours in bed, I heard somebody knocking around in the house. I rolled off the bed—I'd crashed in her spare room—and pulled on my jeans and T-shirt. She was in the kitchen, making coffee.

"How is it?"

"Hurts," she said. She'd gotten cleaned up, as best she could, but said that water hurt the burns. She was wearing loose khaki pants with a long-sleeved cotton peasant shirt, and again I could sense just a dab of the flowery French scent. She smelled terrific, and looked terrific in the peasant blouse, if you didn't know that she was dressed to hide new burns.

Her face was all right; the burn there resembled a bad sunburn, and would heal soon enough. Her arms were the worst of it. The doc had lanced the blisters the night before, to relieve the pressure, but they were filling again.

"The anesthetic doesn't help?" I asked. She'd gotten a spray-on topical anesthetic at the hospital. The doctors had said it was stronger than the Solarcaine.

"Helps for a while," she said. "Then it starts to hurt again."

"I'm sorry."

"Not your fault," she said. "But I don't think I could do what you do. . . . For a living, I mean."

"This usually isn't a part of it," I said.

"Sometimes it must be . . ." She looked me over, and I couldn't deny that there'd been trouble in the past.

"Nothing like fire," I said. "Fire scares me."

"Me, too, now." She reached toward her neck as though she were going to scratch, stopped herself and smiled and said, "I'm going to be a really bitchy patient."

I went out and got a sack of bagels and some cream cheese, and we toasted bagels and drank coffee and talked about Jack and the Jaz disks. When we finished, she said she was going to try to lie down again—"The pain really isn't terrible; it just makes me want to scream. It's giving me a headache."

"All right. Point me to your computer first. You got a Jaz drive?"

"No. But we're about two minutes from a CompUSA."

She showed me her office, with its standard beige desktop Dell, and then went off to lie down. I walked out to the CompUSA, bought an external Jaz drive and a bunch of disks, lugged it all back, hooked up the drive, and got the disks we'd taken from Jack's house.

I started with the top one, and the first thing I found was a file called, simply, *notes.* I opened it and found a couple of random e-mails, apparently picked up from somewhere else on the disk. Jack had been picking out things that might be significant; making notes.

The first one said, *Add CarlG, RasputinIV to list. High correlation on both.*

CarlG and RasputinIV were on the list of Firewall members mentioned in the Web rumors, and now being investigated by the FBI.

The second note said, *check: endodays, exdeus, fillyjonk, laguna8, omeomi, pixystyx.*

More hacker names? They sounded right. Was this some kind of security thing? Was AmMath worried about Firewall, or *dealing* with Firewall? Or maybe it *was* Firewall.

I started browsing the rest of the files, all under the general heading of OMS, and twice found the heading "Old Man of the Sea." They'd gotten the Hemingway title wrong, if that's what it was meant to be. Anyway, the only easily comprehensible part of the files was a huge batch of e-mail and memos that Jack had apparently copied out raw. I looked at maybe three hundred pieces of it, out of fifteen thousand or so, and all of it was routine company stuff: days off, raises, complaints, scheduling.

Of the twenty gigabytes of information on the four disks, the most interesting files I couldn't really open at all. They were five hundred megabytes each and Lane's computer only had 384 megs of RAM. I looked at the first few blocks of each, though, and figured out that the files were graphics of some kind, probably photographs.

Bored and frustrated, I spent a while making two copies of each of the Jaz disks. As I finished, Lane got up, wandered out to the kitchen and began dabbing anesthetic on her burns. I shut down the computer and went out to tell her what I'd found.

"Did his work file . . . did that have a time stamp on it?" she asked.

"I didn't even look," I said, and we headed back to her office, and cranked the computer up. Lane was standing four inches away from me, looking at the screen, waiting through all the stupid Windows-opening stuff. She was an attractive woman; she looked like she'd feel good. I had the sudden feeling that if I touched her, somehow, something might happen.

But I didn't; I sat looking at the screen, and the moment passed. She moved a little, and wound up a few extra inches away . . . And when we opened Jack's work file, it did have a time stamp. It was last closed on Sunday, five days before he was killed.

"So he *did* go in on Sunday," she said.

"You said the cops said he made a phone call from his house and turned off the security system, a camera, and motion detectors," I reminded her.

"Yes."

"That's something we could check," I said.

"How?" She reached down to her arm, unconsciously, to scratch the burns; and caught herself.

"The phone company has these things called Message Unit Details or Message Unit Records," I said. "We called them Mothers back in the bad-old-phone-phreak days. They'll tell you where all the phone calls from your telephones went."

"How do we get them?"

"That guy I called from St. Paul—Bobby, the one I didn't want you to know about—could get them in two minutes," I said.

"So let's get them," she said.

"I have to go out to a pay phone," I said. "You wouldn't want to call that number from here."

"And if we go out to a pay phone, then I won't know it," she said. "It won't be on my long-distance bill."

"That, too," I said.

We went out to a mall and I hooked up my own laptop at a pay phone using a pair of old-fashioned acoustic-adapter earmuffs. After going through the security rigamarole, I got Bobby online and asked him to get me the numbers dialed from all phones at Jack's house on Sunday night, and then on Friday night, when he was killed. He said it would take a few minutes, but he should have them by the time we got back to the house. I said fine, and then added that I needed a mailing address to send him a package.

WHAT?

4 2-GIG JAZ DISKS. NEED MORE EYES LOOKING AT THEM. COME FROM STANFORD.

SEND TO JOHN. HE WILL BRING TO ME.

Lane was looking over my shoulder and said, "So he doesn't mind calling in, as long as we don't call out."

"If you managed to trace the incoming call, it'd probably go back to the local bagel bakery, or Pontiac dealer, or something. He's weird about telephones," I said.

"What does this guy do for a living? Bobby?"

"Databases. Thousands of them. He still does some phone work, but mostly to cover up his database entries. About the only things he can't get into are the ones without an outside connection, and that's damn few of them, anymore. Maybe some military or national security computers; stuff at that level would be pretty tough, though I know he's in some of them. He's been there forever. He's like an unknown, unofficial systems administrator."

The phone was ringing when we got back to the house. Not Bobby—it was an air freight place: Jack's body would arrive the following day, and would be taken to a local funeral home. Lane put the phone down to say something, but it rang against almost instantly. Again, not Bobby.

"*Yes, this is Lane . . . yes? What! What do you mean? Burned down? Well, how much is left? Did it get all of his personal stuff? Well, how bad? Aw, jeez. I told you guys—I hold you guys responsible, I'm gonna talk to an attorney, you never let me in there and then I told you somebody killed my brother, and now they burned his house, and you guys didn't even have time to look into it . . . Bullshit. BULLSHIT! I'm gonna come there, I'm gonna come there as soon as the funeral is over, and I'm going to want to talk to whoever is in charge . . .*"

"Was I good?" she asked when she hung up.

"You were *very* good," I said.

Bobby called ten minutes later. We got the tone, I hastily slapped the muffs on, and two columns of numbers popped up. Between six and midnight Sunday, Jack made three phone calls. On Friday, he made a long-distance call to California at seven o'clock, that lasted twenty minutes: "That's our ISP, I have the same one," Lane said. He made another call at nine forty-five, and nothing later.

"So the nine forty-five call must be the one to the security computers," I said. "We can check that."

"But he didn't call that number on Sunday night," Lane said.

"Which means he didn't turn off the camera on Sunday night," I said.

"Which means that maybe he hadn't found the security system. I wonder if the camera's out in the open?"

I scratched my head and thought about it for a couple of minutes, and finally said, "You know, I think maybe they killed him."

"I've been telling you that."

"Yeah, but I didn't believe you," I said. "There was too much weight on the other side. But if Jack knew about the security system on Sunday, he would have turned it off before he went in. If he found out about the system between Sunday night and Friday night, he'd have known he was in trouble—that the camera would have picked him up. If he knew all that, then why didn't he add anything to the letter he sent me? If they scared him, and he *knew* he was in trouble . . ."

"I just thought of something else," Lane said. "They say he broke into the secure area on Friday night. Well, if he went in there on Sunday night . . . why didn't he have to break in that time? Why was the first break-in on Friday, when we know he was there on Sunday?"

"One of the first things we do is try to figure out how to get into a place without anybody knowing," I said. "LuEllen and I talked to Jack about that, a little, about not leaving a mark . . . that's why I looked for the house key at Jack's place. Better to ease your way in, than to break something, and he knew that." I took a turn around the kitchen, working it through, finally shook my head. "I can see how they could have set it up. It'd take two guys, but they'd have to be brutal assholes to shoot that old man, the guard."

"Two guys came to burn down the house," she said. She said it quietly, like a scholar making the killing point.

"Goddamnit," I said after a while. "I think they killed him."

7

We sent the second copies of the Jaz disks off to Bobby's friend John Smith—also a friend of mine, and an artist himself—and I spent the next two days trying to find something that made sense on the Jaz disks, and working along the edges of the bay, with watercolor. Salty water has a different quality from fresh water, a heavier, more viscous feel. The heaviness was compounded by the light, which was very green and hard. I never got it quite right.

Lane stayed at the house, getting ready for the funeral, doing a little telecommuting and some restless reading. She also spent some time poking through the Jaz disks, but neither of us found much.

Three days after the fire, the blisters on her arms were drying to unsightly splotches of itchy dead skin, while the redness under her neck had begun to fade to brown. I brought in meals during the day, and in the cool evenings we walked out to dinner at a dimly lit Italian place, where the burns wouldn't be visible.

The funeral took place on a beautiful California morning, fifty people gathered in an old-fashioned Spanish-style stucco chapel, where an Episcopalian priest said all the right words with the right dignity. The women cried, the men shook hands and Harry Connick Jr.'s "Sunny Side of the Street" played through the sound system as Jack's childhood friends carried his casket out the side door.

LuEllen walked in the door a few seconds after the service started. I almost didn't recognize her in the New York black dress, hat, and wraparound sunglasses. She lifted a hand to me and slipped into a pew across the way. Lane didn't notice—she was out of it, struggling through the worst week of her life, struggling to get her older brother into the ground.

At the end of the service, Lane went to the front door to shake hands. LuEllen drifted over to me and said, "Bummer."

I said, "Yeah," and then, "You're looking nice. The black dress."

"I was working in New York," she said. LuEllen was something of a chameleon. In black, without lipstick, with her close-cropped frosted-blond hair, she could have been a London model, except that she was too short, and her shoulders a tad too wide. When she put on Western shirts, the kind with the arrows at the corners, and cowboy boots, you'd swear she'd come straight back from hauling hay out to a horse barn in Wyoming, a rosy-cheeked good-time country girl. In Miami, she could have been a drug dealer's bimbo; in San Diego, a slightly used Navy wife on the lookout for a Coronado Island admiral . . .

But she was a lot more than all of that.

"Anything good?" I asked.

"Coin dealer. Let it go. Way too much protection." She looked around with the kind of eye-drooping, stand-back attitude she tended to develop after a couple of weeks of pushing her way around Manhattan.

"Not like you need the money," I said.

"Not yet, anyway," she said. She nodded at Lane. "Who's the chick? Jack wasn't married, was he?"

"His sister. Lane Ward."

"Oh, yeah; when you look at her close, you can see it." She looked at Lane and then back up at me: "Too much makeup for my style," she said.

"There's a story behind it." I told her about the house and the fire. "So she's flash-burned on her neck and arms and the cops want to talk to her. We're trying to bullshit our way through the funeral, then get her out of sight until she's healed."

"Gotta hurt," she said. LuEllen was unimpressed by pain; her own or anybody else's.

"It does. The doc said it'd take eight or ten days to heal, so we've got a while to go."

"Can we talk with her around?"

"I think so; but I haven't given her anything on you at all, except your first name, and I'll keep it that way."

"All right," she said. Then: "You getting laid?"

"Not by Lane, if that's what you're asking."

"By who?"

"Software lady back in the Cities. We're building a computer together." I couldn't see her eyes, but I could tell they were rolling.

"Nerd love," she said.

"Nerd love," I agreed. "How about you?"

"Nothing right now. I've been working pretty hard. I did a hundred and seventy thousand in Miami a couple of months ago, scared myself brainless."

"Come close?"

"Not to getting caught, but the people . . . bunch of peckerwood meth manufacturers. If they'd figured me out, they would've cut me up with a chainsaw, and I shit you not."

Sometimes LuEllen and I were in bed, sometimes not. She had a taste for slender, dark-haired Latin men with big white teeth. I'm not any of that. We hadn't been in the sack for a while, but I expected that she'd be back. Or I would, or something. We'd probably be buried next to each other, sooner or later: funeral thoughts.

On the way out of the church, I introduced her to Lane, who smiled and nodded, and we went outside. I'd driven Lane to the church in her car, but she'd ride to the cemetery with friends. I decided to go with LuEllen, and pick up Lane's car on the way back.

"You know what wouldn't be a bad way to go?" LuEllen asked, on the way out to the cemetery. "You know your time has come, it's all over. Go up in the North Woods in the wintertime, where there are wolves around. You sit down, take your coat off, and chill out. Wouldn't hurt. You'd just go to sleep, and instead of rotting, you'd be a dinner for the wolves. Something useful—and you'd wind up as a wolf yourself, sort of."

"Wouldn't hurt as long as the wolves didn't get there early," I said.

"That's really romantic," she said.

"Or you'd probably wind up getting eaten by field mice. Voles."

"Shut up, Kidd."

Half the people at the church followed to the cemetery. Jack was buried in a smoothly curving piece of the earth framed by a dozen small redwoods; nice spot. The funeral was one of those where, after the coffin is let down into the ground, the bystanders walk by and toss a handful of dirt into the grave. We filed past, LuEllen a step ahead of me, and when I turned past the top of the grave, saw a thick-necked man in a suit and sunglasses standing a hundred yards away, half concealed behind a granite gravestone.

I'd seen him once before, I thought: outside the house in Dallas, his face silhouetted by a streetlight.

"Got a problem," I muttered to LuEllen. "You got your cameras?"

"In the car," she said. She looked right at me, too smart to look for trouble.

"I'm gonna turn, and if you look past my shoulder, you'll see a guy in a gray suit and black sunglasses, about a hundred yards off. What are the chances of getting a shot?"

I turned and she turned with me, smiling, saying, "Yadda yadda yadda," and then, "All right, I got him. He's not a cop, unless he's some kind of federal spook that I don't want to know about."

"He's not a cop," I said. "He could be private security. He could be a major asshole."

The people at the funeral were starting to look around, ready to start moving as soon as the last handful of dirt was dropped in the grave. LuEllen said, "Let me give you a peck, say good-bye," and I leaned over and she gave me a peck on the cheek and started for her car, lifting a hand to wave good-bye as she went.

She was the first to go; her car was only fifty feet down the cemetery lane. She popped the trunk with a remote key, pulled out a shoulder bag, tossed it across the front seat, started the car and drove away. I turned, casually, saw the man in the gray suit still standing there, but faced in a different direction, looking ninety degrees away from us. The last handful of dirt went in the grave, and Lane shook hands with a couple of people, and took the arm of a guy who, with his wife, had driven her to the cemetery: their oldest friends, Jack's and Lane's, and from what I'd seen, nice people.

As Lane started moving toward the car, the man in gray started to move, down away from the stone where he was standing. I couldn't see a car—it was apparently behind an evergreen-covered knoll, out of sight. LuEllen had only had a couple of minutes to set up, and I wasn't sure if she was ready yet. Nothing to do about it, and since I'd come with her, I had nothing to do but wait. The man in the gray suit came to watch? Couldn't be that simple.

Everybody was moving now, but Lane, about to get in the backseat of her friends' car, saw me standing, watching, and called, "Kidd? Where's your friend?"

I strolled over and said, "Give me a hug?"

With a question on her face, she stepped over to give me a hug and I said, quietly as I could, "One of the people who burned Jack's house is here."

"Oh, no." She took my arm and led me a few steps away from the car, looking up at me earnestly, as if giving comfort. What she said was, "What's he doing? Do you see him?"

"He left as soon as you started to. I gotta get back to your house. I'm afraid he might have been here to keep an eye on you while the other guy broke in. Are Jack's disks . . ."

"On my desk. Both copies."

"Shit."

"But we sent a set to Bobby . . ."

"Yeah, but if they get the others, they'll know that we've at least looked at them," I said. "Or that you have, anyway."

"But we don't *know* anything. Not really," she said.

"They don't know that."

LuEllen's rental car whipped around the knoll, moving too fast on the narrow black-topped cemetery lane. She pulled up, popped the door and said, "Got him, and got his plate."

"Good. We've gotta get back to Lane's place. Like now."

"Call the police," Lane said. LuEllen and I glanced at each other. She caught it and said, "Okay. I'll call the police. We'll find a pay phone on the way out. The guy who was here knows we can't get back there for half an hour. If there *is* another guy, maybe the police could still catch him."

"Worth a try," I said.

"Wait for me."

She went back to her friends' car, leaned in the back, said something, got her purse, and hurried back to us. "I'm riding with you," she said.

We drove out to a gas station, spotted a drive-up coin phone. LuEllen dialed 911 and passed the phone to Lane, who said, "Look, I don't want to get involved in this, but I think I saw a man breaking into a house. No, I don't want to get involved . . ." She gave the address, hung up, and we were gone.

LuEllen would not have anything more to do with any cops: "I'll drop you at the church so you can get Lane's car, and I'll call you from a motel."

"Sure."

LuEllen looked at Lane: "If the cops are there when you get there . . ."

"I'll be surprised."

"Tell them that you were at your brother's funeral. Right up front. First thing."

"Why?"

"That'll fit you into a slot, for the cops. Dopers hit houses during funerals. The neighbors have gotten used to people coming and going, and during the funeral itself, the house is usually empty, so it's a good time to go in. It's like a *thing.*"

"Like an MO," Lane said.

"Right, exactly," LuEllen said. "Like television."

The cops *were* there, two squads, four officers. We pulled up and one of them came trotting over. Lane got out and asked, "What's wrong?"

"Do you live here, ma'am?"

"Yes, it's my house."

"We think it may have been broken into. We got an anonymous nine-one-one call and when we checked, we found the front door had been forced."

Lane's hand went to her throat and she said, "Is the man . . ."

"We don't think he's inside. We talked to one of the neighbors and he said he saw a man exit the back door, and walk away down the street—that was just about the time we got the nine-one-one call. He had a fifteen-minute start on us by the time we talked to the neighbor, so he's miles away. His car was probably right around the corner."

"Oh, my god," Lane said, and she started walking toward the house. I said to the cop, "We were just at her brother's funeral."

"You're not her husband?" One of the cops asked, as the others started after Lane.

"No, I'm just a friend of her brother's; I drove her car to the church."

"We better check the house, just in case," he said.

Inside, as the cops moved from one room to the next, Lane looked at me and shook her head, silently mouthed, "They're gone." Also gone: her laptop, a jewelry box with a few hundred dollars worth of jewelry—and a lot of memories, Lane said—a Minolta 35mm camera and three lenses, a checkbook, a couple of hundred English pounds that she kept in a bureau drawer, and a broken Rolex watch given her by her ex-husband.

"Making it look like they were here for the high-value stuff . . . laptops, cameras. Making it look like junkies," I muttered.

"Goddamn animals."

The cops were decent about it. They told her there wasn't much they could do, absent any indication of who might have broken in. They apologized, as though it were their fault, told her to get better locks, and left.

Lane and I spent the next ten minutes teasing out the consequences of the burglary. There were a couple. If the people who took the disks were worried about what Jack knew, and were willing to kill him to keep his mouth shut, then the same might apply to Lane. On the other hand, they might look at the disks and conclude that nothing on them was worth killing for—that another death would just draw attention to them. Flip a coin.

LuEllen called, and I told her about the burglary: "The cops are gone, we're gonna have a war council."

"I've got a room at the Holiday Inn," she said. "I'll change clothes and come over . . . listen, you don't have a package, do you?"

"No."

"Maybe . . ."

"Yeah."

LuEllen had reverted to her usual dress by the time she arrived at Lane's: jeans and cowboy boots, and an orange silk blouse under a jean jacket. She had the figure of a gymnast to go with the jeans: she looked spectacular, if you like cowgirls. She brought along a roll of 35mm Polaroid color slide film, a compact Polaroid film-development machine, a single-slide cabin projector, and a box of empty slide holders. She popped the film out of the camera, and we sat around the kitchen table while she developed it, cut out the individual frames, and snapped the frames into the plastic slide holders.

"If she's gonna be around here, she's gonna need somebody looking out for her," LuEllen said, talking to me as if Lane weren't there.

I nodded. "You know who I'm thinking about? I'm thinking about John Smith. He's in on this already, and he lived in Oakland. I bet he'd know somebody."

"Who's John Smith?" Lane asked.

"He's a guy, an artist," I told her. "He was a young kid in Oakland back in the early seventies when the Black Panthers were going. He's still out there on the left, still knows a lot of hard people."

"How'd you meet him?"

"We helped him organize a Communist revolution in the Mississippi delta," I said.

"Unsuccessfully, I take it."

"No, no, it worked out fine," LuEllen said. That might have been an overstatement. Bobby had convinced us that there might be some money involved in overthrowing a little strong-arm dictatorship in a small town of the Mississippi River. By the time we finished, we'd made some money, all right, and our friends were running the place, but there was blood on the ground, and some of the dead were good people. LuEllen doesn't always seem to remember that part of it; or she does, but finds no point in dwelling on it. She looked at me. "So we call him." She'd finished with the film, got the little cabin projector, plugged it in, and projected a slide against the white front of Lane's refrigerator.

"That's the guy," I said. "I'd bet on it."

Lane shivered and said, "He looks mean."

She was right. He had that thick-necked, tight-mouthed line-backer look, with a crew cut to make the point. "I'm sure he is," I said.

The next slide showed the same man caught as he climbed into a red Toyota Camry with California plates. I jotted down the number: "Who does Camrys?" I asked LuEllen.

"Hertz," she said.

"Time to make some calls," I said.

LuEllen and I drove out to the pay phone again, and I hooked up my laptop, called Bobby and gave him the tag number for the Camry: *"Rental car, could be Hertz. Need to know the driver's name and anything else you can find. Driver probably lives in Dallas area, probably flew into San Francisco in the last day or two. Dump to my cache site, I'll pick it up later. Plan to call John Smith for some help, talk to him."*

Then we called John.

"Kidd, goddamnit, it's been a while . . ." He pulled his mouth away from the phone long enough to yell, "You guys be quiet for a minute, okay? Daddy's on the telephone—hey, Marvel, it's Kidd." Then he was back: "What's up?"

Then Marvel picked up, and I said, "How's the commie state senator?" and she laughed and the bullshit rolled on for a few minutes. Then LuEllen wanted to talk, and we had a long-distance old-home week. I finally took the phone back and said, "Listen, John, we've got a problem out here in California—we're in Palo Alto—and I was hoping you might be able to hook me up with somebody."

"What kind of trouble?"

I gave him a quick and slightly vague answer, and mentioned

Bobby. He didn't press for details, since he knew what we all did for a living, and finally said, "I don't know a guy, but I know a guy who'd know a guy."

"That's cool. We can pay whatever."

"Probably be at least two hundred dollars a day, don't ask, don't tell." Cash, no tax.

"Fine. Let me give you the phone number . . ." I gave him Lane's number and John said somebody would call that afternoon. "Listen," I added, "if *you* need to get in touch, drop mail at Bobby's. But don't call that number yourself; things could get tricky."

H ome?"

LuEllen shook her head. "We need to go into San Francisco . . . the Jimmy Cricket Golf Shop, and Lanny Rose's Beauty Boutique. I got directions."

"Golf shop?"

"Yeah. I'm taking up the game. And I want to look good while I'm playing."

J immy Cricket—he claimed that was his real name—was a nicely weathered gent wearing a black Polo sweatshirt over a golf shirt and jeans, with tassels on his loafers. He was regripping a Ping driver when we came through the door. He smiled and asked, "What can I do for you folks?"

"Weenie called you earlier today," LuEllen said.

"The Gray twosome," he said, as though we'd just shown up for our tee-time, "I thought you were a single."

"Nope," LuEllen said, "Mr. and Mrs. Gray. Weenie said to tell you that all cats are gray in the dark."

"Okay. Well, Weenie's word is good with me. If you'll step into the back . . ."

We went through a flip-up countertop into the back room. Cricket extracted a tan duffel bag from a pile of empty golf-club shipping boxes, placed it on a workbench, and dug out five rag-wrapped hand guns: four .357 Magnum revolvers and a 9mm semi-auto. "I brought the auto just in case," he told LuEllen.

"We're not gonna need it," she said. She picked up one of the guns, flipped out the cylinder, pointed it at one of her eyes, and held her thumbnail under the open chamber, to reflect light back up the barrel. Picked up another and did the same thing. "Can't tell much, but they look okay."

"They're all perfect mechanically," Cricket said. "They are clean and cold."

LuEllen looked at all five, then pushed one at Cricket and asked, "How much?"

"Six." He wouldn't come down on the price but he threw in two boxes of shells, one of .38 Special and one .357. On the way out the door LuEllen spotted a pair of shooter's earmuffs, and gave Cricket another ten dollars.

"Now we can play guns," she said.

anny Rose's Beauty Boutique looked like it was permanently closed, with fifteen-year-old pastel green "Walk-Ins Accepted" signs fading and badly askew in the windows. LuEllen insisted on banging on the door anyway, and a minute later, Lanny peered out from behind the "Closed" sign. He saw us, popped the door, and said, "Jesus Christ, you almost knocked the front of the bidnis in."

"Weenie said the world looks better through rose-colored glasses," LuEllen said.

"Yeah, yeah, fuck a bunch of weenies," Lanny said, but he pushed the door open a bit, and LuEllen and I followed him through the gloomy beauty parlor into a back room. When we got there, he was hanging a pale blue drape on a wall, using pushpins.

"Stand there. Smile, but only a little," he said.

I stood, and he took my picture, twice, with a Polaroid passport camera. Then he took two pictures of LuEllen and said, "I'll be back in a minute."

LuEllen said, "I think I'll come along and watch."

She had her hand in her pocket, and Lanny said, "Weenie promised you wouldn't be no trouble."

"We won't be; I'm just coming along to watch," LuEllen said. "My friend will sit out here in front and read a magazine."

They were gone for twenty minutes. I sat in a dusty beauty-parlor chair and read a story in a four-year-old *Cosmo* about how women can keep their men interested by learning the latest in blow-job techniques—the techniques themselves were described blow by blow, so to speak, by a panel of successful New York advertising and media women. I was not only convinced, I was supportive.

When LuEllen and Lanny came back, Lanny was complaining. "I never make copies of *any* faces. Weenie knows that."

"I don't trust Weenie," LuEllen said.

Back in the car, she handed me four cards: two Texas driver's licenses, and two credit cards. One credit card matched each license. "Will they stand up?"

"Unless you're busted, in which case they'll get your prints anyway," she said. "They're both real people, and the accounts are real, although we don't know the credit limits or the billing dates. We could use them in an emergency, but then they'd only be good until the guy's next bill came in."

"Bobby could get us credit limits and billing dates," I said.

"Might be worth doing . . ."

On the way to Lane's, LuEllen launched a little philosophical discussion.

"You know, Kidd, you told me once that revenge doesn't make any sense, because the dead guy won't know what you're doing and won't care, because he's dead. So what I'm wondering is, *What are we doing?* Jack won't know, and Jack won't care."

"We're not really doing it for Jack anymore," I said. "We never were, really. We're doing it for us. They just pissed us off by killing Jack."

"Not me, especially. I only met him that once. Nice guy, but . . ."

"Then *I'm* pissed about Jack, and you're coming along because of *me*. And I don't have much choice. I'm involved in this somehow, and I've got to find out what's going on. I don't want that crew-cut asshole and his pal showing up at my house someday, tidying up some loose end that I don't even know about."

"So I'm involved only because you're involved—and because you say so."

"That's right," I said.

"That's pretty smug. What if I opted out?"

"You won't. You couldn't stand not knowing what happened," I said.

"You'd tell me."

"No, I wouldn't. I'd never say a single word about it. I'd deny all knowledge."

"Bullshit," she snorted.

"So you're in?"

She let her eyes float to the tops of her eye sockets, and then said, "For a while."

A t Lane's, we ate Lean Cuisines—I had three of them, an appealing mix of Teriyaki Stir-Fry, Swedish Meatballs, and Mesquite Beef—and then LuEllen took Lane and the revolver down to the basement.

"I hate the goddamn things," Lane had said, when LuEllen showed her the gun.

"They're the ubiquitous tools of modern life. Even if you don't like them, it behooves you to know how to use one," LuEllen said.

"Oh, boy."

Fifteen minutes after they went down the basement, a single shot cracked through the house. I jumped up, peeked out the windows all around. Nothing moving. I stuck my head down the basement door, "Jesus, LuEllen . . ."

Bang! A second one, and I nearly jumped out of my shoes.

"All done," LuEllen called. The smell of burnt gunpowder coursed up the stairwell, and a minute later, LuEllen appeared at the bottom of the stairs. "Had to squeeze off a round or two so she'd have a sense of the recoil."

"Well, knock it off, for Christ's sakes, it's louder than hell up here," I said.

"Aw, once or twice, no problem," she said.

They were still down the basement when the phone rang. I picked it up and a soft male voice said, "Could I speak to Mr. Kidd?"

"Speaking."

"This is Lethridge Green. I'm a friend of a friend of a man named John. I was told you have a body to guard?"

"Yes. In Palo Alto, although there might be some travel."

"I get two hundred fifty dollars a day plus any expenses," Green said.

"That's fine."

"How long would the body need to be guarded?"

"I don't know. Not just a couple of days, though—anything from a couple of weeks to a couple of months."

"Good. Don't ask, don't tell?"

"Exactly," I said.

"I can be there in two hours, if you'd like me to start tonight."

"That'd be a relief," I said. "We're sort of afraid to leave the body alone."

"Then I will come directly."

*T*hen *I will come directly.*

Not exactly what I'd expected from hired muscle, but then, with John, you never knew exactly what you might get . . .

A few minutes after talking to Green, I went out and checked my cache with Bobby, to see if he'd gotten anything on the guy at the cemetery. He had. He'd run the plate back to Hertz, dug through their computer, and come up with the credit card and license information on the renter: A Lester Benson, of Dallas, using a corporate American Express card issued to AmMath. The car had not been checked in yet.

Lester Benson: hadn't seen that name before.

There was no hint of a second man in any of the Hertz information, but Bobby was looking through airline reservation files to see if he could spot Benson's seat from Dallas to San Francisco, and then determine who might have been sitting next to him.

I left a note asking him to find everything he could on AmMath and to dump all the information to my mailbox.

L ethridge Green was standing on Lane's porch, knocking on the door, when I pulled up. Green looked like a big Malcolm X—tall, too slender, intent, with round gold-rimmed glasses, short hair, and a solemn, searching intensity.

"Mr. Green?" I pushed through the door. "Come on in."

"You're Mr. Kidd," he said, as he stepped inside. His eyes took in the room, and LuEllen and Lane on the couch, and the .357 on the end table next to LuEllen's hand. "I see a gun. What's the situation here?"

"Somebody killed my brother, and somebody burglarized my house this afternoon . . ." Lane started.

"Did you call the police?"

"Yes. They think it was burglars attracted by my brother's funeral."

"You don't think so?"

"I know it wasn't. We even know who it was; but not exactly why."

Green held up a finger: "Before you tell me anything else, maybe we should take the first security precaution."

"What?" Lane asked. We all looked at him expectantly.

"Pull the drapes," he said.

A fter we'd pulled the drapes, Lane gave him the story—not all of it, but most of it: her brother being killed in Dallas in suspicious circumstances, the funeral, the burglary at her home. She told him about the fire, but didn't mention that we were there. She told him about our record search through Hertz, and the two names we had so far: William Hart, mentioned by Jack, and Lester Benson, from the Hertz records. "We're afraid they might come back—that they might think that Jack passed information to me, or computer files."

"Did he?"

Lane looked at me, and I nodded. "Yes. He sent me some Jaz disks. A Jaz disk is a high-capacity storage . . ."

"I know what a Jaz disk is," he said. "What's on it?"

"Everything from memos to computer games to a lot of gob-bledygook that we haven't had time to figure out. That we might not be *able* to figure out," I said. "Whatever it is, we think Jack might have been killed to keep it private. The shoot-out might have been a setup."

"The guard took a slug as part of a setup?" he asked skeptically.

"The guard didn't see anything," I said. "As far as he knows, he might have been shot by the Easter Bunny. He opens the door and, boom, he's down. The other guy supposedly fires four times and Jack's killed. The guard didn't see a thing."

"Why didn't you just give them back? The disks?"

"That might not help; because we know about them, and we can't erase that. Then there's this group called Firewall . . ." I explained Firewall, as much as I knew about it.

"You're starting to scare me," Green said. "If this is some kind of government thing, the FBI or the CIA or one of those other alphabet agencies . . . I mean, I don't want to be protecting a bunch of terrorists or spies or something."

"Do we look like terrorists? I'm a college professor," Lane said.

"A lot of terrorists start out as college professors," he said.

"Well, I'm not one of them," she snapped. "I'm just scared."

"We're not asking you to crawl down a sewer pipe with a bomb in your mouth," I said. "Just keep her healthy."

"That's it? All I do is keep them off her?"

"That's it. And if it gets heavy, call the cops. We already did that once, and these guys ran for it. Which tells you where *they* are."

"For how long?" he asked.

"For a while. Two or three weeks, anyway. She's gonna have to make a trip to Dallas. In a couple of weeks, these guys should have figured out that if she had anything, they'd know about it, one way or another."

He looked at me for a few seconds, a steady gaze, and finally nodded: "You're lying a little. But if that's the basic idea of what's going on, I'll take the job."

Green got a hard-shell suitcase out of his car and I cleared out of the guest room. "I'll get a room in LuEllen's motel tonight," I said. "It'll have a clean phone line. I'll get with Bobby about AmMath and we'll start looking for Firewall."

"Okay," Lane said. She reached out and touched the .357 on the table. Green asked, "You know how to use that?"

"I just shot a big stack of phone books down in the basement," she said. "LuEllen told me if I need to, just point it and keep pulling the trigger until I run out of bullets."

Green sighed and said, "Nuts."

I wasn't sure I liked leaving them alone in Lane's house. If they were targets, they were just sitting there. It's easy to get lost in America, for a few days or weeks, anyway, and if you try hard enough, *nobody* can find you. But sitting ducks . . .

There was a momentary awkwardness while I was checking into the motel. LuEllen and I had spent quite a bit of time together, and probably would again in the future, and she wasn't involved with anybody and I wasn't *that* involved, but the awkwardness went away and I checked into a separate room. She came down ten minutes later with a couple of beers while I was talking to a guy named Rufus Carr in Atlanta.

"How's Monger doing?" I asked Rufus.

"You're talking to a pentamillionaire," he said.

"I don't know what that is."

"I got five million bucks in the bank, m' boy," he said. Rufus was a fat red-haired man who affected a bad W. C. Fields accent. "Until I have to pay taxes, anyway."

"It works?" I asked.

"Of course it works; I told you it'd work."

"I knew that," I said.

"Yeah, bullshit. You were one of the naysayers. You were one of the guys who said Rufus was going to be eating frozen cheese pizza for the rest of his life. Well, I'll tell you what, pal, it's nothing but order-out pepperoni and mushroom from now on. And a private booth at Taco Bell."

"I've got a favor to ask. Could you mong some stuff for me?"

"On what?"

"You know about Firewall?"

"Yeah?"

"The rumors are weird. Could you just pick up a few of the bigger sites where you see the rumors, and mong them?"

"Is there any money in it?" he asked.

"Fuck, no. But I won't burn your house down."

"Well, thank you, General Sherman. Am I going to get in trouble?"

"I doubt it," I said. "But this whole Firewall thing is getting totally out of hand."

"You're right; it's my patriotic duty. Besides, I'm not doing anything else."

"Can I call you tomorrow?"

"Sure. I'll put it on the trail right now, and get it back tomorrow morning," he said.

W hat's 'mong'?" LuEllen asked, when I hung up. She was sitting on the bed with a beer bottle.

"Monger. It's a rumor-tracking program," I said. "Rufus built it for some securities companies. They use it to bust day traders who try to spread rumors to move the stock market."

"It works?"

"Hell, he's a pentamillionaire," I said.

N ext I got back onto Bobby: he had some preliminary company stuff on AmMath, mostly public information pulled out of various open databases. More interesting was his news on Firewall.

Got a new list supposedly with Firewall. They are: exdeus, fillyjonk, fleece, ladyfingers, neoxellos, omeomi, pixystyx. Friends give me two hard IDs near you. Fleece is Jason B. Currier, 12548 Baja Viejo, Santa Cruz. Omeomi is Clarence Mason of 3432 LaCoste Road in Petaluma.

We'd gotten a map with the car; I went out and got it, and checked. Mason was maybe an hour or an hour and a half away, up north of San Francisco in Marin County. Currier was practically across the street. All part of the Silicon Valley culture that's grown up around San Francisco like a bunch of magic mushrooms.

"So we're gonna find these guys," LuEllen said.

"First thing tomorrow."

I 'm not an easy sleeper; I kicked around the bed overnight, getting a couple of hours here and another hour there, with fifteen minutes of wide-awake worrying in between. I don't like big, arrogant organizations that push people around, or manipulate them, or extort them—but I don't see it as my personal obligation to stop them. I just go my own way. I fish and paint and lie in the sunshine like a lizard. I might steal something from one of them, from time to time, software or schematics or business plans, but I'm very careful about it.

The whole AmMath business was not my style. I liked Jack Morrison. He was a good guy, as far as I knew, but I really didn't know that much about him. Maybe that whole thing about "k" was bullshit; maybe he made it up to pull me into whatever he was doing at AmMath. Maybe *he* put the rumors out. And Lane herself was a computer freak: maybe she was involved with Firewall.

But if not, "k" was cause for concern. It was not a computer identity as such, it was just an initial, and there may be ten thousand people on the Net who sign themselves with a k. The same with Bobby and Stanford—there are probably a thousand Stanfords out on the Net. And I would imagine that there are quite a few people calling themselves Fleece, although omeomi is not quite as generic. The troubling thing was the *grouping*. I had heard most of those names at one time or another. I even knew what a couple of them did, although I didn't know who they were.

Computer people, a lot of them, have the same attitude I do toward bigness, toward bureaucracy, toward being pounded into round holes. They don't like it. Maybe there was a Firewall, and maybe some of these people were in it, and because *they* were, then *I* was suspect . . .

Paranoia is good for you, if you're a crook; but it doesn't make life any easier.

9

ST. JOHN CORBEIL

Corbeil was intent. Not angry, not stunned, not confused. Focused.

"I don't know where she got them, but she apparently knew they were important because she made copies," Hart was saying. His voice was distant, tinny, with traffic in the background. He was calling from a payphone in San Jose.

A television was mounted on the wall opposite Corbeil's desk. One of the talking heads on CNBC was chattering about the newest disaster on the NASDAQ and the New York Stock Exchange. "MUTING" was printed across his face in green letters, like a TV-chip editorial.

"If she had access . . ." Corbeil began, speaking to Hart.

"We know she had access . . . goddamnit, nothing is clear," Hart said.

"Make it clear," Corbeil snapped. "What's the problem?"

"She had four Jaz disks that probably came out of our supply room," Hart said. "They have that blue OEM tint to the cases, and we assume that her brother stole them to make his copies. But on the other four disks, the cases are clear plastic—not ours. We looked in the wastebaskets and found a receipt from CompUSA, which shows that she bought three three-packs of Jaz disks. Nine disks. We found one set of four disks in clear cases—the copies—and one blank disk in a clear case . . ."

"Which means four are missing, and that's the exact number you'd need for another set of copies," Corbeil said, picking up on it instantly. "Goddamnit. Where are they?"

"That's the problem. We don't know. I can only think of one reason that she even made another set of copies."

"For security reasons. She ditched them somewhere."

"Yes. That's what we think," Hart said. "We don't know exactly why she'd go to the trouble, though. The thing is, you can't load an OMS file unless you have five hundred megs of memory. Not without making the computer go crazy. Her home computer had three hundred eighty-four megs, and her laptop has one hundred twenty-eight. Neither one had any of the files from the Jaz drive on it—not even the small files."

"So what are you saying? That she never looked at them?"

"Not at home," Hart said. "She could have taken them to her university office, except that we've been cruising her place almost since she got here, and as far as we know, she hasn't been to the university. So the question is, if she doesn't even know what's on the disks, why'd she make all those copies? If she did?"

"Could you take a look at her office?"

"Doubtful. It's right off a college computer lab, and there are *always* people around there, day and night. Not right in her office, but up and down the hall and around the lab."

"We've got to get those disks, before she does something with them."

"We don't know what to do, other than watch her. We could snatch her, and squeeze the disks out of her, but, man . . . if she disappeared, that might be one too many accidents even for the Dallas police. Also, there's been a guy hanging around with her, maybe a boyfriend or something. It's like she doesn't want to be alone."

Corbeil thought for a long time, Hart waiting through the pause. As he thought, with the CNBC mimes doing their silent chat opposite his desk, it occurred to Corbeil that he'd like to fuck every single one of the reporting women, but as for stock information, he wouldn't trust any of them as far as he could spit a rat. That was not a coincidence, he thought. That was marketing. He wrenched himself back to the problem: "So keep an eye on her. Monitor her."

Hart was disappointed; Corbeil could hear it in his voice. He didn't say "That's it?" but he wanted to. Instead, he said, "We can't really hang around her neighborhood, but if you want to cough up a couple of grand, in cash, I can put a bug on her car. At least we'll know where she goes."

"Do it. I'll send the cash through American Express. I'll find out where the local office is out there, and you'll have the money in a couple of hours. How long will it take you to get the bug?"

"Probably tomorrow. I'll have to call around."

"Good," Corbeil said. "One other thing. I want you to start e-mailing reports to me. I've set up a new account called, um, *Arclight*. A-R-C-L-I-G-H-T. Regular number. Tell me that you're monitoring them, that you're watching them, and ask for advice. I'll send one back that tells you to watch them for another week, to see if they make any contacts that seem to reflect an association with Firewall. We can discuss the feasibility of going to the FBI. Don't be overly dramatic, but mention something about national security. We want to sound ethically challenged in the defense of the good old USA."

"Building a paper trail?"

"Exactly. Give me a note or two every day, reporting on the surveillance. Maybe even suggest that we might want to get an ex-FBI guy to do a black-bag job, but I'll turn you down on that."

"All right. I'll get Benson to chip in a report."

"Read it first. He's not the brightest bulb in the chandelier."

When Hart was off the line, Corbeil leaned back in his chair, made a steeple with his fingers, and thought about it. Hart's memos would be useful in a couple of different ways. If everything went smoothly, and they either recovered the disks or discovered there was no second copy, then the memos could stay in the files just as Hart sent them.

If, on the other hand, the situation got out of control, the memos could be altered to show an illegal operation running inside Am-Math. The memos could be altered without changing the time stamp on them, and a check of the phone records would show the matching calls coming and going . . .

Since the Arclight file had been opened from the computer in Tom Woods's office, it would be at least credible that Corbeil didn't know about it; especially if Woods wasn't around to testify.

That's all Corbeil would need: a level of credibility, and the silence of contrary witnesses.

And a good lawyer, of course.

10

Since I couldn't sleep anyway, I kicked LuEllen out of bed at six-thirty and we went to look for Clarence Mason. We stopped at a diner for cholesterol and caffeine, got clogged in traffic heading into San Francisco, crossed the Golden Gate at eight o'clock, and after a bit of wandering, LuEllen ran into a gas station and got a guess on the location of LaCoste Road. Mason's place was a small dark-green bungalow with an old-style two-track drive. Nobody home.

"Why didn't I think of that?" I said, back in the car. "Most people work during the day." We went out to a phone, and I hooked up the laptop and got online with Bobby. Mason, he said, had his own photography business in Santa Rosa. We found him on the second floor of a downtown building, above a flower store: Mason Restorations.

The office door looked like it might open on a detective office from a noir movie—textured glass with a gold-leaf name. Inside, it was all windows, blond hardwood floors, and high-tech machinery. The place had two rooms—a big working space behind the counter at the entrance, and a small glassed-in office at the far end, along the window wall. The working space was occupied by a half-dozen top-end Macs, a number of film and flatbed scanners and several large color printers. Three women were looking at a computer screen when we pushed through the door; one of them straightened and walked over to the counter.

"Can I help you?" she asked.

"We're here to see Mr. Mason."

"Do you have an appointment?"

"No, but it's fairly urgent." A thirtyish blond man had looked up from a computer inside the glassed-in office; I was willing to bet he was Mason. "Could you tell him we're friends of Bobby?"

"We really need to talk to him," LuEllen said from my shoulder, with a smile.

"Just a minute, please."

She walked back to the glassed-in office, stuck her head inside, and said something; I could see the blond's head bobbing. She motioned to us, and we pushed through the counter gate and down to the office. The woman rejoined the other two, who were looking at the yellowed image of an old woman, apparently scanned from a paper photograph.

Mason stood up, looking unhappy. "I'm not sure if we know the same Bobby . . ."

"If you go online and call him, he'll tell you we're all right," I said.

He swallowed and said, "I'm not online much anymore. . . . Who are you?"

"You saw the list of the people in Firewall? I'm k."

He sat down, and sat perfectly still for a moment, except for his bobbing Adam's apple, then said, "I've heard a couple of things about you . . . if you're really k. Did you once have a contract with a wine company to help straighten out their distribution system?"

"Yes."

"Then you know my friend Clark," he said.

"Miller," I said. "He lives in St. Helena in a redwood house with a real redwood hot tub in back, and his wife's name is . . . Tom."

"Ex-wife," Mason said. "She got the house." He looked at LuEllen and said, "Close the door." LuEllen pushed the door shut and we sat down in a couple of wooden visitors' chairs. Mason pushed both hands through his hair and said, "This Firewall—I don't know anything about it, but my name is all over the place. It's driving me crazy. What's going on? I keep waiting for the FBI to show up."

I looked at LuEllen, who shook her head. To Mason, I said, "Goddamnit. You don't know *anything?*"

He spread his hands: "Honest to God, I was sitting at my kitchen table reading the paper and eating shredded wheat and scanning this article on the Lighter killing, and all of a sudden I see this list with my name in it—omeomi. I almost choked to death. I never *heard* of Firewall before this thing. Now I'm supposed to be some sort of terrorist."

"Yeah. Me, too. And Bobby. We're trying to figure out what's going on."

Mason looked at LuEllen again. "Are you on the list?"

"No. I'm just a friend. Of k's and Bobby's."

Mason shook his head. "I don't know what to do. I've thought about calling the FBI and identifying myself, but . . . I don't know, I don't think that's a good idea."

"I don't know your history," I said. "I might wait a while before dragging in the law."

"Yeah. So would I." He wasn't a tough-looking guy, but the way he said it suggested a need to stay away from the feds. As a matter of privacy, ethics, and personality, I didn't ask him what he did; LuEllen wasn't so inhibited.

"So what'd you do as omeomi, hold up banks?"

She can be so perky, when she wants, that it works an odd magic on men, especially technics, who have residual fantasies about cheerleaders. That's what I hear anyway. Mason showed a small grin and said, "No, nothing like that. I do . . . specialty photography."

"Jeez. When people say that, I usually think porno," LuEllen said.

"It's not porno," he said.

"You guys should talk sometime," I said to LuEllen. "You could trade tips."

"You do photography?" Now he was a little more interested. "What kind?"

"Specialty," she said.

He actually chuckled, leaned back and stretched. "That's the best kind, isn't it?"

We sat in silence for a couple of minutes, and then I said, "Well . . . we better go."

"What are you doing?" he asked. "Just checking out whoever you can find from the list?"

"That's the idea. Between Bobby and me, on the original list of names, we knew a few people. None of us are involved with Firewall. Then Bobby tracked down you and one other guy . . . through friends, I guess. We haven't checked with the other guy, but your story is like the rest of ours."

"What're you gonna do if you find them? Firewall?"

"I don't know. Bobby thinks we ought to turn them in. If they did the Lighter thing, anyway."

"Do it," he said. "Find 'em, and fuck 'em."

Currier lived in an apartment in Santa Cruz. Again, nobody home, and Bobby hadn't been able to find a job for him. I checked with the manager, telling her that I was an old friend in the area for a day. "He's gone to Mexico, on vacation," she said.

"When did he leave?"

"Last week. He said he'd be gone for three weeks. Too bad you missed him."

Now what?" LuEllen asked, as we walked away.

"Back to Rufus. He's three hours ahead of us—let's see if Monger worked."

"What do you think about Currier?"

"He might be running. He's on the list; maybe he's got reason to run."

"Like you."

"Like all of us."

Monger *had* worked. "A lot of the traffic was out of individual computers from about ten major sites—all colleges, all easy to get into," Rufus said. "It looks like somebody went looking for on-line computers, planted a rumor message in a virus that dumped it into AOL message boards and other places like that. In the days before the rumors started, a lot of those ten sites had some extended traffic with a server in Laurel, Maryland."

"How *much* before the rumors started?"

"Week or so. That's about as far back as I can get, before the universe gets too large for Monger."

"A week or so."

"That's what it looks like. Does this help?"

"I have to think about it," I said.

B obby came back with some info about AmMath, and the guy who ran it.

St. John Corbeil was a smart guy, a guy who quit the Marine Corps as a major and moved to the National Security Agency. He worked for the NSA for another five years, doing nothing that Bobby could find out about, except getting an advanced degree in software design. After a five-year hitch at NSA, he quit, moved to Dallas, and started his own high-tech encryption-products firm. He'd taken a half-dozen NSA encryption, math, and software specialists with him. The company had done well, coming along with its product line just at the beginning of the Internet boom. Corbeil was reasonably rich, with his ten percent of AmMath stock and his CEO's spot.

I don't understand any of that encryption shit," LuEllen said.

"Like this," I said. "Suppose you wanted to send me an Internet note that said, 'Let's sneak into Bill Gates' house and steal his dog.' If strong encryption is allowed, you could run the message through a software package—you'd just push a button—and it would be impossible for anybody to break. *Anybody.* Unless he had the key. No matter how hot-shit somebody else's computers were, they couldn't break it."

"But with the Clipper chip . . ."

"There'd be two keys. I'd have one, and the government would have one. You could send the message, and I'd get it okay, but so would the government. If they were watching."

"We'd get to Bill Gates's house and we'd find a whole bunch of cops waiting."

"And we'd be standing there with our dicks in our hands."

"Or a can of Alpo, in my case," she said.

Jack had had a small house in Santa Cruz, about a mile from Currier's apartment. After he was killed, the FBI had gotten a warrant to go through the place, and Lane told them where to find the keys. The day after the funeral, she'd called to see if she could get back in, and the feds had no objection: they'd turned the place over, and had taken out everything that appeared to be computer-related, along with all his old phone bills, personal correspondence, and so on.

While LuEllen and I were looking up Firewall names, Lane and Green had gone over to the house to look around, and to start cleaning up. That's what Lane had called it. Cleaning up.

What she meant was, throwing away anything that couldn't be sold or given away. All the small pieces of a life—posters, notes, letters, unidentifiable photos; like that. Jack had never had children, so there was nobody to get it, except his sister; nobody to wonder who this ancestor had been, and to sit down in 2050 or 2100 and paw through the remains . . .

When they got back, Green said, "Somebody was there before any of us. Somebody spread the lock on the back door."

"Gotta be the AmMath guys," I said. "Maybe they're happy, since they got the disks from you . . ."

111

What'd you find out about Firewall?" Lane asked.

"Nothing," I said. I ran it down for her.

"This guy who went to Mexico," Green said. "He could have gone for more than one reason. You're assuming he went because he was scared because he was on the list, like Mason. But what if he's running because he *is* with Firewall?"

"I mentioned that," LuEllen said. "Kidd didn't buy it. He's got a theory."

"What's the theory?"

"There is no Firewall," I said. "It's bullshit, made up out of whole cloth."

Then we launched into one of those circular arguments in which you almost feel as though you can grasp what's going on, but there's always one critical piece missing from every possible logical construction. Lane started it.

"Exactly what would that do?" Lane asked. "If somebody made up Firewall, why would they do it?"

"To cover some other reason for killing Lighter?" I suggested.

"They didn't have anything to cover. The police thought it was a mugging. They weren't happy, but I've never heard there was any other big investigation going on, before the Firewall thing came up."

"Clipper II was dying. *Is* dying. Maybe they thought if one of the Clipper II people was killed by hackers, there'd be some kind of groundswell . . ."

"There's not going to be any groundswell," Lane said. "The feds might want Clipper II, but it's too late. Everybody knows it's too late. It doesn't have anything to do with preferences or laws. Trying to get rid of strong encryption and replace it with the Clipper II would be like trying to get rid of pi or the Round Earth Theory. It's *too fucking late.*"

"Then how did all of those names come up all of a sudden? Mine and Bobby's and Jack's and omeomi and the others," I asked. "We *are* linked. If you look at it from the right direction, we *are* a conspiracy, because a lot of us sure as shit have conspired with each other . . ."

"I don't know; I don't know why Firewall came up. I don't know how it ties in. But it seems to. There's something out there, and it's not *totally* made up. Something is happening. And Jack is dead and Lighter is dead . . ."

"But it might just be coincidence . . ."

"How could it possibly be?" She ticked it off on her fingers. "Jack is connected with Clipper II and AmMath and Firewall. Firewall kills Lighter who is connected with Clipper II and AmMath."

"But we can't find a single person who is really connected with Firewall," I said. "Not a single one."

Green asked, "Did Jack know Lighter?"

I shook my head. "Not as far as we know."

"Might be something to check."

I turned to LuEllen, who'd kept her mouth shut during the argument. "What do you think?"

"Three choices," she said.

"Yeah?"

"Look at AmMath. Keeping digging at Firewall. Get the fuck out."

L ane wanted to go after AmMath because of her brother. Green didn't much care; his job was to take care of Lane, which he would do one way or the other. LuEllen was edging toward the door.

"You can't fight a bureaucracy," she said. "You just become a *goal*. They put the goal in memos. It's like trying to argue with the IRS."

But I couldn't quit, not yet. The names were out there, and once the cops started unraveling a few identities, they would probably get them all—and we could get hurt without ever knowing why, or what was happening.

"I *have* to find out more about Firewall," I said. "Just for self-protection. If AmMath's involved, then I'll look into AmMath."

"You're giving up on Jack?" Lane asked. "It sounds like you're giving up."

"No, but we've got to be careful. From what it looks like, Am-Math may be more than some mean-ass private company. Jack may have been messing with something serious—big-time trouble, of the kind we really don't want to know about."

"What does that mean?"

"That means that the only way to get at them would be politics. We find some paper, we sic your senator on them, they do an internal investigation and cough somebody up and disown him. But if Jack was killed by some kind of *operation* . . . that's gonna be tough."

The best thing we could do, I thought, was to run down the Monger information in Maryland. Maybe, with luck, we'd find some fourteen-year-old computer hack at the bottom of the Firewall conspiracy. We could dump him in the lap of the local sheriff, get a good laugh out of the press, and go home.

"Fat chance," LuEllen said.

"It could happen," I said. "It's better than trying to crawl through AmMath's basement window."

"What about Lane?" Green asked.

"Call the Dallas cops and tell them that you're coming out to pick up Jack's computers and whatever other property they seized, that they don't want anymore. But that you've got to close down his home out here first."

"And you guys will be in Maryland doing what?" Lane asked.

"You know," I said. "Looking around."

We flew out of San Francisco the same night. Before we left, when we were at the motel, packing, I went back out to Bobby and told him that we'd be moving to Washington. He booked us business-class seats on an evening flight into National, and a car under one of the phony IDs LuEllen had been using in New York. That ID was more solid than the two we'd picked up in San Francisco, and the credit cards that went with them were definitely good. Bobby had also developed more stuff on Corbeil and AmMath.

Corbeil was a smart guy, but he was also nuts. He spent way too much time thinking about godless socialists, mindless bureaucrats, confiscatory taxation, black agitators, the yellow peril, the red menace, the International Jewish Conspiracy, and the New World Order. He'd been known to allow in public that Hitler had done a lot of good things.

I've never been much interested in politics, but once wrote some do-it-yourself polling that allowed low-rent politicians to do their own telephone polls. I eventually sold off the business, but before I did, I got to know quite a few politicians. They were a pretty lively bunch, no more or less corrupt than schoolteachers, newspaper reporters, cops, or doctors.

Anyway, it didn't take much exposure to politics for me to realize that there are as many nuts on the left as there are on the right, and in the long run, the lefties are probably more dangerous. But in the short run, if you find a guy on top of your hometown clock tower with a cheap Chinese semiauto assault-weapon lookalike, that guy will be one of Corbeil's buddies, dreaming of black helicopters and socialist tanks massing on the Canadian border, preparing to pollute America's vital fluids.

Smart and nuts: Corbeil's description sounded a little like an advertisement for breakfast cereal, but wasn't.

B obby had more about Corbeil's lifestyle, as portrayed by the local city magazines. Corbeil's salary was modest for a CEO, running about $150,000 a year, but then, he also owned a big chunk of AmMath stock. He liked fast cars and blond women; he made a point of being seen with Dallas's flavor-of-the-day model. One of them had been a *Playboy* playmate of the month. Bobby included the centerfold picture.

"Why do they shave their pubic hair into those little stripes?" LuEllen asked.

We contemplated this mystery for a moment; then I said, "Maybe they don't wear OshKosh B'Gosh brand bathing suits, like some people."

"You think?"

LOTS MORE STUFF, I'LL SEND IT AS SOON AS I WEED THROUGH IT. HAVEN'T PICKED OUT AMMATH COMPUTER LINES YET, WILL GET BACK LATER.

ANYTHING ON THE JAZ?

YES. OPENED THE BIG FILES, GOT PHOTOS, VERY HIGH RES. ALL THE SAME PARKING LOT. DON'T UNDERSTAND.

CAN YOU MAKE JPEG, LEAVE IN MY BOX?

YES.

ALSO, COPY OUT JAZ DISKS, OVERNIGHT THEM TO WASH HOTEL.

OK

On the flight, we talked about *What Next*. We didn't know what AmMath was doing, in anything more than a general sense, or why Jack might have been killed, if he wasn't killed exactly like the Am-Math people said he was. I still suspected that Firewall was a phantom.

"Gonna have to spend some more time with Jack's Jaz disks," I said.

"There're only four . . ."

I looked at her. "Four Jaz disks at two gigabytes each," I said. "You could put two thousand pretty fat novels on one of them. We're dealing with as much text as you'd get, say, in eight thousand Tom Clancy novels."

"Whoa."

"A bigger *whoa* than you think." I closed my eyes and held up a finger to indicate that I was thinking. A minute later I had it. "If you broke everything up into texts the size of Clancy novels, and looked in each one of them for one minute, and worked forty hours a week at it, it'd take you better than three weeks to look in all of them."

"For one minute each."

"One minute," I said.

"You're a mathematical fucking marvel," she said.

"That's not the end of the problem," I said. "The biggest part of it is, we don't know what's bullshit and what's not."

We thought about that, and she said, "I see a light at the end of the tunnel."

"Yeah?"

"Yeah. Jack looked for less than a week, and *he* apparently found something."

"Unless they just killed him for trying to take it . . ."

An hour out of Washington, with nothing to do, I got out the tarot deck and did a couple of spreads. LuEllen watched with mixed skepticism and nervousness, and finally said, "Well?"

"Just bullshit," I said. "Confusion."

"Let me cut the deck." I gave the deck a light shuffle, and let her cut it. She cut out the devil card. The devil represents a force of evil, but not usually from the outside, not a standard bad guy. The devil is usually *inside.* He sits on top of you, controlling you, without your even being aware of it.

"That's bad," she said. "I can tell by your face."

11

In the course of my life, I'd spent maybe six months in Washington. Though it might not be fashionable to admit it, I like the place. Usually portrayed as a mass of greed-heads packed liked oiled sardines inside the Beltway, Washington has nice places to walk and good art to look at. People who like central Italy, the *campagna*, would like the rural landscape out in Virginia.

We got into National late, and picked up the car and a map. We wouldn't be right in Washington. According to Rufus, the server we were looking for was in Laurel, which is actually closer to Baltimore—not far, I noticed on the map, from Fort Meade, headquarters of the National Security Agency.

I'd had some dealings with the NSA when I was in the military and I'd always been impressed by two things: their employees' technical expertise and their arrogance. I hadn't had anything to do with the agency for a couple of decades, but because it was so heavily involved in computers, there was always a lot of back-and-forth between NSA computer geeks and the outside computer world.

Word got around, and the word was that the NSA was rapidly becoming obsolete. Once upon a time, agency operatives could tap any phone call or radio transmission in the world; they could put Mao Tse-tung's private words on the president's desk an hour after the Maximum Leader spoke them into his office phone; they could provide real-time intercepts to the special ops people in the military.

No more. The world was rife with unbreakable codes—any good university math department could whip one up in a matter of days. Just as bad, the most critical diplomatic and military traffic had come out of the air and gone underground, into fiber-optic cable. Even if a special forces team managed to get at a cable, messages were routinely encoded with ultrastrong encryption routines.

The NSA was going deaf. And the word was, they didn't know what to do about it. They'd become a bin full of aging bureaucrats worried about their jobs, and spinning further and further out of the Washington intelligence center.

LuEllen and I checked into a Ramada Inn off I-95 near Laurel, Maryland. Separate rooms, under separate IDs, gave us some easy options if there were trouble. In the burglary business, you never know when you might need a bolt-hole.

The next morning, after pancakes and coffee and *The New York Times* for me and *The Wall Street Journal* for LuEllen, we went looking for the server. The T-1 line it used was located in a suburban office complex called the Carter-Byrd Center, building 2233. We found it fifteen minutes from the motel, two rows of four, two-story yellow-brick buildings, facing each other, behind small parking lots, on a dead-end street.

The tenants were professional services companies: accountants, financial advisors, a legal publishing firm, a title company, and several law firms. Most of them occupied an entire floor or building wing. The company we were looking for, Bloch Technology, was one of the small companies, grouped with other smaller companies, in a suite of offices in the end building on the right.

LuEllen, dressed in a dark blue business suit and navy low heels, clipped her miniature Panasonic movie camera into her briefcase, gave me a hot little kiss on the lips—going into a job always turned her on—and headed for 2233 to do the first reconnaissance. I waited in the car.

The idea was, she was looking for one of the other companies in Carter-Byrd, but got the building wrong. She'd be inside, we thought, for two or three minutes.

Fifteen minutes after she'd disappeared through the double glass doors, I was about ready to go in after her. Then she walked back outside, with a guy in a short-sleeved white shirt, who pointed up the hill toward the first building. She nodded, and they talked for a few more seconds, she laughed, patted his arm, and started for the car. I slumped a little lower in the passenger seat. The guy watched her go; he wasn't watching her shoulders.

As she came up to the car, I slumped another six inches. She climbed into the driver's seat, fired it up, backed out of the parking space, and we headed up the hill. "He's back inside," she said, as we pulled away.

I pushed myself up. "That took a while."

"I knocked on the door—it's got a Vermond combination pad, not alarmed—and asked where Clayton Accounting was, and we got to chatting," she said. "Those computer people are amazing. They've got all these interesting machines."

"Really."

"Really. He's got five of them. They look like air conditioners, all lined up in the back room."

"Two rooms?"

"Three. One is a standard office, one has the computers, one has a futon on the floor and a miniature refrigerator where he keeps his Cokes."

"Is he in there alone?"

"There're two desks, but one of them looks pretty unused—like maybe a part-timer. I got the phone number."

She'd pissed me off a little by casually talking to the guy. "We're gonna have to do a really light break. If we screw anything up, he'll remember talking to you. He'll remember your face."

"I thought it was worth the effort. And you know what? There is *no* security. The rest rooms are on the second floor. I went into the ladies' room, and there's a drop ceiling, but it's a mess above it. If we went up, and anybody came in to clean up . . . they'd know."

"So what do we do?"

"I'm thinking about it."

"All right." I looked at my watch. "Let's go get some deodorant, and then we can hang out for the day. You can think."

We found a drugstore, and I bought a travel-sized can of a woman's deodorant, the kind that advertises actual freshening powder in its spray, and a couple of Cokes. We drank the Cokes on the way back to Carter-Byrd. This time, LuEllen slumped in the seat while I went inside, carrying her briefcase so I looked like I had a reason to be there.

The building was essentially a long string of business offices opening off central hallways that ran the length of the building.

There was nobody in the hall when I walked inside, and I made a left, slipped the deodorant can out of my pocket, and gave it a couple of shakes. Bloch Technology was the third door on the left. I spotted the keypad as I came up, looked both ways, and then gave it a thorough spraying with the deodorant. I waved my hand in the air a couple of times to disperse the smell as best I could, then headed back out. Total time in the building, less than one minute. Total people encountered, none.

"So let's go hang out," I said.

We hung out, more or less; I took her to a driving range, where she hit golf balls, and very well, with a five-iron older than she was, and with a three-wood that was not only wood, but was no bigger than her fist. I did some quick sketches of her swing. Later, we caught a movie, and in between, I got back to Bobby, who had what he called a curiosity: a sudden spate of rumors on the Net that Firewall was planning a major attack. Bobby knew about Rufus and the Monger; I suggested that he call Rufus and have him trace the latest round of rumors. And I had a new question of my own, that popped into my head just as we were signing off. Bobby said:

WILL TRACE RUMORS SOONEST.

OK.

CALL TONIGHT.

YES. NEW THOUGHT: LOOK AT AIRLINES. SEE IF JM FLEW IN DAYS BEFORE HE WAS KILLED.

YES. WILL ALSO CHECK GAS CARD. ALSO, JPEG IN YOUR BOX.

THANKS.

I downloaded the JPEG, which is a picture format, and saved it to examine later. After the movie, which sucked, LuEllen pointed me at a sporting goods store, where she bought a spool of black monofilament fishing line called Spider Wire. We went back to the motel, looked at the movies she'd made that morning at Bloch—five Dell servers sitting on heavy plastic benches with a monitor and keyboard off to the side—then had a slow dinner at a fast diner. The nerves were getting on top of me, like they always do. After dinner, we went back to the motel, picked up her bag, and at seven o'clock, when it was good and dark, we were back at Carter-Byrd.

There were maybe forty offices in 2233. Seven or eight still showed lights—Americans work all the time, no getting around it. Bloch Technology was not one of the lighted offices; Bloch's futon was only a tiny cloud on the horizon.

We took the end space in the parking lot, and LuEllen tied one end of the Spider Wire around the steering wheel, led the line out through the window, across the lawn to the door. She checked to make sure that nobody was coming from inside; she did a quick knot on the outside door handle, cut the line at the spool, and strolled back to the car. When she was back, and inside, she pulled the line tight, until it stretched, absolutely invisible, directly across the sidewalk to the door.

"Now, if somebody wants to use the sidewalk, they'll simply have to go around," I said. "Either that, or garrote themselves."

"If somebody comes, we cut the string. It flies halfway back across the yard, and nobody sees it."

"Did you ever do this before?"

"No, but I read about it."

We sat in the lot for twenty minutes before the door opened: and the rest worked just like LuEllen thought it would. The guy pushed through the door and walked away, headed toward his car in the parking lot. She put pressure on the door as it slid closed . . .

"Gotta hurry," she grunted. "I don't know if the line'll hold. The door's heavier than I thought."

"Hang on, hang on . . ." I didn't want the guy who was leaving to see me get out of the car. When he was up the hill, I hurried across the lawn. She'd stopped the door just as it touched the doorpost. I pulled it open, and snapped the line off the handle. We were in.

LuEllen had programmed Bloch's phone number into her cell phone earlier in the evening, and dialed the number as she got out of the car. The hallway leading past Bloch Tech was empty. I walked to the door, LuEllen close behind, and mimed a knock: we could hear the phone ringing inside. No answer.

As I mimed another knock, LuEllen turned off her phone and pointed a little battery-operated black light, the kind teenagers used to buy in head shops, at the keypad. The powdery crystals in the de- odorant fluoresced in the light—except for the three that had no powdery crystals.

"Four-six-seven," she said. "But there are four digits in a Ver- mond lock. In this model. So they repeated one of them."

Nobody in the hall: I took a dime notebook out of my pocket and began scrawling number combinations as quickly as I could write, calling them out as I jotted them down. The thing about number pads is, with ten digits, there are 10,000 possible combinations. Get- ting inside with a brute-force attack is tough. And a few locks, but not this one, were alarmed, or would lock up, after a certain number of incorrect combinations. Then they could only be opened with a key.

But if you know the four digits involved in the combination . . . ah, then there were only twenty-four possible combinations. If one of the digits is repeated, like it was here, and you don't know which, the number goes up to thirty-six. But most people start their combination with the lowest number, in this case, a four. We started with four- four-six-seven, and went to four-four-seven-six, and to four-six-four- seven, and so on. We were lucky, hit it on the eighth combination, and pushed into the darkened office.

125

"Gloves," LuEllen said.

We pulled on vinyl gloves, and followed the hair-thin beams of the flashlights into the server room. The Dell servers looked like five little dwarfs, lined up for breakfast; the room was windowless, and windowless was good. The futon was rolled into a corner of the third room, with a fuzzy blue blanket tossed carelessly on top of it. LuEllen, using her flash, found a roll of tape in the outer office, and brought the blanket into the server room. We taped the blanket to the wall so it covered the door, and then LuEllen slipped under the blanket into the outer office, and closed the door behind her. I pulled the blanket so it covered the door completely, and turned on the light.

"Light's on," I said. Then I turned if off, and LuEllen pushed back inside.

"Almost perfect," she said. "There was a little tiny dot of light near the right corner . . ."

We rearranged the blanket and I went to work on the machines. Servers are nothing but specialized computers, optimized for communications and storage. If you've got a relatively modern home computer, you could use *that* as a small server, with the right software. In this raid, we wouldn't be going after the content inside the servers. We wanted access, rather than content. I spent twenty minutes pawing through Bloch's software and service-maintenance manuals, and then got into the servers themselves. They were running on a standard off-the-shelf UNIX server package. I had root in five minutes, with an outside maintenance account. Then I dumped in a little access program of my own; I've done this before. After checking it, I shut down local access, turned the light off again, pulled down the blanket, and cleaned up the tape.

While I was working on the machine, LuEllen had been going through paper files in the outer office, using her flash. "All bullshit," she said. "Tax forms, bank statements, advertisements."

One of the forms listed Toby Bloch as owner of 100 percent of Bloch Technology stock. "Is that the guy you talked to?" I asked. I crumpled up the blanket and tossed it back on the futon, more or less as it had been.

"That's the guy. Toby."

"All right. Nice little business he has here . . ."

With everything back in place, we listened at the door, heard nothing, and walked out; out to the car, and we were gone. Nothing to it.

B ut there was trouble back at the ranch. I wouldn't go online with the server until after midnight, when there was less chance that the real system operator was online. Instead, I checked with Bobby, to see if he had anything more on Jack Morrison or Firewall.

He did.

> LOOK AT NEWS PROGRAMS. FIREWALL ATTACKS IRS WITH DoS. BIG TROUBLE NOW. ATTACK MAYBE STARTS IN SWITZERLAND. STYLE FEELS GERMAN.
>
> **WILL LOOK. ANYTHING ON JM?**
>
> JM FLIES TO BALTIMORE-WASHINGTON INTERNATIONAL ON MONDAY BEFORE SHOOTING, RETURNS SAME NIGHT. RENTED HERTZ, 64 MILES. NO MORE DETAIL. ALSO FLIES TO BWI ON THURSDAY AFTERNOON BACK FRIDAY MORNING. NO CAR, NO HOTEL ON CARD.
>
> **THANKS. WILL LOOK AT NEWS.**
>
> THIS IS *VERY* DANGEROUS.
>
> **LATER.**

I thought about that until LuEllen said, "What?"

"Jack Morrison was in town the night Lighter was killed," I said.

"That's not good."

"No. But Lane's lecture about Jack and guns . . . that's still pretty straight. I still can't see Jack shooting anyone."

"What's this about the IRS?"

"I don't know," I said.

"Bobby seems more worried about that than about Jack."

"Jack's dead," I said.

I checked the *Times* and *Washington Post* online editions, but they had nothing on the attack on the IRS. CNN had a story, but like a lot of CNN stuff, most of it seemed to have been garbled by a mentally challenged paranoiac; I clicked over to *The Wall Street Journal,* which had a short item.

> A DENIAL-OF-SERVICE (DoS) COMPUTER ATTACK AIMED AT THE INTERNAL REVENUE SERVICE HAS CAUSED A MAJOR DISRUPTION IN THE HANDLING OF END-OF-QUARTER BUSINESS TAX FILINGS, AN IRS SPOKESMAN CONFIRMED THIS AFTERNOON.
>
> THE ATTACK, WHICH BEGAN THIS MORNING, IS CONTINUING. THE ATTACKING GROUP HAS IDENTIFIED ITSELF AS "FIREWALL."
>
> A DENIAL-OF-SERVICE ATTACK ATTEMPTS TO FLOOD THE TARGET WITH HUGE NUMBERS OF LEGITIMATE-LOOKING TRANSACTIONS, EVENTUALLY OVERWHELMING THE TARGET COMPUTER'S ABILITY TO COPE WITH THE NUMBERS.
>
> WHILE OFFICIAL DEPARTMENT OF JUSTICE SOURCES SAID THAT THE ATTACK IS LIMITED, ONE HIGH-LEVEL IRS OFFICIAL, WHO ASKED NOT TO BE IDENTIFIED, SAID THAT THERE HAS BEEN A MAJOR DISRUPTION OF END-OF-BUSINESS-QUARTER TAX FILINGS. HE SAID THAT "TENS OF THOUSANDS" OF BUSINESS QUARTERLY RETURNS WERE INVOLVED AND SAID THAT THE ATTACK SEEMED TO BE SPREADING.

AN FBI SPOKESMAN SAID THAT MANY OF THE DoS CALLS APPEAR
TO BE COMING FROM SMALL-COLLEGE COMPUTER LABS.

"WHAT APPARENTLY HAPPENED IS THAT SOME INDIVIDUAL OR
GROUP PLANTED SMALL ATTACK PROGRAMS INSIDE THESE OPEN
COMPUTERS, AND DESIGNED THEM TO GO OFF AT THE SAME TIME. WE
ARE GETTING IN TOUCH WITH THESE SCHOOLS AS WE IDENTIFY THEM,
ASKING THAT THEY GO OFF-LINE LONG ENOUGH TO REMOVE THE
PROGRAMS FROM THEIR COMPUTERS. MOST OF THEM HAVE NO IDEA
THAT THEIR COMPUTERS ARE PARTICIPATING IN THE ATTACK," FBI
SPOKESMAN LARRY CONNERS SAID.

CONNERS SAID THAT THE ATTACK PROGRAM IS AN
UNSOPHISTICATED ONE, BUT THE IRS OFFICIAL SAID THAT IT TAKES
ADVANTAGE OF THE FACT THAT THE IRS COMPUTERS MUST BE OPEN TO
THE OUTSIDE TO RECEIVE LEGITIMATE TAX RETURNS. THE ATTACK IN-
VOLVES SENDING AND RESENDING HUNDREDS OF LEGITIMATE-LOOKING,
BUT SLIGHTLY FLAWED RETURNS, WHICH THE IRS COMPUTERS THEN
ATTEMPT TO RETURN TO THE SENDER. AS THE VOLUME BUILT, THE
COMPUTERS WERE NO LONGER CAPABLE OF HANDLING THE FLOW OF
TRAFFIC.

"INDIVIDUALLY, THE ATTACK FILINGS WOULDN'T BE A PROBLEM;
THE PROBLEM IS THAT THEY JUST KEEP COMING, OVER AND OVER,
FROM SO MANY DIFFERENT SOURCES," THE IRS SOURCE SAID.

THE FBI'S CONNERS SAID THAT THE ATTACK MAY HAVE STARTED
IN SWITZERLAND, WITH THE ATTACK PROGRAMS PLANTED AS LONG AS A
MONTH AGO . . .

"If the attack isn't sophisticated . . ."

"It's not sophisticated, but a fire ant isn't sophisticated either," I
said. "But you get a few thousand of them swarming up your shorts,
and you've got a problem. If the feds get really pissed, and start ham-
mering on that list of names, who knows where it'll end?"

"There've been other attacks like this. I read about one in *Newsweek*."

"Yeah, but there's a huge difference," I said. "Before, they were messing with private businesses. The politicians' public attitude was, well, that's too bad, but the real feeling was, *fuck a bunch of private businesses*—those guys got too much money anyway. But now, these guys are messing with the *politicians'* money . . ."

"Ah."

"Yeah. Big 'Ah.' "

The JPEG photo that Bobby sent me was still on my hard drive. I opened it, and took a look. A parking lot, apparently taken from a fairly high angle. Three men in suits were walking across a parking lot full of pickup trucks. All three of them were carrying briefcases, and one had his face turned up toward the camera. The resolution of the JPEG was not high enough to make out the faces. All of the photos, Bobby had said, were the same.

"So who are they?" LuEllen asked.

"I don't know."

"If the picture's important . . . it must be that the three shouldn't be together. You know, like a gangster and a cop."

"Or a Chinese and an American," I said. "Look at this guy . . . there's something about him that looks Oriental."

"Shape of his face . . . unless it's a woman."

"Huh. I don't know." And I didn't.

Late that night I went into Bloch Tech's server. There's so much stuff in a server, even a small one, that there's no real-time, hands-on way to sort through it—it's not like flipping through a book. It's like flipping through a library, like trying to make sense of Jack's disks.

I did a search for references to Firewall, and found several hundred in saved e-mail and in postings on Web sites. Six accounts seemed to have a lot of traffic about Firewall. I went into the administrative files, pulled the accounts, and copied out names and addresses. As I finished, I noticed a peculiarity: they were all new accounts, they'd all signed up in the last two weeks, and they'd all paid the up-front minimum of three months by check, rather than opting for credit-card payments.

"Damn it, I'll bet the names are fakes," I told LuEllen. I saved the names. I could ship them to Bobby later, and have him look them up.

Since I had the administrative files up, I checked for Jack Morrison and came up empty; then, on the off-chance, I checked Terrence Lighter, and got a surprise. Lighter had an account on this server, and better yet, his e-mail had dozens of letters. A few were encrypted, so I skipped over those. Most of the rest were letters to and from collectors and dealers in antique scientific instruments, apparently a hobby of his.

And there was one letter that said, unencrypted and in the clear, the Sunday before last:

MR. MORRISON. I WILL SEE YOU TOMORROW AT MY OFFICE AT 8:30. PLEASE BRING THE FILES WITH YOU. THANK YOU. T. L. LIGHTER.

12

At three in the morning—midnight Pacific time—I called Lane. Green answered the phone and said, "We got somebody on us."

"What do you mean?"

"Somebody watching. Not close, but they're around. It's almost like being paranoid, but I've seen one car—it's green, and I think it's a Camry—a few too many times, and a face looking toward us. Always a couple of blocks away."

"What do you think?"

"We need to get out of here. If we can lose them, I'd feel a lot easier. Here, we're pinned like butterflies."

"Okay. We've got a couple more things to do here, but we'll be in Dallas the day after tomorrow. Or the day after that, not later than. You could surprise them somehow, get out to the airport, ditch the car, get on a plane."

"What if they've got people in Dallas?"

"Fly to Seattle first," I suggested.

"All right; I'll talk to Lane about it."

"How is she?"

"Antsy. But here, you talk to her."

Lane came on and I told her about Jack and Lighter, that Jack may have found something at AmMath that needed Lighter's attention. She didn't immediately pick up on the problem of the second trip.

"I knew something was going on," she said. "If Jack was talking to this guy, and this guy was killed, then we've got to tell somebody. This proves it. That something was going on with AmMath."

"It doesn't prove anything in particular," I said. "And the second trip—that's a problem."

"I don't see a problem. The guy—"

"They'll say Jack shot him," I said.

That stopped her only for a few seconds: "But we know he didn't," she argued. "He wouldn't do that."

"They've got a gun in Texas that was stolen in San Jose years ago. They've got witnesses who say he was the shooter, and one of those witnesses took a bullet in the chest. Now, if they ever get around to looking, they can show that he flew into Baltimore late in the afternoon—after working hours—and flew back the next morning. His NSA contact was murdered right in the middle of that time period, and he never said a word about it to anyone."

That stopped her for a little longer: "Okay. That sounds bad. When you put it that way. But maybe he didn't even know about it . . ."

"There's another problem. If we pass information to the FBI . . . where did we get it?"

"We could finesse that. An anonymous call from Dallas . . ."

"All right, we could figure something out. Maybe we'll do it. But later. When the information doesn't look so incriminating. Or when there's something else to go with it."

H ow are the burns?" I asked.

"The bad ones are peeling, like a heavy tan. The lighter ones are almost gone. Not much pain anymore. Everything itches like crazy."

"Have you talked to the Dallas cops again?"

"Yup. The lead detective of the case called today and wanted me to fly out. I told him it'd be a couple of days yet and got on his case about AmMath again."

"How're you fixed for cash?" I asked.

"I'm okay. You need some?"

"No. But get Green to use his credit cards when you go to Dallas, and give him cash to pay him back. They don't know who he is, so they won't be able to track him using his credit cards. Take your cell phone."

"Of course. Where're you guys going?"

"We've got some more research to do here and then we'll hook up with you in Dallas. Stay with the phone . . ."

I have never been a particularly good sleeper. My sleep/wake cycle is about twenty-five hours long, so I tend to push the clock around, until I'm sleeping all day and working all night. Then I just keep pushing. In any case, seven hours is about right: anything shorter than that and I tend to get grumpy.

I got fairly grumpy when LuEllen ran her cold fingers up my spine at eight o'clock in the morning; I nearly bounced off the ceiling, which she thought was moderately hilarious.

"You're gonna give me a fuckin' heart attack some day," I snarled at her, and there were some teeth behind the snarl. I didn't like her sneaking up on me. "How'd you get in?"

"The lock is shit," she said.

"Wonderful, that's just fuckin' great. You give me an aneurysm because you want somebody to talk to at breakfast."

"No, no. I had some seriously bad news to share with you, but you're being such a mean asshole that I'm not going to do it," she said. She crossed her arms.

"What news?"

"Say please."

"Give me the fuckin' news or I'll breathe on you."

"The feds busted Bobby," she said.

"What?" The news left me completely disoriented. "Where'd you get this? Who called?"

"It's on TV. They busted him last night and he'll be arraigned today in federal court in New Orleans. They say he's involved in the attacks on the IRS and that the attacks are continuing."

"Sonofabitch." I fumbled the TV remote off the nightstand and punched up CNN. At the same time, I asked LuEllen, "Did you bring the cold phone?"

"Yeah."

CNN was doing an advertisement for itself. When they got back to news, they were doing the weather. I hopped out of bed, got my notebook, and used the cold phone to punch up John Smith's phone number in Longstreet. John answered on the first ring; he was wide-awake.

"This is the guy from upriver," I said. "Is it true?"

136

"We don't know. I don't think so, but this guy, whoever it is, is gonna be in court in two hours, so we'll know for sure, then. Our guy's off-line, though. All his numbers are down."

"They wouldn't be down unless he took them down," I said. "If the feds grabbed him, they would have left the lines up, to see who called."

"There's something else: if they busted him at his place, they'd most likely be taking him to court in Jackson, not in New Orleans."

"I don't know where his place is at, but I'm glad to hear you say it," I said.

We talked about it for another minute, poking through clues from a TV broadcast neither of us had seen yet. "I'll get back," I said.

How much trouble are we in?" LuEllen asked.

"Depends on whether they really got him, and if they did, what they got. And if he's willing to deal. I've never met him face-to-face, but if he wanted to deal . . . he could hurt a lot of us. He knows all about Anshiser . . . He knows about Longstreet. He knows about Modoc and Redmond." All jobs involving what we lightly call industrial espionage.

"Maybe you ought to back away from this thing," LuEllen said. "Get back home and maybe pack a suitcase."

"Something to think about," I said, "Though I wouldn't be good at running."

"How does ten years in the federal penitentiary sound?" she asked.

"There've got to be other options. Gotta be."

We looked at each other and I realized how hooked up I really was. I'd always thought of myself as something of a loner, going my own way, doing what I wanted when I wanted to do it. But Bobby knew about me—knew where to find me—and so did LuEllen, and John Smith, and now Lane Ward knew a couple of things, and so did twenty or thirty other people. If the feds somehow managed to get them all in the same room, they could hang me.

"*You* can get stubborn," she said. "But I *still* reserve the right to split, you know that."

"Anytime," I said. That'd always been the deal, and she'd always been protective of her identity, background, and home. Nobody knew much about LuEllen; not even me.

We watched television for a half hour, and I got cleaned up. We saw one item on Bobby, which said just that he'd been caught, and was believed to be a leading member of Firewall, and was coordinating the attack on the IRS. The attack was still going on, and the government was considering an extension of filing dates for quarterly business returns. Congress was squealing like a herd of stuck pigs.

"You were right about what gets them excited," LuEllen said.

We went out to breakfast, but neither of us said much. I spent the time trying to figure out what to do next, and one thing kept coming up: call the cops. The problem would be to get the cops to listen, especially since (a) they thought they knew what was going on, and (b) we were the bad guys.

"Not having Bobby to do research is like . . . I don't know. Like going blind," I told LuEllen as we walked back to the hotel.

"What more research do we need?"

"Anything that would get the bureaucracy running in a different direction. They're tearing up the world looking for fifteen or twenty of us, and we haven't done anything—I mean, nothing that they think we did. Somebody has to talk to them."

"Not me."

"Of course not; you're not in jeopardy. But I might try to find somebody *I* could talk to. I *could* find somebody, if I had Bobby."

B ack at the hotel, I changed to shorts and a T-shirt, and went for a run, the cell phone clipped uncomfortably into the shorts. LuEllen went shopping. I did three miles, fairly hard, and the exercise felt good after all the time cooped up in cars and planes and small rooms. When I got back, I jumped in the shower again, for a quick rinse, and was just toweling off when John called.

"It's not him," he said. He sounded bubbly, which was not usually the case. "The guy they busted is white. They just had a picture of the cops walking him into federal court."

"Ah, Jesus. I hope our guy's okay."

"So do I. He can't run—not literally, anyway. He needs to stay at the . . . business."

"If he calls, tell him I need him."

"Do that," he said.

After hanging up, I turned the television down and went out on the Net. Trying to learn about the NSA and find some names. I got nothing but bullshit. But I have a few mailboxes scattered around, under different names and IDs; and when it became obvious that I wasn't going to get anything useful off the Net, I checked the box at AOL. I found a message: six digits, beginning with 800.

"Bobby," I said aloud. He knew a couple of the boxes. I tried the next one, and found seven more digits. The last box was empty. I picked up my laptop, got the acoustic earmuffs out of my travel bag, and headed for the door.

I called from a drive-up pay phone at a gas station two miles from the motel, using the muffs. Earmuffs are a valuable item, if you travel. It makes no difference what the country, what the phone system, or what the line voltages are—if you can get an audible signal from your home Internet service provider, you can get online. I dialed using the old protocol, and after getting the "?," I typed in "k."

THAT WASN'T ME.

NO SHIT. TELL ME, WHAT DID THE WOMAN DO AFTER THE AMAZING EVENTS ON THE MISSISSIPPI?

I got a couple of seconds of silence, as he thought about it. I wanted some confirmation that I was actually talking to Bobby, and he was quick, Bobby was. He came back with a woman's name. The right one.

MARVEL.

I NEED SEVERAL NAMES OF NSA GUYS THAT I CAN TALK TO PRIVATELY ABOUT FIREWALL. SERVER IN MD HAS NSA CLIENTS. FIREWALL RUMORS MAY COME FROM NSA.

FBI BE BETTER TO TALK TO. NSA MAY DISAPPEAR SERVER MATERIAL.

WOULD PREFER TO TALK TO IN-PERSON. FBI HAS GUNS.

OK. WILL CHECK NSA NAMES.

MAYBE GET FBI NAMES ALSO.

I CAN DO THAT.

WILL YOU BE AT THIS NUMBER?

NO. CHANGING NUMBERS WITH EACH CONTACT, LIMITING CALLS TO 2 MIN. WILL LEAVE NEW # FOR YOU LIKE THIS TIME. WILL DUMP NSA INFORMATION TO SF BOX.

Before I signed off, I gave him the information that would give him system administrator status at the Bloch Technology server, and suggested that he look at the client list.

WILL DO THAT. MUST GO.

TAKE CARE.

YOU TOO.

LuEllen was waiting when I got back. I quickly filled her in on what had happened. "So what do we do now?" she asked.

"Wait. Until Bobby gets us a contact."

"And you want to talk to this guy personally."

"Yeah. If we do it online, or call, as far as he might know it could be some teenaged crank. If we look him up personally, we can be a little more definite."

"It's a risk."

"Yeah . . . And you know, I've been thinking. Bobby thought maybe we should go to the FBI instead of the NSA, because the NSA might just decide to dump whatever's on that server. So if he gets us some FBI names, maybe we should drop a note to them, too."

"Let's think about it."

We went out and hit more golf balls, and went to another movie, which also sucked—there've been a whole line of movies starring old action-adventure stars paired with much, much, much younger women; they're kinda creepy—and kept checking the mailbox. At two o'clock, the SF box, which has an ancient heritage going back to the original Well, popped up with three paragraphs of type.

The recommended NSA contact was an executive in the security section, a woman named Rosalind Welsh. She was high enough up that she could talk directly to the top levels of the bureaucracy, far enough down that she'd not have any minders. And, Bobby said, she was newly divorced, with a son going to college. Her husband was also an NSA exec, but he was showing a new address, while

Rosalind Welsh kept the Glen Burnie address and the old phone number. All of that, taken together, meant that she was living alone.

We also got five names with the FBI, including the personal home phone number of the director. If we used it, I thought, we should get some attention . . .

And finally, Bobby said,

RAN BLOCH SERVER CLIENTS AGAINST NSA ROSTER. OF THREE THOUSAND CLIENTS, 1844 APPEAR TO BE NSA.

AMAZING. NSA IS FIREWALL.

MAYBE.

GET OUT OF SERVER. I MAY TALK TO FBI.

YES.

If I was going to talk to Rosalind Welsh personally, I needed to cover my face and hair. LuEllen recommended a Halloween mask, since Halloween was coming and they should be easy to find, and because from any distance, they don't look like masks. We drove all the way to Philadelphia to get it: a full-face molded rubber mask of Bill Clinton. It worked fine, except that I couldn't talk very well through the mouth slit, and we wound up snipping off the lips with sewing scissors. We got a plastic water pistol from a toy store, and a baseball hat to complete the outfit.

We went to Philadelphia because it was only two hours away by car, and LuEllen had contacts there—a gun guy who I'd met once, and now, it turned out, a phone guy. We got another cold cell phone, guaranteed for a week, for $300. We were back in Baltimore a little after seven o'clock. Glen Burnie is south of the city, and we were scouting Welsh's house at seven-thirty.

"Lights; she's home," LuEllen said.

"So we cruise it a couple of times, and I hit the door."

"You're gonna scare the life out of her . . . and the other problem is, what if there's somebody in there with her?"

"There's a garage window," I said. "I can check the garage on my way up—see how many cars are in there."

"Not perfect," she said.

"Nothing is . . ."

We didn't need to do it, anyway. We were cruising the place for the third time, picking out a place for LuEllen to wait with the car, when Rosalind Welsh walked out the front door of her house, did a few stretches in the driveway, and jogged off down the street. We rolled slowly past, and I got a look at her. She was probably fifty, and ran with the earnest, hunched-up stance of somebody who hadn't been running long, but was determined to lose the armchair ass.

"Let's do it on the street," I said. "Stop ahead of her and let me out in front of a house without lights. I'll bend over the car like I'm saying good-bye, and when she comes up, I'll stop her."

"She'll see the car. Maybe get the plates."

"Pull into a driveway, so we're sideways to her. When I stop her, I'll turn her around, and you pull out and go around the corner. When I'm done, I'll get her jogging the other direction."

"This worries me."

"Yeah, well. It's better than the door."

"If she screams?" LuEllen asked.

"I'll run."

This was the only part of what I do that bothers me—the involvement of innocents in ways that might hurt them. For the most part, when I'm working, I'll take information from one place and deliver it to another. In most cases, I can make at least a thin argument that what I do benefits the population as a whole—encourages competition, saves jobs, etc.

But sometimes, although I regret it, I involve an innocent. Like this lady, a bureaucrat, a little too heavy, earnestly chugging off the pounds on a quiet suburban street. Whatever else came out of it, I was about to scare the hell out of her. I wouldn't do it, if not for the Firewall thing . . .

I pulled the mask over my head, put on the cap, and got the plastic gun out. LuEllen guided us past her again and pulled into a driveway a half block ahead. I got out, and bent over the open door: LuEllen said, "A hundred feet, seventy-five, fifty, forty, shut the door and make your move."

I stood up, slammed the door, and turned to the sidewalk. Rosalind Welsh was twenty feet away and smiled reflexively as I turned toward her. I said, feeling the rubber edges of the mask flapping against my lips, "Mrs. Welsh. Stop where you are. I have a gun pointed at you. Don't scream, just stop, and I won't hurt you."

As I said the words, I moved to block her; she tried to turn, but I said, sharply, "Don't," and when she saw my face she opened her mouth and shrank away, and I said, sharply, "Don't scream: I won't hurt you. I just want to talk."

She looked all around, and I stepped close, directly between her and the car and said, "I have to ask you to turn around. We're going to back the car out of the driveway and we don't want you to see the license plates. If you do . . . well, you don't want to see them. Just turn around and look straight ahead, and when your back is to the car, I'll walk around and face you . . ."

I tried to keep talking quietly, in a nonfrightening way, explaining what was happening: giving her something to focus on. When she was turned, I edged around her and said, "Don't look at the car." LuEllen backed out of the driveway and turned at the corner.

"I'm one of the people the NSA is putting out rumors about— I'm supposedly a member of Firewall, along with several friends. But we are not," I told Welsh. "We began researching the situation, trying to figure out what was going on. Are you aware of the source of the Firewall rumors?"

"Sir, we don't have much to do with trying to find Firewall. That's the FBI . . ." She was scared, on the edge of bolting. Calling me *sir.*

"The Firewall rumors are coming from an ISP called Bloch Technology in Laurel," I said. "It's a private server whose clients are almost all NSA employees. We believe that the NSA is Firewall and will inform the FBI of our conclusions tonight."

The fear was receding; I could see it in her eyes. She'd become interested in what I was saying. "You think the NSA is attacking the IRS?"

"We think a group of European morons is attacking the IRS and jumped on the Firewall name because it was already notorious and it sounds neat."

She asked, "Have you ever heard of a man called Bobby?" I hesitated, but in hesitating, answered the question. "So you have."

"Yes."

"The FBI and our security people are debriefing him now," she said. An implied threat, showing a little guts.

Again I hesitated; but they'd find out soon enough what they had. "That would very much surprise me," I said, "since he's the one who got me your name. This afternoon."

Her eyebrows went up: "You're joking."

"I'm afraid not. The guy you picked up may be named Bobby, but he's not Bobby."

"What about Terrence Lighter?" she asked.

Now I had to make a decision; again, a tough one, but what the hell: "Have you heard the name Jack Morrison?"

"Yes." Nothing more.

"Then you know he was supposedly shot to death by a guard at one of your contracting companies—AmMath, in Dallas."

"He was *definitely* shot to death by a guard."

I held up a finger: "We don't think so. We think he was killed by the same people who killed Lighter. Look at Lighter's outgoing e-mail; he's on the Bloch server. Then look at Morrison's travel. He came to see Lighter twice last week, the last time, the night Lighter was killed. The Lighter and Morrison murders go together, and they were coordinated through an ISP that's basically a server used by your people."

She shook her head. "Why should I believe you?"

"Don't. Just investigate. You're a security executive. Do your job."

I glanced back over my shoulder: we'd been talking for two or three minutes, I thought, but it felt like an eternity. "I've got to go. I will call you, to find out if you're moving on the case. If you are, we won't have to. If you don't, we will, and we make no guarantees about who gets hurt. We will call the FBI, tonight, about the Bloch Technology server."

I took a step back, and she said, "Would you have shot me if I screamed?"

I looked down at the pistol in my hand, shook my head, and tossed it to her. She picked it out of the air as I jogged away. "It's not loaded," I said as I went. "I didn't want it to leak on my pants."

She was still standing there when I turned the corner. She called after me, "Nice talking to you, Bill."

A little guts.

So are you going to call the FBI?" LuEllen asked, as we rolled away.

"Absolutely. If we get two bunches of bureaucrats fighting over the server, it'll be harder to keep it hushed up."

I made the call from a pay phone, working down Bobby's list of FBI agents' names and home phone numbers. The first two weren't home. The third guy was named Don Sobel, and he answered the call on the first ring. He sounded like he was talking through a mouthful of shredded wheat; in the background, I could hear the Letterman show.

"Mr. Sobel," I said. "I'm a member of the computer community. I'm calling to tell you that this group, Firewall, which is supposedly attacking the IRS, was invented by the National Security Agency . . ."

"Who *is* this?" The way he asked, I knew what he was thinking: *crank.*

"I'm calling several different people," I said, "So if you're interested in keeping your job, you should write down this name. Bloch Technology. B-L-O-C-H. The company has an Internet server in Laurel, Maryland, at the Carter-Byrd Center . . ."

"Just a minute, just a minute, let me get this down," he said.

I spelled the name again, and then said, "The server is the source of the Firewall rumors. If you check the client list, you will find that most of the clients are NSA people. You will also find that the first mentions of Firewall all come from this computer, several days before the name went public. The rumors were planted by an NSA contract company called AmMath, of Dallas, Texas. A-M-M-A-T-H. AmMath is also involved in the murder of an NSA official named Terrence Lighter. L-I-G-H-T-E-R. Are you getting this . . ."

"Give me that name again, Lighter . . ."

I spelled it again and then said, "NSA security people are on the way to Bloch Tech right now. There may be nothing left to discover if the FBI isn't there to watch them. You can call an NSA security official named Rosalind Welsh"—I spelled her name and gave him her phone number—"to ask about the server."

"What about . . ." he began.

"Good-bye," I said. I hung up, and we took off.

"Now," I said. *"Something's* got to happen."

13

What the European hacks were doing to the IRS was simple enough—the programming could be done by mean little children—but their organization showed some good old German general-staff planning. They must have worked for weeks, getting into the computer systems of not only a lot of small colleges, but, as it turned out, into the computers of several big retailers.

Without studying the problem, I would have thought that getting at the retail computers would be almost impossible, without a physical break-in to get at security codes. I was wrong. It appears that several of the big online retailers spent all their security money on protecting credit-card and cash transactions, and making sure that nobody could fool with their inventory and sales records.

But they had other computers that specialized in routine, automatic consumer contacts—computers, for example, that would do nothing but send out standardized e-mails informing the customer that his order had been shipped. For these computers, no great security seemed necessary.

They were perfect for the hacks. They were optimized for sending outgoing mail, and once the hacks were inside them, they could easily be set up to ship the phony IRS returns. At the peak of the attack, the bigger online companies were sending out thousands of phony returns per hour.

That would have been bad enough, but the hacks had taken it a step further: they didn't have the returns sent directly from the retailer to the IRS, but rather bounced them off the customers. When the retailer sent an acknowledgment of a purchase, the IRS file was automatically attached, but would not show up on the customer's computer screen. What would show up was a legitimate receipt or other message, plus a message from the hacks that said, "For auditing purposes, and your shopping protection, please acknowledge receipt of this message by clicking on the 'Acknowledge' button below. Thank you."

Every customer who clicked on the "Acknowledge" button was actually sending a message, but not to the retailer. The message was one of the phony returns, and went to the IRS. When the IRS tried to track the messages, they'd find they came from thousands of individuals all over the country, all of whom denied knowing anything about it.

The attack was continuing the following day when LuEllen and I loaded into the rental car and went for a noon-rush-hour drive on Interstate 10. We picked the Interstate because if we were moving fast, we'd be switching phone cells every few minutes.

"Hate to waste a perfectly good phone," LuEllen grumbled.

"That's why we got it," I said. Using one of the new cold phones, I direct-dialed Welsh at her NSA number. Nobody answered.

"Not there," I said, hanging up.

"What does that mean?"

I thought for a moment, and then said, "I told her I'd call her. But it's Sunday, and maybe she thinks we've only got her home phone. I'll bet she's home, sitting on the phone."

"With a bunch of FBI agents."

"Yeah, well . . ."

I dialed her home phone and she picked up on the fifth ring. On the fourth ring, I said to LuEllen, "Maybe they don't fuckin' care." I was about to hang up, when I heard the phone shuffle, and then her voice.

"Hello?"

"This is Bill Clinton. I spoke to you last night. Did you go to Laurel?"

"Yes, we did. Is this a cell-phone call?"

"Yes."

"Then we will have to be circumspect. We looked at the account you were speaking about, but there wasn't any traffic of the kind you described, between the gentleman here and the gentleman from Dallas."

"There was last night . . ."

"We think that the file in question may have been altered. Did you place an administrative account named B. D. Short on the Laurel installation? For your own uses?"

"No, we didn't."

"Then someone unknown has been burning files."

"I told you who it was . . ."

"We are looking into that," she said. "We want you to stay in touch, though, and we also want to send you a file and have you look at two photographs. Can you take a quick transmission if I switch over?"

"Just a minute." I wasn't ready for that; it seemed uncommonly cooperative. I turned in the car seat, reached over the back, got out the laptop, and turned it up. "I'm just bringing it up," I said.

"I'll have to say, to be honest, that I didn't appreciate your approach last night. You scared me."

"I regret that," I said. I had the line that would go from the modem to the phone wrapped in a bundle, and fumbled it as I tried to pull off the rubber band while still talking on the phone. The bundle dropped between my legs and I had to lean forward to get it. As I did, with my head at a low angle, I noticed a helicopter a mile or so ahead, hovering above a line of buildings. I picked up the bundle of wire, undid the rubber band, and clipped it into the laptop and the phone, and called up my communications program. A moment later, I was ready.

"Switch over anytime," I said.

"It's about a hundred K, so it'll take a minute or two," she said. "If you're ready, here it comes . . ."

I got a tone and hit the enter button on the laptop; a moment later, the download began.

"What's going on?" LuEllen asked.

"They're shipping a couple of pictures they want us to look at," I said.

"An unusual show of cooperation," she said wryly, echoing my own thoughts.

"Yeah, I . . ." And as I started to say it, I looked right out the passenger window. There, a half mile away and running parallel to us, was another helicopter. "Shit!"

"What?" She'd picked up the tone in my voice as I plucked the wire out of the computer and shut down the phone.

"We were set up. They're tracking the call and they've maybe got us isolated. See that chopper straight ahead? We've got another off to the right . . ."

"Aw, man, Kidd, what do we do?"

"Don't do anything, yet; keep the speed steady," I said. "In case they haven't spotted us."

"The front chopper is sliding this way."

"So's the side guy," I said. An exit was coming up, with signs for a shopping center. I could see it to the north, a big one, with what looked like an enclosed parking garage. "Take the exit, take the exit."

She cut right and took the ramp, "What next?"

"Take a left. There's a shopping center over there with a covered ramp. If they've isolated us, we won't be able to run from them as long as they can see us."

It was a cool day, and I was wearing a light sweatshirt over a golf shirt, and had a jacket in back. I peeled off the sweatshirt and began wiping down every surface I thought we might've touched, and at the same time tried to look for the choppers. The one that had been to the right was closing fast.

"I think they've spotted us," I said. "Get in the parking ramp."

LuEllen ran a stoplight, took a hard right into the shopping center, went the wrong way up a one-way drive and into the parking ramp, under cover. "We were in the backseat," she said. "We were in the back, we've got prints. We used the radio . . ."

I'd spotted a parking space: the inside end of it, against the wall, was slightly lower than the outer end. "Right there. But don't go in head first. Back into it."

"Why?"

"Do it, goddamnit."

I crawled over the seat into the back, wiped down everything, stuffed the laptop back into my briefcase, and got out my old

Leatherman tool as LuEllen maneuvered the car. When she killed the engine, I said, "Pop the trunk. Get out. Don't touch anything."

She did, pulling her hands inside her jacket sleeves, wiping frantically along the way. I hopped out, wiped the handles, then ran around behind the car, dropped to the ground between the barrier wall and the back of the car. I got the Leatherman out of my pocket and unfolded a long pointed blade with a serrated edge. After a couple of timid attempts to do it by hand, I pulled off a shoe, stuck my hand in it, and smashed the blade through the gas tank. Once I got a hole, the rest was easier, enlarging it to the size of a dime. A steady stream of gasoline flowed out and began pooling under the car and I slid out from under and stood up.

As I did, LuEllen said, "Kidd, I hear the chopper—the chopper's coming in."

"You still carry a lighter?"

"Jesus, you're gonna blow up the garage." But she got it out of her shoulder bag, a cheap blue-plastic Bic, and handed it to me. I stooped and fired it into a finger-wide trickle of gasoline. The flame caught and we ran.

Ran for fifty feet, until we were away from the car, then slowed to a walk. There were people further down the structure, but they were paying no attention to us. I could hear the chopper, somewhere, the beating sound seeming to come from all around. Then the fire jumped up from behind the retaining wall, and I heard somebody yelling; and then we were inside.

A mall is a mall is a mall. We either had to get out of this one in a hurry, or hide. I said so to LuEllen. Run or hide.

"This way," LuEllen said, grabbing my arm.

"Where?"

"Backside exit . . ."

We walked across the width of the mall, to the far exit. "Look for somebody, a woman, getting out of her car. Spot the car. Spot the woman."

How many people have you seen getting out of cars in parking lots? A million? But try to see somebody getting out when you need to see them, and they don't. We could see that there was excitement on the other side of the mall. A couple of people running, but they were the best part of a block away. I was looking toward them when LuEllen said, "There."

I looked where she was looking. A woman was climbing out of a deep-red Dodge minivan. She was wearing a hip-length teal-colored jacket and carrying a purse. When she passed the back of the minivan, she casually turned and pointed her hand at it, and the tail-lights blinked. Then she dropped the keys in a side pocket of her jacket.

"That's her," LuEllen said. "That's her. Now do what I tell you. You gotta do it exactly right . . ."

What I did was, I hurried halfway down the mall, until I was standing in front of a Victoria's Secret store. The woman in the teal jacket came through the inner door a second later. I started toward her, carrying my briefcase open and across my chest, digging in it with one hand. LuEllen was behind her, four or five feet back, pacing her. As we closed, I suddenly crossed in front of her and stopped abruptly, bowing over the briefcase, and she almost ran into me. She put her hands up to fend me off, and I said, "Oh, jeez, I'm sorry," but she was already past.

When she'd swerved to avoid me, then ricocheted off my arm, LuEllen had dipped her pocket for the keys. As the woman went on down the hall, LuEllen nodded at me, turned, and headed out. I was a step behind.

"We might not have long," LuEllen said, as we crossed the parking lot. She was tight. We could still hear a chopper, but it must've been on the other side of the building. Then there were sirens and for a moment I thought the cops would be blockading the place, but the sirens were fire trucks, coming in from off the mall.

We got in the van, LuEllen driving, and headed out; from the corner stoplight, we could see the parking ramp, and a fireball in the near end. Two big choppers were down in a vacant area of the lot, and a couple of hundred people were standing around, looking at the fire.

"If they get any prints out of that, they'll have earned them," I said.

"You think there were any left?"

"I don't think so. But why take a chance? And the fire got people looking that way."

"You think that woman saw your face?"

"Yeah, probably," I said. "A slice of it. Not all of it."

We took the van to the airport, trying not to touch anything. At the airport, we wiped it and left it in a reserved slot. I put a sheet of notebook paper on the dashboard with a note: "This car was stolen." A cab took us back to the motel.

A t the motel, LuEllen took advantage of me. She tends to do that when there's trouble, when things have gotten tight. She went to her room, did a couple lines of cocaine, then, her eyes all blue and pinpointed, came down to mine.

"You need some exercise," she said, pulling her shirt off.

LuEllen's a good-looking woman and an old friend. It would have hardly been polite to say no.

The first round of sex all done with, I was tracing some of her more interesting contours with my fingertips, and she said, "Tell me what they did."

"They must want us fairly badly," I said. "But then, we're right where they've got all their equipment. I think they probably put up several pairs of helicopters around Baltimore and probably Washington, with radio direction-finding equipment—cell phones are radios . . ."

"I know that . . ."

"Then, with the access the NSA has to phone call-tracing equipment, they probably picked up the cell our phone was using, spotted it, vectored in the nearest helicopters and fed them our signal at the same time. They'd get us pretty close just with the one cell, and our speed would probably tell them that we were on the Interstate. Then, if we switched to another cell, they'd have our direction, and from the time of change, a pretty good location. From that point, with their direction-finding equipment, it was only a matter of time. That's why they were downloading those pictures. They were keeping our signal going back and forth, and getting us to focus on what was happening."

"Smart," she said.

"Yeah. We fucked up. Sorry, *I* fucked up. I forgot who we were dealing with. If I'd been using my brain, we could've taken the train to New York, which they would never in a million years have been covering, and we could have called from midtown at lunch. Instead . . ." I spread my hands. "We have a major screwup. Hertz is gonna be pissed at Nancy M. Hoff."

She giggled: "Their car is a puddle of plastic."

"We hope."

Then she sighed and rolled over and said, "This was fun; both the running and the fucking. But we've got to be smarter."

"I don't see anything more for us here," I said. "Welsh told me that they'd gone into the computer in Laurel, so maybe they'll take care of everything."

"Back home?"

"You want to go back home?"

"Where're you going?"

I thought for a moment, then said, "Texas. Just to look around."

"I've been to Texas," she said. "I sort of like it there. I like the way they dress."

"You're welcome to come along."

Late in the afternoon, we checked out of the motel, took a cab to BWI, and flew to New York. We stayed overnight in Manhattan, sharing a room this time. Monday morning, before we left for La Guardia, I called Welsh at her office from a pay phone. Her secretary answered and when I asked for Welsh, said Mrs. Welsh was in a meeting.

"This is Bill Clinton. If she wants to talk to me again, right now, you have ten seconds to get her on the phone. After that, I'm gone."

Five seconds later, Welsh picked up. "This better not be a joke."

"This is no joke. This is a threat. If you come after us again, or threaten us, we'll tear major new assholes in all those bright and shiny computers you keep buying out there."

"Your threats don't worry us too much, Bill. We're only about one step behind you now."

"Oh, yeah? Get a lot of prints off that car? Listen, lady, I'm telling you. If we feel threatened, we'll take you down. If you want a demonstration of what we can do, we'll put your internal phone book on the Internet, with all the names and home addresses listed, so people who don't like your brand of bullshit can call you up at any time of day or night. Would that convince you?"

Her resolve seemed to waver: "I don't think you could . . ."

"What phone do you think I'm talking to you on?" I asked. "Jesus Christ, woman, take a minute to think about it."

"So don't do that . . ."

"Look at those computers, find out what happened with Lighter and Jack Morrison and AmMath and Clipper, and stay the fuck away from us."

I hung up. We were headed toward the airport, five minutes later, when one of LuEllen's cell phones rang. The taxi driver was chanting to himself in Arabic, and apparently paying no attention. LuEllen dug the phone out of her purse, punched the Talk button, said, "Hello?" listened for a moment, then handed the phone to me. "Green," she said.

Green was calling from a phone at a gas station in San Francisco. "I couldn't figure out how they were tracking us, when they were always so far away, always two or three blocks," he said. "So I drove over to my brother's place—he's got a garage—put the car up on a lift and guess what?"

"You had a bug."

"Still got it," he said. "But I moved it inside the car, and duct-taped a big alnico magnet to it. When we get to the airport, I'll stick it on a car that's leaving. That ought to confuse them for a while . . . then we'll fly the Seattle-to-Houston route, and drive up to Dallas."

"Good. We're on our way now. We'll be in Dallas tonight."

"We'll probably stay over in Houston, see you tomorrow."

We talked for another minute, and then he was gone.

And we were gone. Seven hours later, we were in Dallas.

14

ST. JOHN CORBEIL

Corbeil was sweating. In the cold air-conditioning of his office, he could feel the dampness under his shirt collar and despised himself for it. Not good clean sweat, the kind you got lifting weights. This was nervous sweat, the kind you got when a hard-nosed NSA security officer cornered you with unexpected questions, while some FBI faggot sat in the back smiling and playing with his tennis bracelet.

Strunk—the security officer's name was Karl Strunk—had questions about the Bloch Tech ISP, about the emergence of Firewall, about the deaths of Lighter and Morrison. Corbeil managed to finesse the questions, to play dumb. He hated having to project even the appearance of ignorance, but it had been necessary. And it had been a close-run thing.

How had they gotten onto Bloch Tech and the connection between Bloch Tech and the Firewall rumors? That was the last thing he would have expected . . .

Hart knocked once and pushed into the office. "What happened?" he asked. "Trouble?"

"I'm not sure. Something's going on. They know about Bloch Tech, and they suspect that Lighter and Morrison are connected. But they don't seem to have any idea what the connection might be. And I don't understand *that* . . . how they could suspect a connection without having any idea what it might *be* . . ." He stopped, pulled himself in. He'd almost been sputtering, like some striped-tie civil service asshole who'd lost a box of paper clips.

"We took care of that with the Morrison plane tickets," Hart said. "Did they find the tickets?"

"I wasn't asking any questions—but I assume they did. I came down hard on the idea that we were monitoring everything, that we were afraid that we'd been penetrated by Firewall. I suggested that Firewall had penetrated Bloch Tech, recognizing that it was the biggest ISP in Glen Burnie, and figuring that there must've been a lot of NSA people in it . . . Probably in there looking for anything they could get."

"What'd he say?"

"The idea didn't surprise him. I kept talking about his IRS attack. That has them confused, too."

"That has *me* confused."

Corbeil smiled: "I think it's absolutely wonderful. They're going to find some people who profess to be Firewall, and they'll have *nothing* to do with us. If you've ever dealt with those little cocksuckers who infest the Internet these days, you know that they'll probably take credit for every bit of damage that gets done. They think it's glamorous."

"It'd still be nice to have an . . . overview."

Corbeil nodded. "I'll go up to Meade and tap the old-boy line. See if I can find out what's happening . . ."

"I can make a couple of calls," Hart said. "Ask a couple of guys to keep an eye out—tell them that if there's trouble, I want to get out while the getting is good. That might produce something."

"Do it," Corbeil said. "And tell Woods to keep an eye on the computers, just in case the people at Meade have a backdoor into it."

W hen Hart was gone, Corbeil made a half-dozen calls and managed to wangle an invitation to visit NSA headquarters to talk about Firewall and AmMath. Once inside, it'd be usual enough to visit old pals, an ordinary thing to pick up on the gossip. He'd made a lot of money on the outside, and had jobs prospects to dangle . . .

Somewhere, somebody was working a vein of information, and if he couldn't find out who, he might get hurt.

He spent another half-hour online, using an encrypted spreadsheet to move money between offshore accounts: from the "in" account to, eventually, the "invest" account. Corbeil had a number that he had taken out of *The Wall Street Journal.* The head of a big arbitrage fund had set aside twenty-five million for his own use, the *Journal* said, and with the rest of his fortune, he simply played. Twenty-five million, the man said, was enough to take care of any realistic need.

Corbeil made that his number: twenty-five million. When he reached that number, he would shut down the Old Man of the Sea, find a way to seal himself away from Woods and Hart and Benson. Then find something else to do, in a softer climate. Ibiza would be a candidate ...

He thought about Ibiza for a while, and then again about Woods and Hart and Benson. If something were to happen to Hart and Benson, and if Woods were to disappear with a large amount of cash, then conclusions might be drawn. Then, if Clipper died, as it appeared that it would, he could liquidate and find that something else.

That would be a couple of years, yet. He was not yet halfway to his number ...

H art came back. "Talked to some guys, they'll keep their ears open, but right now, nothing. The only talk about us, is, most of them have heard that Clipper is going down."

"Common knowledge," Corbeil said. "I've been thinking about this whole problem. There is either a source of information about us, or the Ward woman knows something that we don't. Maybe she had more files than we know about. Maybe Morrison made more than one entry. Maybe they were working together ..."

"Possible. But if all that was true, and if she's giving her stuff to the NSA, why are they so confused? Why are they just sniffing around? They don't really seem to know much. Maybe she's just jacking us up, and is gonna come in with an offer ..."

"Doesn't feel like it. If you two hadn't lost her."

"Listen, when they made that switch, that was professional," Hart said. "Where does a college professor get off spotting a beacon the size of an ice cube? I'm telling you ..."

Corbeil waved him off. "We've been through all that and she's out of sight for the time being. The police say she's coming here to look at the house and to pick up some of Morrison's equipment and personal effects. You found MasterCard and American Express receipts in her house—maybe you can pick her up through her cards."

Hart nodded. "I'll check."

Corbeil leaned back in his chair. "Somebody is working on us, William. Possibly the NSA, but it doesn't feel like them. Strunk knew a few things, but there were holes in everything he knew. Questions didn't follow any reasonable logic. He had bits and pieces, only bits and pieces."

"Gotta find Ward," Hart said.

"Find her, and look at her."

15

Dallas was hot.

Hot enough that the newspapers were whining about it. Unnaturally hot, for the time of year. When we got to the DFW car-rental building, which was a couple miles from the airport, a chunky red-headed woman dragged a bulky black suitcase up to the Hertz desk with a complaint about her bill. I didn't hear the details of the complaint, but noticed that her blouse was soaked with sweat from the fifty-yard walk across the parking lot.

We rented a thoroughly air-conditioned car, using one of LuEllen's IDs, and got two rooms at the Ramada Inn. When we were settled, we drove to something called the West End Historic District, which turned out to be a fern-bar shopping district injected into a bunch of aging warehouses.

The TrendDirect building, once a big, old red-brick warehouse, had been dressed up with modern black windows and new tuck-pointing. It stood alone on its own block. Part of the ground floor had been given over to an imposing lobby, with a glass wall separating the street from an interior done in old brick and new marble, with huge wooden beams crisscrossing overhead. A guard and reception desk sat to one side, a half circle of marble. We could see two heads behind it, but no details of the security.

Except for the lobby, the front part of the building's first floor was all retail—a couple of boutiques, a men's formal-wear store, a sports-collectibles shop, a coffee shop and a beer-and-steaks restaurant on the corner.

TrendDirect, a direct mail advertising company, occupied floors two through five, plus the back part of the first floor. Six and seven were a single law firm, eight was occupied by an ad agency. Nine and ten were AmMath.

LuEllen had her game face on. "Ten stories," she said, as we cruised the neighborhood.

"Ten stories."

"Exactly."

The front of the building was on a wide street, but faced a grassy square, and most of the traffic was local. Both side streets were narrow, showing walls of black windows. There were three window wells on each side.

The rear of the building was on a wider, busier, dirtier street, smelling of truck coolant and exhaust. A half-dozen truck-parking bays backed up to a loading dock, with steel overhead doors opposite each truck bay. A windowless standard door, of steel, was at the center of the dock, between two of the big overhead doors. A smaller, street-level garage door, also steel, and just big enough for a small truck, was located at the end of the building. A video camera monitored the dock.

"What do you think?" I asked her. She was looking straight up through the windshield.

"I'd like to see the roof," she said.

"LuEllen . . ." I'm just the tiniest bit afraid of heights.

"It's gonna be a tough building," she said. "That guard desk is a twenty-four-hour operation, and we know there are guards wandering around at night. Jack supposedly shot one who was making a routine round of the building. We could probably crack one of the doors in back, but then, the question is, could we get up? We can't tell without going inside."

"Gotta be a way."

"Probably. The fact that there's some kind of government top-secret connection makes me extra nervous. If we came down from the top . . . look, the building across the street from the south side is an office building. Turn here, I'll show you."

The building across the street was just as she said: another old warehouse, renovated, with glitzy neon-signed shops on the bottom floor, and what must've been offices on the floors above.

"The thing is, the security'll probably suck. There's no lobby, it's a little shabby, so it's probably a lot of individual offices. We could get access during the day, hide out inside, and get onto the roof at night. It's twelve floors—two higher than TrendDirect," LuEllen said. She looked back and forth between the two buildings. "Narrow streets here . . . I bet it's not more than forty feet between the two cornices. We heave a climbing line across, slide down, and the TrendDirect roof's probably got no security at all. It'd be really unusual if it did."

"Why don't we get fake IDs and fool the guards," I said. "Or keys for the back doors?"

"Those are options."

"Or we could do a sneak." *Sneak* is private language. It amounts to doing an easy reconnaissance, like a phony delivery, to look over a target. LuEllen has done them twenty times. I usually go on public tours—most big companies have them, and they are very informative, if you know what to look for.

"That's another option," she admitted. But she liked the roof idea. She'd like the rush it'd bring, swinging out over the street at three o'clock in the morning. We spent another fifteen minutes looking at the building, and LuEllen shot a couple of rolls of color-slide film. She also got out of the car and looked into one of the window wells.

She came back, shaking her head. "Why would you put glass brick all the way up and down?" she complained. "People working in there have to *breathe,* for Christ's sakes. It's inhuman."

"LuEllen, the voice of the working man," I said.

"But you know what? It all looks *very* secure," she said. "Somebody went out of their way to be secure . . . and something else I just thought of."

"What?"

"How often are building guards armed? Like the old guy who got shot?"

I thought about that and shook my head. "Not often."

"The place is tough," she said. "I'd turn it down, if I were working on my own, unless I had a very tight inside connection."

"Huh." We both thought about that as we rolled away, leaving the building behind. Neither of us had ever spent serious time in Dallas, and it turned out that the West End Historic District was historic not only because it was old, but because that was where John Kennedy was assassinated. We went past the memorial, not knowing exactly what it was until LuEllen spotted a Dealy Plaza sign.

"Do you remember Kennedy?" she asked, her face turned to the memorial as we passed by.

"Sometimes I think I do," I said. "But I think I mostly remember my folks telling me about him."

"I've only seen him in old TV shows," LuEllen said. "He seemed like an okay guy for a president."

On the way back to the motel, we found a phone and got online with Bobby. He'd been doing research on AmMath, knowing that we might try to go in. I said:

> TREND**D**IRECT LOOKS TOUGH. ANY ONLINE OPTIONS?
>
> CANNOT FIND ONLINE OPTION BUT DID LOOK AT CORBEIL HOME.
> HE HAS T-1 LINE.
>
> EXCELLENT. GIVE ADDRESS . . .

Corbeil lived in a snazzy glass-and-brick low-rise apartment building on a North Dallas golf course; a gated community called Lago Verde. The T-1 line meant he was probably working from home on his downtown computer system.

"This is the place to do a sneak," she said, as we rolled past the gate. "I'll bet you dollars to doughnuts that all the security is out here, on the fence, with maybe some drive-by guys in golf carts at night."

"So let's go in," I said.

"Let's call Bobby again," she said. "We need to nail down Corbeil's exact address, and we need the name of a single woman who lives in there, anywhere. Maybe he could check elevators—don't elevators have to be inspected or something?"

"I think so."

Bobby came back and said that Corbeil, according to the local phone and electric companies, lived on the eighth and ninth floors of a nine-story building called Poinsettia. All of the apartments in the building were two stories—on two and three, four and five, six and seven, eight and nine. He couldn't find out what was on one, nor could he find anything about elevators. There was a state elevator data bank, but you had to know the serial number to find the right one; the bank was not searchable by address.

He did get the name of a single woman, an Annebelle Enager who lived in the Primrose building.

"That's a start," LuEllen said.

"We're gonna do a sneak?"

"An easy one," she said.

One thing the movies never tell you is that burglars spend about half their life shopping. We bought a small paint brush and jars of red and black water-soluble poster paint at a kids' store. At an office supply place, LuEllen picked up a bottle of rubber cement, a roll of duct tape, an X-Acto knife, and one of those roller-receipt boxes with a roll of receipt paper to go with it. The receipt paper went on a spindle-bar inside the top of the box—like a toilet paper holder— fed to the outside, across a plate where a customer would sign, and then back inside the box to a take-up spindle.

We rented a white van from Hertz, took the van to a mostly vacant parking lot outside a thirty-six screen theater, and I used the poster paint to create a business on the side of the van: Rose's Roses.

"That looks great," LuEllen said, when I'd finished. "You missed your calling. You should have been a sign painter."

"Yet, I think I would be unfulfilled," I said. I'd painted two intertwined red roses, with black stems, above the name, in red. You had to hope nobody looked at both sides of the truck, because the roses were not exactly the same.

While I was painting, LuEllen sat on the back bumper and used a screwdriver to rip the guts out of the roller-receipt box, and the X-Acto knife to cut a quarter-sized hole through the plastic side. Her JVC miniature camcorder fit snugly inside, held in place with the duct tape; she used the rubber cement to glue a receipt across the face of the box.

"We ready?" she asked, as I finished up the roses.

"If you are."

"Let's go."

I didn't have to do anything, truth be told. LuEllen drove the truck up to the gate, said something to the gatehouse guard, who pointed, and let her in. I waited a block away, in the car.

She was inside for exactly twenty-two minutes, about ten more than I thought reasonable. She waved at the guard as she left, took a left, and five minutes later, we met in a weedy, litter-strewn strip under a freeway. When I got there, she'd already gotten out a gallon jug of spring water and a roll of paper towels, and was wiping Rose's Roses out of existence.

"No problem," she said cheerfully, as I walked up. "I even got a date, if we need it."

"Who with?"

"Guy named Ralph Carnelli, he's an office guy there; some kind of low-level manager, I think."

Inside the compound, she'd driven around until she spotted the Poinsettia building. The first and basement floors were parking, she said. That was as much as she could see. Then she found the club-house, which sat on the edge of the golf course. The clubhouse included a receiving area, the upstairs management offices, and a lounge and exercise room for the residents.

"I got lost," she said. "I wandered all over the place . . ."

"An easy mistake to make, in such a big building," I said.

"Yeah. I went up these stairs and eventually I found Ralph and he took me back downstairs and showed me the reception desk. I left the flowers for Annebelle and we got to talking. He came on to me a little and I gave him a little shine. I wouldn't give him the phone number, but I took his."

"Nice guy?"

"Good-looking, forty-two, divorced. Big shoulders."

"With that skirt and your ass, the poor guy never had a chance."

"Exactly. And . . ." She paused for dramatic effect.

"What?"

"The clubhouse is open all night. Twenty-four hours. The door that connects the clubhouse to the office suite can be slipped. At the back of Ralph's office is a big wooden flat file that has the names of different buildings on different drawers, four names to a drawer."

"Architect's drawings?"

"That's what I think. Couldn't see for sure. But the office has something to do with maintenance."

"Tonight. We cross the fence onto the golf course, watch the building; when it's open, we go in."

"Absolutely," she said.

We got a call from Green at eight; they were in Houston, and he and Lane would be heading for Dallas as soon as it got light.

LuEllen and I replayed the movies she'd made at Lago Verde, until I knew my way around the place as well as she did.

We went into Lago Verde at ten o'clock, carrying nothing but a thick woolen Army blanket we got at a salvage store, a dinner knife I stole from a Denny's, and a penlight. We parked on a residential street a block off the golf course, after spotting a convenient tree along the edge of the course; the course was bordered by an eight-foot chain-link fence, but without any guard wire at the top. We both wore jeans, black gym shoes, and crimson jackets. Dark red is as good as black for concealment, as long as nobody throws a light on you. If a light *is* thrown on you, you look a lot more innocent in red than in black.

The tree at the edge of the golf course was halfway between two streetlights, along a commercial strip. Across the street from the tree, a paint-and-wallpaper place closed at eight o'clock, and the adjoining high-end stereo place at nine. At ten, with a good space between cars, we jogged across the street. LuEllen tossed the blanket over the top of the fence, and I lifted her up to it, and she was over. I did a quick climb, pivoted on my belly on the blanket, and dropped to the other side. We both squatted behind the tree, to look at the passing cars. Nobody slowed. We waited, out of sight, for ten minutes, and then headed across the golf course.

Once we were away from the strip, the golf course was dark as a coal sack. I'd never had a mental image of Dallas as a place with trees, but it has about a billion of them: from the air, the city looks like a forest. Golf courses are even denser with them, and most of them seem to have thorns. We crossed a fairway, moving slowly, I stepped into a thorn bush, backed out, fell in behind LuEllen, and we groped our way toward the apartment light three hundred yards away.

Fifty yards out of the clubhouse, we found a soft patch of grass between two trees, spread the blanket, and hunkered down. We could see lights both at the front of the clubhouse and at the back. The upstairs windows were dark.

The back of the clubhouse was framed by a wall of floor-to-ceiling windows. We could see a line of soda and snack machines along one wall, and a bunch of soft leather chairs, like the first-class lounge in an airport. There were a half-dozen people in the lounge. Two had apparently just come out of the exercise room; they were putting on tennis shoes. The other four were sitting in a group of chairs, talking.

"Could be a while," LuEllen said.

About three hours, in fact. The group in the lounge stayed for an hour and a half, an animated conversation that seemed to go on forever. When they finally left, a couple of other people had settled in. More came and went from the exercise room. Traffic slowed down after midnight, but every time we thought to move, somebody else would show up. At one-fifteen, we hadn't seen anybody for fifteen minutes.

"Let's try," LuEllen said.

We left the blanket and started through the dark to the clubhouse door. Twenty yards out, at the edge of the golf course, we came to a line of head-high shrubs. After we passed them, we'd be out in the open and committed. We stopped, looked around, then LuEllen touched my arm and we moved.

Slowly, LuEllen on my arm. We got to the clubhouse, stepped inside. No sound, except a refrigerator gurgle from one of the soda machines. We waited another second; then LuEllen slipped the dinner knife out of her pocket, walked to the door connecting with the executive suite, slipped the lock with the knife blade, and we were in. And up.

Ralph's office door had the same crappy lock. We slipped it and LuEllen led the way inside. I shut the door behind us and she turned on the penlight. The flat files were not locked; didn't have locks. The architect's drawings for Poinsettia were right where they were supposed to be, in the Poinsettia drawer, with drawings for Wild Rose, Black-Eyed Susan, and Hollyhock. The drawings for Poinsettia made up a pad a half-inch thick, and probably three feet long by two and a half wide.

"Take the whole thing?" she asked.

"Might as well. Hope nobody goes looking for them."

"They're dusty; we should be okay," she said.

We put the room back together, and walked out. As we crossed the paved area toward the parking lot, another couple was coming off the parking lot, carrying a blanket, but not ours. We never got closer than fifty yards, but they waved, and LuEllen waved back, and then said, "Jesus Christ, Kidd, the golf course is the local lover's lane. We're lucky we didn't trip over somebody."

"Better cover for us," I said.

We saw nobody on the course. We crossed the fence, strolled back to the car, and were out of there.

16

uEllen tends to wrestle herself around pillows, and wind up in odd positions. When I woke up the next morning, her bare bottom was sticking out of a tangle of sheets, and a glorious sight it was, like a new peach, round and firm and slightly pink. I will confess to an inordinate fondness for that portion of the female anatomy, and after a few minutes I reached over and gave it a little pat. A little *stroke*.

"If you touch me, I'll rip your fuckin' heart out," she groaned.

"But it's so interesting."

"Shut up."

"Can't. Time to get up."

She propped herself on her elbows and looked at the bedside clock. "Bullshit," she said, and dropped straight down. "Be quiet. I need another hour."

I went to the window and stuck my face into the crack between the curtains. "Nice day out. Blue skies, no clouds."

"This is Dallas, you moron, it's supposed to be like that," she said. "Now go away."

N ot a morning person. I got cleaned up, humming to myself. Thought about LuEllen's ass—all right, I'm not just fond of it, I actually contemplate it—and remembered Clancy.

Clancy's the woman back in St. Paul, who was building a computer with me. Very nice woman. Smart, interesting, sexy. Too young for me—I'm eight years older than she is—and the difference troubled me, though it didn't seem to bother her much. And we weren't finished with each other; there was more to say.

Clancy in St. Paul, LuEllen in Dallas. Hmm.

When we were done in Dallas, LuEllen would most likely take off again. She had a tendency to winter in warm places, like Mexico, Venezuela, or the Islands, and to hang with the indolent rich. I, on the other hand, would be back in St. Paul, in snow drifts six feet deep, with wolves, and would need the comfort of a woman like Clancy.

I would probably try to hide this moment with LuEllen. Given my past track record, I'd probably succeed. The thing was, LuEllen wasn't just sex: she was a *friend*. Our time in bed was an expression of *friendship*. I worked over that line of thought as I shaved. This whole sex thing with LuEllen would take some seriously hypocritical rationalization, I thought, if I wanted to keep my feet warm over the winter.

———

LuEllen was still in bed when I finished cleaning up, so I went downstairs to the restaurant, had eggs, bacon, and toast, read the paper—Firewall was *still* on the attack. The IRS had no idea of how to screen them out without losing billions and billions. In Germany, the cops raided the apartment of a kid who had an Internet handle that translated as Cheese (so said *USA Today*), but Cheese had been in the bathroom at the time and that apparently gave him some kind of immunity from prosecution: he wasn't actually hacking when they came through the door. In any case, *USA Today* said that Cheese was the rat in the DoS attack.

When I got back upstairs, LuEllen was dressed: "Green called. He and Lane are checking into a Radisson Hotel up in Denton, which is like twenty miles from here."

"Why there?"

"Because Green plays golf, and it's a golf resort."

"Silly goddamn game," I said.

"You don't know the first thing about it," she said.

"Chasing a white ball around a cow pasture . . ."

"Look at a list of people who play it, and tell me they're chasing a ball around a cow pasture. If you gotta brain in your head, you gotta suspect that there's something else going on, even if you don't play yourself."

My eyebrows went up: she actually sounded a little passionate on the subject. Not like LuEllen, eternal cynic. "Mmm," I said.

"Fuck you."

LuEllen drove. I sat in the passenger seat, looking through the architect's drawings and trying not to get carsick. Eventually, I gave up; but I'd found one interesting thing.

"There's a silent alarm wired into Corbeil's apartment. The console is in a closet."

"Can you trace the out lines?"

"Nope. The lines go into an indicated junction box along with lines from some other rooms, and then they all go down to the first floor."

"Either to a security service or over to the reception area in the clubhouse. Or both."

"Clubhouse would get a quicker response," I said.

"Yeah, but if you wanted a little more weight, some pros with guns, it might go out."

The Radisson sat on a hill on the west side of the highway; it took a while to find the driveway in, but we got it sorted out eventually and went up to Lane's room. Green answered the door. He was wearing a golf shirt and loose, pleated, tan slacks and had his hand in his pocket. He took it out when he saw us. "There you are."

Lane was lying on a bed, watching a movie on HBO. LuEllen, who'd come in behind me, looked past me and said, *"Emma.* I didn't know that was on."

She went over and dropped on the bed next to Lane.

"I think we're gonna go into this Corbeil guy's apartment," I said to Green and Lane. "We've got some . . ."

"Shhh," Lane said. "They're gonna kiss. This only takes a minute." Emma and her friend were standing under a spreading oak. Lane and LuEllen were totally focused.

"I think we gotta . . ."

"Shut up, shut up, just one minute." LuEllen held a finger up.

I went over to look: "Christ, that woman's got a long neck."

"They all did back then," Lane said.

"This wasn't made back then, this was made . . ."

"SHUT THE FUCK UP," LuEllen said.

I looked at Green, who shrugged, and we went over to a corner of the room, sat down, and shut up.

A fter Emma and her friend were married, and the movie ran down what happened to everyone else, Lane sighed and turned off the TV. "God, I love that movie."

"So do I," LuEllen said. "But you know what? I don't think they did a very good job with Frank. They needed to make him more attractive in the beginning and worse in the end, and show why Emma was attracted to him."

"I didn't think he was very attractive at all," Lane said. "I don't see how he could possibly compete with . . ."

"Could we talk about what we're doing?" I asked.

"I think that would be good," Green said, "Since we're in these guys' hometown."

W e brought them up to date on what we'd done, without providing any details that might be used against us in a court. We would have to trust them at some point, though, and I said, "We're seriously considering going into Corbeil's apartment. He has a T-1 phone line, and we think he probably uses it for rapid access into the company computers. There's a good chance that I can tap into his computer line, and that'll give us a door into their mainframe."

Lane said, "We've been looking at the photo you sent us, and I can't see anything in it. If we knew who the people were . . ."

"It's a blank wall," I said. "Jack must have gotten something out of the computers that went with the photographs. That's what we need to find."

"I really, mmm, I had some problems back home and if I got caught going into a place, I could be looking at a long time," Green said. He sounded apologetic.

"You couldn't go in anyway," I said. "It's not an area where a black guy can wander around. We could use a couple of eyes, though."

"We could do that," Green said. "Do we know anything about the place?"

"We came up with these," I said, touching the drawings. "I've seen a couple of things in them; everybody ought to take a look, and see if we can spot anything else."

We did that, spreading the drawings around on the beds like pages from *The New York Times* on a Sunday afternoon. LuEllen said, eventually, "Look at this." She was pointing at a blank box.

"It's a blank box," Green said.

"It's a safe."

"Yeah?"

"Bet your ass it is," she said. "Let me look at the drawings for that wall . . . and for the opposite wall. Where are the materials specs, anyway?"

After a while, Lane and LuEllen went out for Cokes, and Green and I continued to look at the blueprints.

"You're pretty good at this," Green said after a while. It sounded like a statement, but there was a question inside of it.

"I've done it for a while—not exactly this, but related stuff."

"I know a little bit about Longstreet," he said. I looked up at him: Longstreet was supposed to fade away into the past—a political seizure of a small town in the Mississippi delta, engineered with several tastefully chosen burglaries and a few bad moments at the dog pound, to say nothing of the weeks of hospitalization and physical rehab that followed.

"I wish people would forget about all of that," I said, finally.

"Most of them are forgetting, but not everybody," Green said. "What I'm saying is, my friends tell me that I should go all the way with you. That it's important."

"I'm not sure how important it is outside our little group," I said. "I wouldn't want you to be misled."

"Not too worried about that," he said. He stood up, stretched, looked out the sliding glass doors toward the golf course. "What I'm worried about is, I'm getting bored. Hard to stay sharp when you're bored, stuck in hotel rooms."

"Do you play golf?"

"Does a chicken have lips?"

"Why don't you take LuEllen out for a round? She's getting antsy herself. I'll read though these drawings for a while longer, keep an eye on Lane."

"Okay." He chewed on a lip for a minute, then said, "Think Lane has a little thing for you."

"Yeah?"

"A little thing," he said.

"I thought, maybe, you guys have been hanging around for a week or so . . ."

He shook his head: "I'm not from the right social-educational strata."

"She's a bigot?"

185

"No, no. Never that. She's got a Ph.D. and I never quite went back for my GED, if you know what I mean. She's got this thing about . . . diplomas. Degrees."

"Huh. Don't know what to tell you," I said. And I didn't.

We spent some more time looking at the architect's drawings and when LuEllen got back, I said, "We go in through the garage. I can get us up to Corbeil's floor, but after that, I've got no guarantees. If we want to make it a quiet entry, I don't know. You'd need some lock picks or something. I don't think we could use an auto-pick. There are three other apartments up there."

"How are you going to get us up? If we don't know how long we're gonna be up, I don't think it'd be a good idea to take the elevator apart."

I explained it, and she said, "That means we need more scouting trips. And some more gear."

"I was thinking we'd go in Saturday night," I said. "That article that Bobby found said he was a big social guy. Saturday night in Dallas?"

"About ten o'clock?"

"If it's possible at all," I said.

"I wish I could get a look at his door," she said.

For each of the next three days, Green and LuEllen played thirty-six holes of golf on the Radisson course, while Lane and I hung out, sometimes together, sometimes separately. I got a lot of drawing done, and she was online with her business in Palo Alto.

LuEllen, it turned out, was a near-scratch golfer. "I'm damn

good," Green said one night, "But she's better. I think if she was a little younger, and worked on it, she could probably go on the women's
tour."

"Can't putt," LuEllen said.

"You could if you had a little patience," he said. "You never
look . . . " And they'd go off on a long, twisted argument about
putting—or chipping or pitching or whatever—that would leave
Lane and me nodding off.

The nights were more interesting. LuEllen and I scouted Corbeil's apartment from the golf course, with Green and Lane circling
the course, listening to a police scanner, looking for cops. We'd
bought Motorola walkie-talkies, apparently used by hunters—they
were in camouflage colors—so they could call us instantly if anything came up. We'd found a better place to enter the golf course,
where two uneven pieces of fence came together at a corner, next to
a sidewalk. From one direction, you couldn't see us at all; from another, it looked like we'd turned the corner. From the third and
fourth, you could see us plainly, but traffic was light enough that we
could wait for holes.

On Wednesday night, we took a look at the garage. The garage
entry was on the end of the building, and nicely landscaped, which
was a break for us. Coming in from the golf course, we could get
close without being seen. The garage was enclosed with a steel door,
and a key card was used for entry. If I could get fifteen seconds with
a key card, I could duplicate the signal easily enough—you can buy
the parts at Radio Shack—but getting fifteen seconds with a key
card might be a problem. Not an insuperable one, but there appeared
to be an easier way.

When the doors opened, they stayed open for as long the car was
in the garage entranceway, and then for a few seconds longer. The

doors operated on a simple infrared cell; the key card opened the door, and then, if a car was blocking either of two cells, the doors stayed up. All we had to do was block the cell when a car came out. The door would stay up until we unblocked the cell . . .

Once inside, we would head for the freight elevator.

On Thursday, we got a bunch of photos of Corbeil from Bobby; memorized the face, and wiped them out of the computer. That same night, LuEllen found a tree she could climb, where she could look through the floor-to-ceiling windows of an apartment on the second floor.

"If his door is the same, it's a standard solid-wood door set in a steel frame," she told me when she came down. "I couldn't see the locks, but they're probably pretty good."

On Friday night, we were lying out in the grass outside his apartment, listening to a couple make love on a blanket twenty yards away. They continued for longer than seemed probable, then had an intense conversation about two people named Rhonda and Dave, who seemed to have been their respective spouses; then they started again.

"Must be younger than us," I whispered to LuEllen.

"Younger than you," she whispered back. "Unless, maybe, you're entertaining Lane during the day, when I'm playing golf."

"How could you possibly be that full of shit?" I asked. "What the fuck do you mean . . ."

Like that.

At nine o'clock, a white limo pulled up outside the apartment house, and a young woman got out. A very nice-looking young blond woman, with a long neck like the woman in *Emma*. She didn't dress like Emma, though; she dressed like a supermodel. Her short black frock probably cost as much as the average condo and if there'd been any less of it, she couldn't have crossed a state line without committing a felony.

Eight minutes later, a few lights went off in Corbeil's apartment, and two minutes after that, as the improbable couple to our left grunted and squeaked toward orgasm, she reappeared, two steps in front of St. John Corbeil. Corbeil moved in that stiff, upright military-academy way, as though he were holding a golf ball in his crotch as he walked. Not an especially tall guy, but one of those small-headed, wide-shouldered types who probably wrestled in high school.

LuEllen, who had the binoculars, focused on them with that kind of silent intensity that an attractive women gets when she feels she might have become a satellite, rather than the planet. That's what I thought at the time, anyway.

When Corbeil and his date had gone, we lapsed back into the waiting mode, until the adulterers decided they'd had enough. They split up after a last hasty kiss and grope, and as soon as they were gone, we headed across the golf course ourselves. Halfway across, in the dark, LuEllen said, "I'm gonna have to go away for a while."

We signed off with Green and Lane, and back at the hotel, LuEllen started making phone calls to numbers she'd memorized. She was looking for some specific gear, and she needed a nearby supplier. She got the right guy just before midnight, talked to him for five minutes, and dropped the phone back on the hook.

"Find it?" I asked.

"Yeah. We have a slight change of plans. We're not going in quietly; we're gonna go in superhard. We're gonna go after his safe."

"He'd probably suspect something . . ."

"Maybe. But maybe not . . ."

She told me about it as she changed clothes, into black jeans and a black jacket. "I gotta have that piece-of-shit car."

"Where're you going?"

"Out of town," she said. "One of my friends."

"When'll you be back?"

"Really late, or early tomorrow morning," she said. "Actually, there's no reason for you not to know. I'm driving to Shreveport."

"I could take you."

"Nah. Better if I go alone. This guy is okay, most of the time, but he's nervous."

"Most of the time?"

"You know. As long as he's on his meds . . ."

17

That night I stayed in LuEllen's room, and spent twenty-seven bucks on pay TV, waiting, unable to sleep before LuEllen returned. She knows lots of people who do bad business, and not all of them are her friends, and not all of the places she goes to are good places for women to be after dark. That's not sexism: it's the simple reality of the redneck ghettos where she buys her tools.

When I wasn't watching movies, I worked over the architect's drawings, following every wire and line though the building, and everything that went outside. Two of the lines were particularly troublesome: one may have been—probably was—a camera that scanned the inside of the parking garage. No way to tell where it pointed, or whether it was live video only, or if it spooled onto a continuous tape. Another line ended in several vertically stacked switches in the service-elevator shaft, and I thought they almost surely were floor indicators going out to the elevator. If they were something else, like infrared motion detectors, we would have an even bigger problem. LuEllen had night glasses in her scouting bag, along with her cameras, and once we were inside the elevator shaft, could use the glasses to check for security devices.

And we would be in the shaft, going up the cables with climbing gear. It's easier than it sounds, with good gear. The only alternative, with a keyed elevator, was to steal a key, or wreck the elevator getting to the wiring behind the key. That would take time, make noise, and tip anyone who decided to use the elevator after we did. Climbing was easy, and out of sight.

LuEllen was gone for a bit over seven hours; I was at the door when she came in. She was carrying a hand duffel, the same kind I packed for an extended fishing trip. She dumped it on the floor and it clanked.

"Sounds like construction equipment," I said.

"Deconstruction equipment," she said. "There better be something in that safe. This stuff isn't cheap." She was very sharp, each word clearly defined, coming out rapid fire. She was eager, hot, ready-to-go, bright-eyed and . . .

"Ah, man. You got your nose in it, didn't you?"

"Just a little bit. And a little bit for tomorrow. Today."

"Goddamn it." I turned away.

"Hey . . ."

All right; I let it go, like I always did. LuEllen did a little cocaine from time to time—and, from time to time, more than a little. I hated the shit. I might smoke some weed after a long day on the water. I might even do a tab of amphetamine if there were enough reason. But cocaine, heroin, crystal meth . . . that crap will kill you. And if the dope doesn't, the dealers will.

W e stayed in bed well past noon. LuEllen had been bouncing around all night, the residuals from the cocaine. Later in the day, she'd be sleepy. At two in the afternoon, I was up, feeling groggy, looked out the window. Another great blue-sky day. I cleaned up, and as I got out of the shower, LuEllen was finally crawling out of bed.

"You okay?" I asked.

"No." Still coming down.

"Go stand in the shower."

"Yeah."

When she got out, still a little groggy, I put her in the car, along with the equipment, and we went out for food. She began to revive, and we drove to Corbeil's place and sat across the street watching the reception area. The reception area, as shown on LuEllen's movies, had a single guard monitor.

"Look at this," she said. "You see where the guy is standing?" We were two hundred yards away, but I could see him through the glass of the reception center.

"Yeah?"

"The monitor is just to his left. Now watch." She took a cell phone from her pocket and dialed a number. The guard straightened, took a couple of steps to his right, picked up the phone.

LuEllen said into the phone, "Do you have Prince Albert in a can?" And clicked off.

The guy behind the glass shook his head, put the phone down, and went back to where he'd been standing before. He might've been reading something.

"So . . ."

"So when he's answering the phone, he can't see the monitor," she said. "If the monitor is rotating between sites, there's a good chance that we wouldn't be on it, anyway."

"Take us ten seconds to walk inside and get to the freight elevator," I said.

"Mmm."

"But we won't know whether they've seen us or not."

"That's the fun part," she said. "The waiting."

When we left Corbeil's, we drove up to the Radisson, and LuEllen and Green spent time hitting golf balls on the driving range, while I went over the drawings again. Lane, looking over my shoulder, chewing on a raw carrot, suggested that one particular group of rooms in the Corbeil apartment could be for a live-in maid. It was labeled "guest suite," but it could have been either. We debated it for a while, and I finally pulled up the wiring diagrams. We decided that the questionable area had no wiring for a stove or for an electric clothes dryer, so it was probably a guest room.

"We'll have to call," I said. "Every fifteen minutes."

We started calling right after dark. The phone would ring four times and we'd get Corbeil's answering service. I was getting cranked on adrenaline, and LuEllen took a walk around the closed-down driving range and did a little cocaine. At ten o'clock, we left, LuEllen and me in one car, Green and Lane in the other.

I dropped LuEllen on the corner where we crossed the fence, and she was gone in an instant. I took the car around the block, parked, and crossed the fence myself five minutes later. LuEllen was waiting. We'd wrapped all of her tools in towels, and we were decently quiet as we moved slowly through the trees toward Corbeil's apartment. Halfway there, we stopped for a radio check with Green:

"Got us?"

"Gotcha."

We started moving again. There's a technique to the movement— hunters call it "still hunting," and it takes some discipline. LuEllen and I learned it, separately, as a method of staying out of jail. You take three slow steps and stop, and listen. Then five more, and stop. You cover ground more quickly than you'd think, and quietly, and almost always hear other people before they hear you.

We took fifteen minutes crossing to Corbeil's, and it was all worth it, for our own self-confidence. If we were caught with LuEllen's black bag, there'd be no point in explanations.

At the edge of the golf course, we stopped under cover of a low twisted pine, and listened. In twenty minutes, we heard nothing, nor did we see anything move. Corbeil's apartment was dark, except for the IR glow through the night glasses.

"Gonna do it," I said.

"Got the reel."

She had an old Penn level-wind reel filled with fishing line. We'd attached a piece of a black 3.5-inch computer floppy disk to the end of the line, as though we were going to cast it.

What I was going to do was easy enough, but I would be out in the open: a risk. After checking around one last time, I stepped out of the landscape planting and walked up to the garage door, towing the line behind me.

Six inches from the garage door, a small electric eye looked across at its illuminator on the other side of the driveway. I taped the floppy to the edge of the metal case around the illuminator, so it was hinged, and could fall up or down. Then I walked along the side of the building into the back, as though I were heading for the golf course. A minute later, I sprawled out next to LuEllen.

Normally, a driver would pull up to the door inside the garage, and tap his radio-operated garage-door opener to send the door up. Electric eyes both inside and outside the door would make sure that the door would not come down on top of the car, should it stop for some reason. As long as the electric eye's illuminator was blocked, the door would stay up. The normal up-and-down cycle would not give us enough time to get inside, without taking the risk of being seen by driver of the departing car. With the electric-eye blocked, however, the door would simply stay up until we cleared it.

We couldn't just cover the eye, though, because if a car came from the outside, and the eye was blocked, the door wouldn't come back down—and whoever had just driven into the garage would probably notice that. So we needed the hinged cover.

All of that was easy enough: we'd both done something like it in the past. But the wait was a killer. During the week, when we were scouting the place, a car might come out or go in every fifteen minutes or so. The longest we'd had to wait was a half hour. This time, we had to wait for forty-five minutes, but we lucked out. When the door finally went up, the car was inside the garage, heading out.

I put the radio to my mouth, and said, "Up yours."

Green came back: "Sounds good to me."

I pulled the straps for LuEllen's black bag over my back, and got to my knees. The brown Town Car cleared the garage and started around the approach drive, the door still up. As it began to exit, LuEllen pushed the speed-dial button on her cell phone. When the car disappeared, LuEllen whispered, "Go."

We went. As we crossed the drive, she said into the phone, "George? Is this George?" Then, "Don't tell *me* this is a wrong number, buster . . ."

The guard at the reception center, on the other end, eventually hung up, but by that time we'd walked thirty feet across the garage and were sheltered behind a concrete pillar at the freight elevator. The elevator doors were shut, but opened when we pushed the call button. A roof light came on, and I reached up and covered it with the black bag until LuEllen got the doors closed.

"Hatch," she whispered.

I made a hand stirrup, as I had for Lane back in Jack's house, and LuEllen stood up in it and pushed the elevator hatch askew. LuEllen peered up the elevator shaft with the night glasses. Looking for an in-frared motion detector or anything else that might trip us up.

"We're clear," she whispered, and pushed the hatch up out of the way. I boosted her through, handed her the bag, and followed be-hind. Using the light of two needle-flashes, we put our Jumar climbers on the cable, replaced the hatch, and started up in the dark.

A five-minute climb, eight floors. Hanging off the elevator door at Corbeil's floor, LuEllen first took the stethoscope out of her pocket, and listened. Nothing. Then she dialed the next number on her speed dial—Corbeil's apartment. Again, no answer. She patted me on the shoulder. I had her mechanical door-openers ready. I forced the jaws between the doors, and we pried the doors open. LuEllen did a quick peek with a mirror, then clambered into the hallway. I was five seconds behind her, with the bag.

The hallway was arranged like many rich people's hallways—so that the rich people would encounter each other as seldom as possible. A vestibule at the main elevator branched into two hallways, one for Corbeil's apartment, one for the other apartment that shared this entry floor.

Both hallways made a sharp turn just off the vestibule. When we crawled out of the service elevator shaft, we were already on Corbeil's side of the floor, but too far down the hall, past his door.

We went back to his door and LuEllen took the jaws from me and forced them between the door and the steel doorjamb. Then she attached a steel wheel, like a small steering wheel, to a square screw-end at the top of the jaws, and moved behind me so I could turn it. The mechanical advantage was huge: the big wheel must have spun five or six times for every quarter-inch that the jaws opened, but nothing could stand against them. Slowly, slowly, the door moved; then suddenly, popped.

LuEllen had moved around so that she was below me, facing the door, a heavy utility knife in her hand. When the door popped, she shot inside, making for the closet where we thought the alarm console was fixed. As she did that, I began uncoiling 150 feet of climber's rope from the black bag.

As I did it, I was counting to myself. Some of the alarm systems give you as much as two minutes to punch your code into the key pad. Some of them give you less. As soon as she'd gone into the apartment, the keypad began a slow beeping. Then she was into the closet. I stepped in behind her and pushed the door shut.

Twenty seconds. I could hear a scuffling sound, a ripping sound, then quiet, except for the *beep-beep-beep-beep* and then *beeeeeeeeeeeee.* Thirty seconds. The pad was dialing out. Damnit. The shortest possible delay. LuEllen appeared in the doorway, black-on-gray. "We're good," she said, in an almost normal voice.

"I'll rig the line," I said. I was drenched with sweat: I did indus-trial espionage, and went places where I wasn't wanted, but the big-time apartment break-in wasn't my style.

"Look at the rug," she said.

I looked down, in the light of her flash: we were leaving greasy tracks behind us. "Uh-oh." I stepped to the door and looked out in the hall. The tracks came all the way down the hall from the eleva-tor, though they were harder to see in the subdued hall lighting. "Let's get the line rigged. We'll just have to take a chance that nobody'll see them."

Another unforeseen risk.

We did a quick run through the apartment to make sure it was empty. On the way, I stopped for a few seconds to admire LuEllen's work with the alarm. She'd used the knife to cut a hole through the drywall to expose the alarm console—couldn't just pull the wires out, because if you cut a wire, the security service would be auto-matically alerted. She'd then stripped the wire, clipped in bypasses, and then cut the wire between the two bypasses. The top bypass si-lenced the keypad; the bottom one would keep the circuit alive, so the cut-wire call-out would never be made. She'd done it in about twenty-five seconds.

The suite that had worried us, the possible maid's suite, was just a guest room. The computer was in a small purpose-built office. "Don't stop," I said. "Just walk on by."

The balcony ran the width of the apartment. We took a mo-ment, surveying an adjoining balcony with the night-vision glasses, then carefully opened the door and listened. I could hear what sounded like a radio or CD, but it was inside, contained. Above us,

I thought. We looped the climbing rope around one of the support posts on the balcony, and coiled the rope so that a quick kick would launch it down the side of the building. If somebody came through the door, we could be on the ground in less than a minute, pulling the rope after us.

That done, we headed for the safe, which was nicely concealed behind a piece of wooden paneling. LuEllen said, "I'll do this, you get going."

I walked back and forth and around the room, leaving traces of the black grease, while LuEllen started pulling out her equipment. After leaving the tracks, I went back to the door, took off my pants, jacket, shoes, and the dirty kitchen gloves, and walked back to Corbeil's office in my shorts and socks.

LuEllen made a lot less noise than I'd feared. She was good at this, and what she was doing was more a cover than any serious attempt at the safe. As long as Corbeil concentrated on the safe, and not the computer, we'd be cool.

In his office, I shut the door and turned on the light. What I was doing was simple: I was loading a program that would spool anything he typed on the computer to a file on his hard drive. Another program—one of my own design—would send the file to one of my online mailboxes, and then erase its tracks. The only question was, had Corbeil booby-trapped his computer with hardware of some kind, or software, to detect intrusion?

I spent twenty minutes trying to figure that out, and in the end, didn't. I didn't think so, but you can't be sure, not in twenty minutes.

As soon as my software was in, I checked the rest of the desk, found a couple of Zip disks, and copied them to my own Zip disks.

I was just finishing when LuEllen scratched on the door. I turned out the light and opened it: "Almost done," I said.

"I need your help. Hurry, and get dressed."

In the study, LuEllen had done two things: she had taken her heavy bar, which had an edge like a razor, and had cut through the wall around the cylindrical safe. The safe was set in concrete, inside a steel frame that was probably bolted to the building beams. Around the cylinder flange, she'd fitted a five-sided, one-size-fits-all steel collar, with adjustable bolts.

With that in place, she'd gone to the far wall and cut another hole, exposing one of the I-beams that held up the building. The beams had been covered with drywall, so exposing them was no problem. She'd slipped a steel strap around the beam, then hooked the strap to the collar on the safe, using what amounted to a large come-along.

The come-along was essentially a high-ratio pulley, with a four-foot-long handle and a three-foot pipe as an extension; the connection was a steel cable. She'd pumped the cable tight; so tight that I could have walked on it without bending it at all.

"The thing is, the safe is starting to move," she said. "The concrete is cracking up. I can hear it, but I've got so much pressure on it, that when it breaks free, it's liable to come flying out of the hole."

"Jesus."

"It won't fly far—but it'll hit like a ton of bricks. They'd hear it all over the building. I gotta stand right next to it while you pump."

So I pumped the handle of the come-along and she stood next to the safe, watching the concrete deform. "Starting to crumble . . . crumbling . . . crumbling. Stop."

I stopped, and she peered at the safe.

"Give it a little punch." I gave it a little punch, and suddenly, the safe came free.

"All right, all right . . ."

Working as hard and quietly as we could, it still took ten minutes to work it the rest of the way free. When it finally came out, I staggered backward with it and dropped it on a couch.

"No way I can get that down the elevator," I said. "The goddamn thing's gotta weigh two hundred pounds. It'd pull me right off the cable."

"We can't just let it sit here . . . we've almost got it," she said urgently.

"LuEllen, the goddamn thing is like a two-hundred-pound car battery—I can haul it, but it's got too much weight in too small a package."

"Well, goddamnit, Kidd . . ." She walked around it for a minute, then said, "Wait," and walked out of the room, turning toward the back of the apartment.

A minute later, she was back, carrying a black satin sheet. "Let's get the safe. I'll help."

"What're we gonna do?"

"Just help."

We wrapped the safe in the sheet, so we could pick it up by the ends. LuEllen is strong as a horse, and she tied a loop in one end of the sheet so she could get it over her shoulder, and then led me back through the apartment, and out a door onto the balcony.

"What're we doing?" I whispered.

"This way."

"Oh, no."

"Yeah, we can do it. From right exactly here. It'll go right straight down into soft dirt."

"Aw, man." I was scanning the dark golf course. "Somebody's gonna see us."

"Small chance." She was grinning at me; this was what she lived for, and what might send her to jail someday. "C'mon, Kidd, be a good sport."

"Ah, fuck."

Before I became a sport, I called Green: "Anything?"

"Not a peep."

"Drive by and see what you can see."

"One minute," he said.

We waited one minute and he came back, "Man reading a magazine."

"Get out of here," I said.

"Ten-four." He wasn't quite laughing.

I picked up the safe, groaning, leaned over the railing, got centered, and let it go. A couple of seconds later, it hit the ground eight stories below with a dull thud, like a small car hitting a wooden phone pole.

We stood absolutely still, listening. An intake of breath? A cry of surprise? Nothing but a car accelerating in the distance.

"No problem," LuEllen said.

We would have been safer, probably, going down the elevator shaft again. LuEllen convinced me to go over the side of the building. "There's nobody on the balconies. We're good," she whispered.

"Jesus."

"Ten seconds from now, we're gone."

Not ten seconds, exactly. I insisted on a last look around the apartment, staying away from the computer but tracking more grease around. We packed up the black bag, and went over the edge on the climbing rope. On the ground, she gathered in the climbing rope and took the bag, while I tried to take the safe. I managed to carry it a hundred yards or so, before I had to stop. Then we wrapped it in one of the sheets, made a couple of handles out of the knots, and in ten minutes got it to the corner.

I sent LuEllen to get the car, with the sheets. She spread them on the backseat, and when she pulled up next to the fence, I threw the safe over, crawled over after it, then picked it up and humped it over to the car.

No problem.

LuEllen always gets cranked when she's been inside a place she's not supposed to have been. Dealing with her was like handling a hyperactive child: you try to keep her under control, slow her down. Tonight, she wanted the car, the safe, and the tools.

"Where're you going?"

"Back to Shreveport," she said. "If I give him the tools back, he'll cut the safe for free."

"We don't want it blown up or anything."

She rolled her eyes. "Jesus, Kidd, nobody's blown a safe since Bonnie and Clyde. He'll cut it open with a lathe."

She dropped me at the hotel and took off. As I got out, I said, "Cruise control."

"Absolutely."

When you're running, you always want to run on cruise control.

Get out on the Interstate, set your speed two miles an hour above the speed limit, and no cop on earth will look at you. If you're not on cruise control, your adrenaline will eventually get to you and you'll go flying past some cop at a hundred and ten, and it'll feel like forty-five.

With LuEllen gone, I walked six blocks to a drive-in phone on the edge of a gas station parking ramp, checked in with Lane, and afterward got online with my dump box.

Lane was almost as cranked as LuEllen.

"What'd you get? How come you're not up here?"

"We don't know what we got. It's in a safe and we've got to cut it open. LuEllen's taking care of that tonight, but she won't be back until morning."

"How about the computer?"

"We should be online with him. I'm going to check in a few minutes."

"Damn it, Kidd, it freaked me out, even though we were outside. Freaked me out. Something for the memoirs."

"Better fuckin' not," I said. "This is not even for your memories."

The dump box was a mailbox I'd set up especially to take everything Corbeil typed on his computer terminal. There was nothing in the box. I hadn't expected anything. Corbeil, the social butterfly, the model-dater, wouldn't be back until late, if at all, unless somebody found the broken door.

Finally, I went out to Bobby. He had nothing more to offer on Jack's Jaz disks, but was certain that the attack on the IRS was coming from Europe.

GOT SOME NUMBERS IN GERMANY AND ID'D ZOMBIE COMPUTERS
HERE IN STATES THAT ARE FEEDING ATTACK. WILL PASS ALONG TO
NSA CONTACT AND TRY TO STEER HER FROM OLD NAMES.

SHE'S NO WIZARD. YOU MAY BE PUTTING TOO MUCH HOPE IN
STUPID PEOPLE.

MUST PUSH THEM OFF. THEY STILL THRASH AFTER OLD NAMES.

TAKE CARE.

AND YOU.

I got to bed a couple of hours before dawn, still worrying about LuEllen. I got three hours of sleep, and, still groggy but unable to keep my eyes closed, got out of bed and nearly fell on my face. I'd felt a little creaky the night before, but now every muscle in my body was screaming at me. That goddamned safe. I know what muscle-pulls feel like, and I had what some docs called micro-pulls, the kind you get shoveling snow off a sidewalk. No major muscles, but hundreds of tiny pulls.

I hobbled into the bathroom, took six ibuprofen out of my dopp kit, swallowed them, shaved, and then spent fifteen minutes in a scalding shower. You're supposed to use ice, rather than heat, but this was ridiculous: I'd have to bury myself in a snow drift to chill everything I'd pulled. The heat made it feel better, anyway.

I was toweling off, slowly, when I got the sudden feeling—a premonition without the negative vibe—that LuEllen had just gotten back. I walked over to a window, opened a slit in the curtain, and looked down at the hotel parking lot. Yet another wonderful day, sunny, but with that early-morning dryness that we don't see in Minnesota. LuEllen was not in sight.

So much for premonitions. As I finished toweling off, I had another one: I'd just seen something important, but I didn't know what. What was it? I wandered around, looked out the window again, looked at myself in the mirror, looked at the towel. What the hell was it?

I couldn't figure it out, gave up, and got dressed, slowly. My back and underarms hurt the worst, and the inner thighs weren't good. My hair didn't hurt at all, but that was the only bright spot. I was leaving the room, going for breakfast, I had a third premonition, this one about LuEllen again. I went back to the window, looked out, and saw the black Pontiac GrandAm rolling into a parking spot. An accurate premonition—if you have enough of them, and look often enough, you'll always have a good one. I watched her walk into the hotel, and five minutes later, opened the door as she came down the hallway.

"Saw you in the parking lot," I said. "How'd it go?"

"You got a big industrial lathe, cutting a safe is like cutting cheese," she said. She pushed the door shut. "If you can mount it and turn it, you can cut it." Then she stepped up to give me a big kiss, and I winced.

"What's wrong?"

"That fuckin' safe. I pulled every muscle in my body."

"The penis is a muscle."

"It's pulled," I said. Then: "You seem pleased. Maybe even chipper."

She dug in her pocket and took out something glittery, held out her fist, and I cupped my hand underneath it. She dripped a platinum-and-diamond necklace into it. "Remember that model chick we saw going into his place? She wasn't wearing it going in. She kept touching it coming out. Looked too nice to be an outright gift. I thought it might be in there."

"How much?"

"Lots. I called my guy in Georgia, and he said he could probably get me a hundred and a half. They're all small, one-carat, but they're top quality, like the necklace was made to sell. A bank account."

"That was it? The necklace?"

"Nope." She grinned. "He had forty thousand in cash, all in hundreds."

"Computer disks, printouts . . ."

She shook her head. "Nothing like that. Some personal papers—a mortgage, birth certificate, his passport. I brought it all back, but I don't think there's anything for you. There *was* enough to make it worthwhile for somebody like me to hit him."

"So maybe he'll be less likely to look at the computer."

"Maybe. I'll tell you, Kidd, you've gotten me in some shit over the years, but we've always made money, huh? Every time."

"Just lucky, I guess."

She tagged along for breakfast and then said she needed a nap. Having her sleepy made me sleepy, and we went back to her room, put out the "Do Not Disturb" sign, and slept into the afternoon. Green called at three o'clock and asked what the hell we were doing.

We ate dinner together. Green took a look at Corbeil's passport as we were waiting for the meal, and said, "Travels a lot. Extra pages." He folded the extra pages out like an accordion. "Travels in the Middle East. And India."

"One of those been-everywhere, done-everything guys," LuEllen said.

The food arrived and Green started looking at the mortgage, which he said wasn't a mortgage at all, but a contract-for-deed, which I said was the same thing, and LuEllen said, "Not quite."

Finally, during the dessert, Green folded up the mortgage paper, tossed it on the table, and said, "He's got something strange going with a ranch."

"A ranch?"

"Yeah. A private sale, looks like. A contract-for-deed. He paid seven hundred and fifty thousand up front, and then a thousand a year for ten years, and he can pay the last ten thousand anytime."

"That sounds weird," I said. "He paid three-quarters of a million up front, but couldn't come up with the last ten grand?"

"Makes no sense," Green said.

"Sure it does," said LuEllen. She had a glob of ice cream on a spoon and was licking it, like an advertisement for fellatio.

"Well, tell us, Miss Sucking on a Spoon," Lane said.

"If you get a contract-for-deed, the final ownership doesn't pass to you until you make the last payment."

"So?"

"So that means the ranch is still in the seller's name. What's his name?"

Green picked up the contract-for-deed and looked at it: "Fred Lord."

"See, Fred Lord sells it to Corbeil, and Corbeil still has to pay a few bucks to totally own the land, but he gets the full use of it, but only Lord's name appears on tax records, land records, and so on. It's a dodge."

"He doesn't want people to know he's got a ranch?" I asked. "We ought to look at it. Where is it?"

"McLennan County, wherever that is," Green said. "Twelve hundred and eighty acres. Two square miles. Corbeil-land."

Lane wanted to go take a look right away. "What else are we going to do?"

"Monitor my drop box," I said. "We need that computer more than we need a ranch."

"How do we know that?" Lane demanded. "I feel like we're getting bogged down. It's been three weeks since Jack was killed. I don't think anybody cares anymore. Except us."

"And the people chasing after Firewall," I said.

"Ah, Firewall," she said. She batted the thought away, like a gnat. "They'll find these kids, and that'll be it."

"I wish it was true," I said, "But I don't think it is."

We talked about Firewall for a couple of minutes, about the technique of the attack on the IRS and the use of the zombie computers. We also talked for a few minutes about her talks with the cops, which were set for Monday morning, sixteen hours away.

She'd try to pressure them on AmMath. The more pressure that we could apply, the more curious the cops and the FBI and the NSA got about AmMath, the better chance there was that something would break loose. If we could get it into the media, make it a political problem, we had a chance of generating a legitimate investigation.

"I don't see the logic of it," Lane said.

"There is no logic. We just keep bringing AmMath up, hooking them to Firewall, to Jack's killing, to the house burning down, to the burglary at your place . . . we don't have to explain it, we just have to keep hooking them up."

We agreed to meet the next afternoon, after Lane's talk with the cops. When we left, I was still getting a bad vibration from

Lane—for her, Jack was the main question, and it obviously wasn't the same for LuEllen and me.

"She's starting to worry me a little," LuEllen said. "What happens if she decides that the only thing to do is to talk about us, about Firewall, about the NSA, about *everything,* to get the cops to look at Jack?"

"She doesn't know that much," I said.

"She knows we're the ones who hit Corbeil. That's a lot right there."

"Yeah." We drove along in silence for a moment; then I sighed and said, "It's not out of control yet. I think we could talk to her about the damage she'd do, if she dumped on all of us. She'd listen."

"I hope," LuEllen said. "But we've got to keep our options open." She thought a moment, then added, "Too bad she knows where you live."

Corbeil went online that night. There was no way to tell when they found that the apartment had been cracked, but I checked the dump box all day, every hour, and at ten o'clock, it was spooling stuff from an online session between Corbeil's apartment and the Am-Math computer. The software I was using was simple enough—you can buy copies of the heart of it for $99, over the counter. Essentially, it records keystrokes. Everything that Corbeil typed on his keyboard type was recorded, picked up, and sent to my dump box. Sometimes, it can be a little hard to follow, if the guy you're recording is a bad typist, but I've had enough practice that I can read it like a letter.

"What do you got?" LuEllen asked, looking over my shoulder.

"To begin with, we've got the phone number, the sign-on protocols, and Corbeil's password to get into the AmMath computer," I said. "After that, not much."

Corbeil sent company mail to one of his security people, telling him about the break-in.

Where are you? Can't find you. My apartment was hit by burglars. They pulled the safe out of the wall, must have used industrial equipment because they wrecked the place. They got money and jewelry. We need a full alert downtown, and somebody's got to keep an eye on the ranch. We need some over-night temps at the office. I tried to call Nasmith Security but can't get hooked up. We need people downtown tonight!! (I'll go down myself when we're finished here.) I had to call cops about the burglary because the apartment management discovered it. No way around it. Cops on way now. Maybe it was the money & jewelry, Marian wore it Friday & everybody saw it. There's no way to be sure, we have to assume otherwise. We better get low for another week or two. I'll call the paks this afternoon and put them off. Wipe this when you get it & call me.

He also pulled a file. We couldn't see what it was, because the program only recorded keystrokes, but we got the name, OMS2. All he did was read, and then the connection shut down, and he was off-line.

"Let's go," I said. "He's off, and he's going to be occupied for a while."

We went out to a Red Roof Inn—checked in with the fake ID I got in San Francisco, but paid cash—and got online. The dump box was still off-line, which meant that Corbeil's computer was shut down. I went out to the AmMath number, punched in his password, and we were in.

The OMS2 file was short and sweet: a few corporate memos, and a list of names and phone numbers. I then checked for an OMS3, got nothing, went to OMS1, got nothing, and then simply OMS, and again, got nothing—which was odd, because the files we'd inherited from Jack were labeled OMS. They could have been in another sector of the computer, or a different computer entirely, someplace where I didn't have access.

I did find a find a large administrative file called CLPR, which turned out to be internal memos about the Clipper II program. I dumped it to our Jaz disk, which took a while. Too long, actually. When we had it, I closed down the connection.

We'd taken care not to touch any hard surfaces inside the room that we didn't have to, and when we were done, we wiped those we'd had to touch, told the motel clerk that something had come up at home and that we'd have to check out—you could see the *Yeah, right,* in his eyes as he looked at LuEllen—and headed back to our hotel.

"We should have spent a little time fooling around," I said. "For verisimilitude—you don't really have that nice pink postorgasmic look that you get afterwards."

"We could still go for it," she offered.

"Too late to impress the clerk," I said.

The OMS2 file was mostly interesting for the names—military people from around the world, but mostly from the band of Islamic states that stretched from Syria to Indonesia. Only Egypt in Africa; and Turkey was missing.

"Why is that odd?" LuEllen asked, when I commented on it.

"Just the selection of names. If you're doing the Clipper, these people might all be customers, but the main customers would be the bigger states—England, France, Germany, Russia, Japan, China, India, like that. Instead, we have Syria, Iraq, Iran, Kuwait, Pakistan, Indonesia, Kazakhstan—missing Afghanistan, missing Saudi Arabia, missing Turkey."

"It's only one file. If it's OMS2, that implies other numbers, even if we couldn't get them. Maybe they're someplace else, or they erased them."

"Yeah, that's true . . ."

The CLPR file included a couple of thousand memos on routine technical, personnel, and financial matters. We spent four hours reading through them—scanning them, really—without finding a single useful fact.

"You know what?" LuEllen said. "If I had to be an administrative guy, I'd cut my wrists. I can't imagine even writing this shit, much less worrying about it."

"Not a single goddamn thing," I said, discouraged.

"Maybe there is one thing," she said. "Not a fact . . . and I'm not sure, but let's look at the dates on these things."

We looked at the dates, and LuEllen pointed out that two years earlier, there were ten or twenty Clipper memos being filed every week. A year ago, there were ten at the most. For the past six or eight months, there were four or five being filed weekly.

"Like the project is running down," she said.

"Maybe it's running out of time, or money. Maybe they've been stealing from it, and that's what they're trying to cover," I suggested.

"So why would they kill for a picture of three guys in a parking lot? If they did?"

"We'd know, if we could figure out who the guys were," I said.

"How do we do that? Figure it out?"

"I don't think we do. We're not the fuckin' FBI. We're just some guys."

ST. JOHN CORBEIL

Corbeil was in a rage: the necklace was gone, and the palm of his hand itched for it. His space had been violated. He had been so angry about the necklace that he hadn't seen that it was a diversion. And they'd done it so beautifully.

They'd absolutely suckered him. Those greasy footprints all over the living room, with only one track leading past the computer. He could still see the footprints in his mind's eye, could still feel the way he'd relaxed when he realized that the computer hadn't been touched.

He'd been angry about the necklace, but that had only been thieves. Lord knows he'd paraded the stones around enough, hanging them off the necks of half the models in Dallas. But they'd *used* him, they'd known how he'd think.

Then, that same night, they'd looted the computer. They would not have been found out if Woods hadn't been watching, hadn't seen, the next morning, the odd groping-about in the files. He'd come in to ask about it, and Corbeil knew instantly what had happened.

Suckered.

"Lane Ward," he said.

"She wouldn't have the resources," Hart protested. "Whoever went into your apartment was a pro. That safe wasn't ripped out of the wall by hackers. That took special gear. They goddamned near destroyed your apartment and nobody in the building heard a thing."

"Then who is it? The FBI doing a black-bag job? Not anymore, it's not. The CIA? They're the most gun-shy intelligence agency in the West. The NSA? They have fewer resources in the dark than we do. So who? Somehow, it's Ward. Or if it's not Ward, she can tell us who it is. Look at what they did with the bug in San Francisco. She's got help." He turned and looked at Hart. "Find her. Take her. We'll talk to her out at the ranch."

"Mr. Corbeil, if she disappears, the shit's going to hit the fan. I'm already tied to the Morrison killing."

"Look: we can make her out to be a member of Firewall. We've already started the groundwork on that. I'll have Woods do an entry from the outside, using the stuff from my apartment, just like they did it—but they'll go into Clipper files, and we'll call the NSA and the FBI in. We'll lead them back to her, somehow."

"What? She drops her driver's license on the motel floor?" Hart asked skeptically. "And she's got somebody with her."

"Yeah, and that's another guy we want to talk to. I'll bet it's some little Stanford computer genius who happens to know how to hack into anything. One of those goddamned pencil-necked hundred-

and-sixty-IQ smart-asses who might even be able to pull a safe out of a wall."

Hart shook his head, and then Corbeil said, "Fingerprints, maybe."

"What?"

"A computer attack's launched from a motel room. When the FBI investigates, it finds her fingerprints all over the place."

"How're we going to get her to do that?"

"We'll talk to her first in a motel room. Rent a room, talk to her there, make sure there are plenty of prints around, then take her out to the ranch. As soon as she's gone, we have Woods make an intrusion call from the motel room . . . The Agency can still trace that kind of crap."

"Sounds too complicated. If she broke away, if she started screaming . . ."

"So if it's too complicated, take her right out to the ranch," Corbeil snarled.

"Then we can't . . ."

"We'll have her hands," Corbeil said. "She won't need them. Not when we're done talking to her."

"Jesus," Hart said.

"No, he's not here," Corbeil answered.

"I just think, I'm starting to feel . . ."

"What?"

"This is out of control."

"William, you're right. You're absolutely right. We've got to get it back *under* control, or we're dead meat. You did a year in the softest prison in Texas. How'd you like a *real* hard place, the kind of place they reserve for traitors? That's what they'd call us: traitors. William, we would spend the rest of our lives up to our necks in shit."

"But if we just . . ."

"Do nothing? We've been trying that, William. It's not working. We need to know what's happening. If worse comes to worst, we at least need the time to run."

"Run." Hart clasped his head in his hands. "Ah, Jesus. Running."

"So *you* get Lane Ward. And the geek who's driving her around, whoever it is. In the meantime, I'll sit here, behind this desk—" he pointed to the cherrywood desk in the corner— "and try to think of a way to pin the whole thing on Firewall. Pin it hard enough that *we* won't go down for it, anyway."

"We should shut down the Old Man of the Sea."

Corbeil shrugged. "If you insist, but there's really no point. They're not close to it; they have no hint of it."

"I would just feel easier about it," Hart said.

"I'll talk to Woods," Corbeil said.

We slept late the next morning, LuEllen later than I. At ten o'clock, I rolled out, stretched, cleaned up. When I came back into the main room, LuEllen was still half asleep. She'd thrown the blanket off, and from one angle, near the bathroom door, her face was nicely framed by one outflung arm, and was just rising—from that perspective—over a thigh, with her foot in the foreground. Feet are always nice to draw, especially when you get to see them from the bottom. I tiptoed around to my briefcase, got out my drawing book, eased a chair over to the bathroom door, sat down, and drew for an hour.

Finally, growing aware of the total silence, she pushed herself halfway up and looked around. "Kidd?"

"Right here."

"Drawing my butt again?" She pushed herself all the way up, stretched and yawned.

"It's in the picture, but it's not the focus; it's sorta half cut off."

She came to look as I worked some shading in around her toes. "My feet aren't that big," she said.

"From this perspective."

"They're not that big. They're fives."

"From this angle."

"Bullshit. Not that big. And my toe isn't that bent."

"You're right. I'm sorry. I apologize."

"No, you don't," she said. She stretched again. "You don't care whose fragile ego you crush. All artists are like that."

"Somebody once said that a portrait is a painting where there's something not quite right about the mouth," I said. "It might have been Sargent. Anyway, nobody's ever said that about the foot."

"I'm the first."

"Go take a shower," I said.

She went to take a shower and I struggled with the foreshortening of her leg and foot, and with her face in the back, rising over her thigh, and the pillow behind that. When I was done, I took the drawing out, ripped it up, and tossed it in the wastebasket. Something not quite right about the foot. With all that in my head, waiting for LuEllen to get out of the bathroom, I looked out the window down at the parking lot.

And understood what I hadn't understood before.

Why I had looked down at the parking lot and thought I'd missed an important thought.

Understood the AmMath photographs—or something about them, anyway. It all came out of the perspective of LuEllen's foot . . .

The shower was running and I could hear her humming to herself in the bathroom as I brought the laptop up, and one of the photos.

"Jesus." I was right. I sat staring at it, then brought up another one. Ripped a piece of paper out of my drawing book, got a pen, and began making comparative measurements on the computer screen. I was still doing it when LuEllen came bobbling out of the bathroom with a towel around her head. I glanced at her and looked back at the computer.

"Thanks," she said. "I'm here with my nice pink . . ."

"Shut up. I gotta get online with Bobby. Get dressed."

"What?"

"Look at this photograph."

She looked over my shoulder. "What?" she asked again.

"Look how this shadow comes down from this light pole? The shadow from the sun?"

"Yeah?"

"Look how it comes down from this light pole," I said.

"All right."

"And this one."

"I see all the shadows and all the light poles, Kidd. So what?"

"All the shadows are in exactly the same perspective. Exactly, as close as I can measure. Doesn't it look weird to you?"

"No. And so what?"

"It's impossible, that's all. Well, not impossible, if the camera was far enough back."

"We were thinking it might be a surveillance camera up on a roof. It'd have to be, to get that high angle."

"Still not high enough," I said. "I gotta get with Bobby. He could make some better measurements and do the numbers."

"If that's not high enough, what? You think it was made by a plane?"

"Not high enough," I said. "I think that's a satellite photograph."

She still wasn't much impressed; I had to work to get that. "Think what a face would look like if you took it from three blocks away with your Nikon and then blew it up to this size. It'd look like a thumbprint," I said. "Look at those faces. You can't quite recognize them, but you almost can. If that camera's in orbit, it has one unbelievable capability."

Now she was hunched over me, and spotted something we should have seen before. "You know, those cars . . ." There were only a half-dozen of them in the parking lot. "Not a single one of them is American-made. Look at this one . . ." She tapped the screen with a fingernail. "I don't think I've ever seen that kind. It looks like a combination of a pickup truck and a sedan."

"You see those in the Middle East," I said. "Lots of them."

She straightened. "So it's a satellite photo. So what?"

"I don't know, yet. But it seems unlikely that a satellite would take a picture of three guys and the three guys were important," I said. "How could you time something like that?"

"Radios, maybe . . ."

I shook my head. "I bet it's not the guys that are important. I bet it's the photograph. Not the content, just the photograph, that they have it. They're supposed to be working on the Clipper chip, and they have *this*. This has got to be some kind of ungodly high-level secret capability. You could not only see stuff like ammo dumps, you could see what's in them. If they can do something with computers to punch up the resolution—just a probability engine—they might be able to figure out who gets into which car, might be able to track cars through traffic . . . all kinds of stuff."

"They're NSA, right? Isn't that what they do?"

"No, no, that's another group, the NRO, the National Reconnaissance Office. They do all the satellite stuff."

"So let's get online with Bobby, and see what he says."

We got online from a mall. Bobby thought he could figure out the height of the camera by picking out small parts of the original full-strength photos and making some precise measurements on the shadows.

FREAKY IF IT'S A SATELLITE PHOTO. NEVER SEEN ANYTHING LIKE THIS.

MAYBE WHAT THEY'RE HIDING.

BUT WHAT DOES IT HAVE TO DO WITH FIREWALL?

There was the other side of Lane's question. Lane was interested in what happened to Jack; Bobby was interested in how his name got attached to Firewall. Somehow, AmMath was involved in both of those things, but how and why were they related? Or were they related?

We talked about it as we were leaving the mall, and decided they had to be linked. Jack went to Maryland, where the computer that started the Firewall rumors was located. The guy he saw, who was later killed, was a client of that same server. It was all tied. We just couldn't see the knot.

---

ane, it turned out, had been worrying about the same questions all night. We all had breakfast together, and she leaned across the diner table, picked up my glass of Coke, and rapped it on the table. She had a theory, she said.

"Say the photographs are wildly important, for some reason. We don't know why, but let's say that's a given. Jack steals them. They know he stole them, but they don't know why, or who he might have given them to. So they come up with a scheme. They invent this Firewall group, using names that they harvest from the Internet. Legendary hackers. There's all kinds of talk on the Net. Anybody could get a list like that. They make Jack a part of the group, so when the names finally come out, the cops'll say, 'Ah-ah, he was a member of the radical Firewall group, that's why he broke into AmMath and it was only bad luck that he got caught . . .' "

"Why use the server in Maryland?" I asked. "The same one that Lighter just happened to be on."

"You said it was mostly NSA people," she said. "Maybe it was one server they all knew. That they all had access to."

"Sounds weak," LuEllen said.

"But the rest of it sounds pretty good," Green said. "It ties things together."

"What about the IRS attack? That was set up weeks ago."

"But the Firewall name wasn't around weeks ago," I said. "That could have been made up at the last minute. These hacks are ready to attack the IRS, and just at that moment, somebody invents a group with a neat-sounding name. So they say, 'All right, we're Firewall, too.' "

"Goddamnit," LuEllen said, "It's still too hard to think about."

"I'll tell you what, though," Lane said. "When we go back into AmMath's computer, I think we ought to be looking for stuff on

Firewall and satellites. This Clipper stuff is a dead end. Whatever's going on doesn't have anything to do with Clipper."

"When *we* go back in?" I asked.

"Darn right: I know my way around mainframes as well as anyone. I want to be there tonight, when we go back in," she said.

"Gotta find a new motel," I said.

"There's a place called Eighty-Eight right across the street from where we're at," Green said.

"So we'll set up there tonight," I said. "We'll use one of LuEllen's IDs, and call you when we're settled in."

Lane didn't have much to say about her talk with the cops: "They say they don't believe that AmMath had anything to do with anything—but I think they believe there's some kind of government deal going on, and they don't want to know about it. They think *we're* the bad guys—Jack and me."

"You told them about the burglary at your house."

"Of course." Lane said. "We gave them every single detail. We told them we thought Jack's house had been broken into, too."

"They're dead in the water," Green said. "I used to work with a program in Oakland that investigated shootings by cops. Most of the shootings were open-and-shut. But every once in a while, we'd get a shooting and there'd be something wrong about it. No proof, no evidence, just something wrong. We'd try to get the cops to look a little deeper, to ask a few more questions, and they'd say they would, but you could see it in their eyes: they'd signed off. They either believed they knew what happened, or they didn't want to know any more. That's what's happened with this case. I could see it: they've signed off. They're all done. They don't want to know any more."

"Damnit, nobody'll *move,*" I said.

We thought about that; then Lane said, "By the way, I looked up McLennan County, where Corbeil has that ranch. It's about a hundred miles south. Near Waco."

We made arrangements to meet them that night in Denton, and then LuEllen and I took the rest of the day off. We'd been cooped up too long, hanging out in hotel rooms and restaurants. We were the kind of people who liked to move around. I got my laptop and sketchbook, and my watercolor tin and a plastic squeeze bottle of water, and we went out to a driving range and LuEllen hit balls for an hour while I drew the shelter over the driving line. The whole thing with the satellite photos—if that's what they were—had gotten me thinking about perspective. The driving line was sheltered by a fifty-yard-long metal roof mounted on steel poles, and from the corners, made a fairly interesting challenge in three-point perspective.

When LuEllen got tired of hitting balls, we went back to the hotel, talked to a desk clerk who got a map out and drew a six-mile jogging circuit that he ran himself every morning, and we drove out to his starting point and did the six miles in forty-five minutes, just cruising along suburban streets looking at all the pickups.

"Not bad," she said, when we got back to the car. "Let's go buy some boots."

She bought two pair of cowboy boots, and paid six hundred dollars for them. I've never actually seen her on a horse, but she does like horses, and she liked the boots. They put an inch or two on her height, and she liked that, too.

A t nine o'clock, LuEllen checked us into the Eighty-Eight Motel in Denton. We got online, and took a look in the dump box.

Corbeil had been online in the morning, before we'd even gotten up—no rest for the wicked—but hadn't used the computer since then. "Maybe they're fixing up his apartment and he's staying someplace else while they do it," LuEllen suggested.

"I hope not. I'd like to be sure that he's in his apartment, and done for the day, before I sign on with his codes," I said. "If we were on, and he tried to get on, he might see the conflict."

LuEllen called Lane on the cell phone, and told her where we were. We didn't want any calls on the room phone going out to a number that could be connected with any of us, and figured to throw the cell phone away in the next day or two. Lane and Green showed up ten minutes later, having walked over from the Radisson.

I told them about the dump box, and how we were using it as a cut-out, and why I didn't want to go online immediately. "Makes sense," Lane said. "I'd like to look at those files you got . . ."

She spent the next two hours flipping through the administrative files, stopping every fifteen minutes or so to look at the dump box. Green, LuEllen, and I chatted for a while, then LuEllen ordered a pay-TV movie, a hyperviolent science-fiction flick that had all the depth of a comic book. The production values, on the other hand, were great.

Ten minutes after the movie ended, Lane went online to check the dump box, and found that Corbeil was working. The sign-on protocols and codes were the same as the night before. He sent a couple of short memos, one of them berating a guy named John Mc-Neal about a production problem on CDs carrying what apparently were commercial code products. Then he signed off. We waited another half-hour, Lane with increasing impatience, to make sure he wouldn't sign on again, then went out to the AmMath computer.

We looked for anything that involved satellites, photographs,

Middle Eastern nations, the NSA, the CIA, the National Reconnaissance Office; tried all of those things as keywords in a variety of searches, and even threw in oddball stuff—"orbit," "surveillance," "resolution."

After half an hour, I suggested that we shut down. "We need to do more research into what we're looking for," I said. "Maybe just go to the library and get business stuff about AmMath. Trying to flog our way through the computer is like trying to find a two-inch article in ten years' worth of newspapers."

Lane wanted to continue: "Fifteen more minutes," she said. "Twenty minutes. We're in, who knows whether they'll change all the protocols or something?"

LuEllen wasn't doing anything, and bored, said, "I'm going down the street to that Randy's place and get coffee and a doughnut. Anybody want anything?"

"I'll walk along," I said. To Lane: "Fifteen minutes . . ."

"Yeah, yeah."

R andy's was a combination greasy spoon and greasy bakery. We bought doughnuts and coffee and a Diet Coke, and talked about not much at all; two people carrying a couple of white bakery sacks along the highway. We were a hundred yards from the motel when we saw the flashes. LuEllen said, "Did you see that?"

I was already trotting toward the motel. Night-time gun flashes are hard to mistake, and even with the background noise of the highway we could now hear the rapid *pop-pop-pop* of gunfire.

We got closer and saw two men break away from the motel, from the end where our room was. Another couple, young kids, college kids, maybe, both carrying book bags, stopped to look at them as they crossed the parking lot to a waiting car. The shorter of the two men was hobbling. One of the kids broke away from the other, running toward the motel. Then the other one followed, and I ditched the white bags behind a car and the car with the two guys screeched out of the parking lot, fishtailed once in the street and disappeared into traffic.

We turned the corner of the motel and saw an older guy, white-haired in a burgundy windbreaker, walking toward our room, the college kids just coming up. I was ten steps back now, LuEllen a few steps further behind and the college kid, a boy, went inside and then popped back out and started screaming, "Call an ambulance call an ambulance . . ."

I pushed past his white face to the door and saw Lane on the bed. She was dead, her face gone. Couldn't see Green; the bathroom door was mostly closed and shot to pieces. I stepped over to the door and knuckled it open. Green was in the bathtub, looking up at me, a gun in one hand.

"Got an ambulance coming," I said. "Are you hurt bad?"

"Hit twice," he groaned. "What about Lane?"

"Gone."

"Get out of here," he said.

I went back out into the main room. The college girl was inside with LuEllen and I shouted at her, "Go out to the street, wave the ambulance in."

"What?"

"I dunno, I dunno," I shouted at her. She stepped back, frightened of me, and turned and ran toward the street. "Flag the ambulance," I shouted after her. To the old guy in the burgundy windbreaker I yelled, "Two people shot. Run down to the office and make sure that kid's called an ambulance . . ."

He turned and ran. The minute he was gone, I stepped past the bed, not looking at Lane, ripped the phone wire out of the telephone, bundled up the laptop, which had fallen on the floor, and stuck it in the back of my waistband, under my jacket.

LuEllen had stopped to take a close look at Lane—Lane had been hit at least twice in the side of the head, and laid sprawled face-up, eyes open just a crack, on the yellow bedspread. LuEllen shook her head. Lane's purse was lying on the floor. LuEllen rolled it with her foot, took the pistol out, and slid it into her jacket pocket. Without another word, we were out of the room. Two motel people were running toward us, and I waved at them: "In here, in here . . . hurry, hurry, get an ambulance."

More people came running, and LuEllen and I eased to the outside of the group, and then turned, and then were around the corner, and in the car. We went out the back of the parking lot, slowly, onto a service road, down a block, and were out of sight when the first cop car arrived.

"She had no chance," LuEllen said grimly. "Executed."

"Green's alive, but he was hit a couple of times," I said. "He was in the tub. He was still thinking. He said to get out, so he'll cover us."

"Fingerprints?"

"Not from me," I said.

"The only hard surface I touched was the TV remote, and Green was using it after I did, so I should be okay."

"You used the bathroom."

"I was careful. You used the telephone . . ."

"Just plugged into the side, never picked up the receiver. I don't think I touched anything with my fingertips."

"Guys from AmMath," she said.

"Gotta be."

"What is it with them?"

"I don't know; but they must have spotted me coming online last night, and set up to back-trace our entry tonight. Took them an hour to do it and get here . . . Christ, Lane and Green probably thought that was us at the door, coming back with coffee."

21

LuEllen and I had been in jams before. I don't know whether it was simply experience, or some essential defect in our personalities, that allowed us to carry on as efficiently as we did. To get the laptop, to get out. To do it without talking about it or hesitating.

If I've ever been seriously attached to any one person in my adult life, it was LuEllen. But if she'd been in that motel room, and if I'd walked back to find her dead on the yellow bedspread, then, God help me, I believe I would have reacted the same way. And if I'd been dead, and she'd looked in, it would have been the same. No rage, no horror or fear or even sorrow. Efficiency. Get the laptop. Get the gun. Get out. Assess the damage.

The rage and sorrow comes later.

But it comes.

On the way out, in the car, LuEllen kept coming back at me about fingerprints: that's where we could hang up. If I'd left my prints behind, they could put a face with them—I'd been thoroughly and repeatedly printed in the Army—and the other witnesses at the motel would confirm it.

But I didn't think I'd left any. LuEllen and I had done all this before, operating out of remote sites, and you *go in* thinking about not leaving prints. If you get sloppy about it, then you'll always leave a few. The only hard thing I'd touched was the phone and the room key-card, which I still had in my shirt pocket. Still, we both ran the whole night through our heads, picking out each move we'd made. After a while, I let out a breath and said, "I'm good."

"So am I, except that the clerk saw me when I checked in."

"Yeah, but Lane looked sort of Latino and half the people around there looked Latino. I bet the clerk identifies her as the woman who checked in, because she looked like a lot of other women who checked in. And her face is shot up . . . Good thing I didn't check us in, with Green being black. Then they'd *know*."

"Maybe Green won't cover for us."

"He couldn't give them too much. He doesn't know who we *are,* really."

"He could find out. Or give the cops enough information that *they* could."

"I don't know. I think Texas is a felony-murder state. If he says he doesn't know what was going on, that he was simply a hired body-guard for Lane, who was doing something with her computer . . . If he says that, he'll kick clear. If he lets them know that he knew what Lane was doing, then she would have been killed in the course of committing a crime, and that might make a case against him for felony murder."

"So he can't talk."

"He wouldn't—if he knows all this."

"So let's call Bobby; maybe he can get the word back."

We called Bobby from a pay phone. When he came up on the laptop, I wrote:

CALL ME NOW VOICE LINE: EMERGENCY.

He called back five seconds after I was off. I'd only talked to him on a voice line a couple of times. The only thing I knew about him was that he was a black guy, who I thought lived someplace in the Mississippi River South. He had one of those soft Delta accents, and was tied into a lot of interesting black people who, in the sixties, would have been called activists, or maybe, in that part of the world, agitators.

"What happened?" he asked, without preamble.

I gave it to him as succinctly as I could, then said, "Somebody's got to get with Green. A lawyer, who can tell him to stick with the ignorant bodyguard story. If he lets on that he knew Lane was committing a crime, then they might . . ."

"Felony murder," Bobby said. "Bad for you, bad for me."

"Yeah. Somebody's got to get in touch."

"I can handle that," Bobby said softly. "How are you?"

"We're good, but we're clearing out. We don't think anybody will be looking for us too hard, but just in case . . . we're gonna run down, to, ah, Austin."

"Check in from there."

"Talk to you," I said, and hung up.

"Austin?" LuEllen asked.

"It's a big city with lots of people coming and going," I said. "Other than Dallas, it's about the closest big city to Waco."

"Corbeil's ranch." She was quiet for a while, then said, "So now you're on a revenge trip. Forget Jack, you're going to get them because they killed Lane."

"No. If I could, I'd go home right now. But I need to get loose; I can't get loose. The feds have a list of names, they've got murder and evidence of a conspiracy and the IRS attack and maybe what looks like an attack on a major encryption company. They'll eventually start peeling back the names. I've got to figure out what's going on, and get them running that way, or I'm fucked."

She didn't say anything, so eventually I said, "I'm not sure you really need to stay around. From here on out, it's gonna be mostly computer stuff."

"Oh, shit, Kidd. You know I'm not going anyplace," she said irritably.

"Maybe if you . . ."

"Shut up."

So I shut up: I wanted her around.

We stayed the night in Dallas. Given the time the shooting took place, it was too late to make the regular television news. If the papers bothered with it, they wouldn't get more than a few basic facts from the cops. We decided to stay over, and to leave at the peak checkout time in the morning. That's what we did: there'd been nothing on the late-night news and nothing in the morning papers. At eight o'clock, we were headed down I-35 to Austin.

"Hope Bobby got somebody to Green," LuEllen said, partway

down. Neither of us was talking much. The images from the motel were too clear, the kind of images that push you back into your own head.

"He said he would, and he's got good contacts," I said. "I hope."

A ustin used to be a small-town pretty place. Take away the heat, and it's more like Minnesota than the rest of Texas. Twenty years ago, I could have imagined living there, except that the landscape colors weren't mine. Now, there're too many people, and the city has gone from a Great Place to a Pain in the Ass.

Somebody else's problem. We checked into a Holiday Inn and started making phone calls.

WHAT HAPPENED?

ATTORNEY TALKED TO GREEN THIS MORNING. GREEN'S IN INTENSIVE CARE / WOUNDED LEGS/THIGHS / WILL BE OKAY. GREEN KNOWS FELONY LAW, TELLS COPS HE DIDN'T KNOW WHAT WAS GOING ON EXCEPT CLIENT HAD BEEN ATTACKED SEVERAL TIMES, HAD BEEN BURGLARIZED, BROTHER SHOT. HE WAS HIRED TO DO BODYGUARD WORK. GREEN SAYS HE WAS IN BATHROOM WHEN DOOR KNOCK CAME, SHE SAID THEY'RE BACK AND HE SAID STAY AWAY BUT SHE OPENED DOOR AND SHOOTING STARTED. HE SAYS HE HIT ONE, COPS FIND BLOOD TRAIL.

HE DID GOOD. MUST PLAY DUMB.

HE DOES THAT. COPS PUSH HIM HARD BUT ALL HE HAS IS HIRING ON RECOMMENDATION OF FRIEND — FRIEND WILL COVER. TELLS COPS HE DOESN'T KNOW LW, DOESN'T KNOW COMPUTERS, SAW NO TROUBLE UNTIL SHOOTING STARTED.

OK.

YOU STILL WORKING?

YES. IRS ATTACK CONTINUES?

CONTINUES, BUT CLOSING DOWN NOW. RUMORS: FEDS HUNTING FIREWALL NAMES, MAKE SOME BUSTS; NOTHING IN PAPERS. WASH POST: FBI, NSA IN CONFLICT OVER FIREWALL. RUMORS: GERMAN CALLED COPERNIX DOES IT.

OK. YOU MONITOR, WE WILL CALL DAILY.

YES. ONE MORE THING. THE FIVE DATA STRINGS WITH THE PICTURES INCLUDE VARIOUS 125–200 (APPROX.) BYTE FILES FOLLOWED BY DISTINCT 512-BYTE/4096-BIT FILES FOLLOWED BY VARIOUS 350–600 BYTE FILES. 4096-BIT FILES ARE LIKELY ULTRASTRONG KEYS, BUT DON'T KNOW LOCK. POSSIBLE PHOTOS ENCRYPTED/DECRYPTED WITH KEYS?

WILL LOOK.

GOOD. BYE.

"What?" LuEllen wanted to know.

"Those goddamned files. As soon as we got them, we should have gone to Mexico or someplace and hid out, and figured them out. If they're killing for them, there's got to be a reason; they must think we can figure them out."

"Why don't you just mail them to the NSA and let them figure them out?"

"Not until I know what they are. If they're important enough to kill for, then they might be important enough that the NSA or the CIA or somebody else would just keep coming after them. Anyway, I've got a new theory."

"Lane had a theory."

"But I have another one. The theory is that AmMath screwed something up so badly that they figured they had to cover it, and the whole thing got out of control when Jack was killed. Now they're killing to cover up the killing."

"Sounds like a bad movie."

"That's what I got," I said.

That afternoon, we got something else. After looking gloomily through the files—I saw how Bobby isolated the 4096-bit file, and there wasn't any question that it was distinct from the garbage before and after, and it did look like a key—I noticed the OMS tab again. The Old Man and the Sea. No, that wasn't right: everyplace I'd seen the whole name, it was Old Man *of* the Sea: either a mistake, or not Hemingway.

"Let's go," I said.

"Where?"

"Down to the university library. See if I can get somebody to tell me about this Old Man of the Sea."

"Kidd . . . this is the University of *Texas*."

"And a damn fine university it is," I said.

"Really?"

"Yup. It is."

"But then if it turns out to be something important, whoever you talk to will probably remember you."

"I think it's a chance we've got to take."

"Couldn't you just look it up on the Internet or something?"

"Well . . ." I scratched my head. I could try, of course, but I'd become so accustomed to thinking of the Net as a large sewer clogged with crap, that it hadn't occurred to me. "We can try."

I plugged "Old Man of the Sea" into the Alta Vista search engine and got back 756 Web pages; most of it was junk, but it became pretty clear that the original Old Man of the Sea was a character from the *Voyages of Sinbad the Sailor.*

According to the story, Sinbad was stranded on an island—he never learned—where he came across an old man who he believed to be crippled. The old man asked to be carried to a pool of water, but when Sinbad got him there, the old man wouldn't get off Sinbad's back.

In fact, he grew something like spurs, and claws, and dug into Sinbad's neck. For days, Sinbad was forced to carry him around the island and feed him. Sinbad himself, in an excess of pain, hollowed out a gourd that he found, and filled it with grapes. In a few days, the grape juice had become strong wine, which he drank to kill the pain.

The old man noticed him doing this, and demanded some of the wine. Sinbad gave it to him. The old man became drunk, and Sinbad was able to throw him off his shoulders. Not being a major moralist, Sinbad then beat the old man to death. When he managed to get a ship off the island, he was told that the old man was a famous devil, who would beg to be carried, but then would ride his victim to death, eventually eating the body . . .

"Nice story," LuEllen said.

"I should have remembered it," I said. "I read all the Sinbad stories, but a long time ago."

"So . . . what does it mean?"

"There are some very heavy social and psychological implications to it."

"You have no fuckin' idea what it means," she said.

"Why do you think we've been cutting the devil card out of my tarot deck?"

She opened her mouth to crack wise, and then shut it. And kept it shut.

Actually going out on the Net suggested something else to me. I did a quick search, found a site, and plugged in www.dallasnews.com. *The Dallas Morning News* had one of the better newspaper sites, and on page one, it carried a teaser: "One Killed, One Wounded in Denton Shooting."

I punched it up and after a minute, a brief story trickled down the laptop's screen.

A California woman was killed and a man who told police that he was her "bodyguard" was wounded in a shooting at the Eighty-Eight Motel in Denton late Saturday night. Denton police say the shooting may be drug related.

Lane Ward, an assistant professor of computer science at Stanford University in Palo Alto, California, was pronounced dead at the scene, while her "bodyguard," identified by police as Lethridge Green, of Oakland, California, was in fair condition at Mount of Olives Hospital.

Police said that both Ward and Green had prior drug-related arrests, Ward in 1986 in San Francisco for possession of marijuana, Green in 1977 in Oakland for possession of cocaine.

Witnesses said the gunmen were two white males, one of whom was wounded in the shooting. Neither gunman has been found.

Police said Green was being held for questioning at the hospital.

"Ooo. Little Lane was smoking dope," LuEllen said.

"In 1986," I said. "She was a college kid."

"But it sounds bad, doesn't it?"

"Not unless the cops dropped some dope in the room, and the paper doesn't mention any dope being found," I said. "Of course, there's the other possibility."

"Yeah?"

"That it's all bullshit from start to finish; that the FBI or some-body is mixing in with the cops, and don't want reporters asking any more questions. I mean, right now, it's another dope-related shooting. Nobody'll give it another look."

"Good for Green . . ."

"Probably," I said.

So we didn't go to the library. We didn't go to Waco, either; not that day, or the next. If there was anything going on at the ranch, they might be looking out for conspicuously nonrancher cars, for at least a couple of days.

So we spent Sunday and Monday wandering around Austin; bought a basketball at a Wal-Mart and played a little one-on-one at a local playground, hit some more golf balls, did some drawing. Checked the *Dallas Morning News* Web site a couple more times, but the story was dead.

Talked to Bobby. The FBI had interviewed Green, pretty much cutting out the local cops. He'd convinced them that he was hired muscle: he had all the background, plus the attitude. They left with a few threats, but both Green and his lawyer thought it was all over.

I also spent some time calling around Austin, and found a place I could rent a pickup—"I need to help my daughter move some fur-niture from one house to another," I told the guy at Access Car Rental, who didn't care one way or the other—and picked up the truck. On Monday night, we watched movies on pay TV. The next morning, at eight o'clock, we left for Waco.

Or Whacko, as LuEllen pronounced it.

22

When we were killing time in Austin, we hardly talked about Lane Ward. We were working at pushing her away, the image of her dead on the motel bed. Instead of talking about that, we were technical: How did they find us so quickly? When did they detect the intrusion, etc.?

On the way up to Waco, LuEllen, who had hardly spoken at all that morning, asked, "Who's going to take care of her?"

"What?"

"Who's going to take care of Lane? Who's going to take care of the funeral and her stuff at her house? What's going to happen with all that? Does somebody just haul it to the dump?"

"Don't start," I said.

"I can't help it. I woke up thinking about it. I mean, she was about my age, and she doesn't have any kids, and her parents are dead, just like me. Then, all of a sudden, she's killed—and who takes care of her? The state? I mean, do they just cremate her and throw her ashes in a dump somewhere? Do they take all of her books out and throw them away, or have a garage sale, or what?"

"If she's got a will . . . I mean, that should take care of it."

"That's just legal," LuEllen said. "I wonder if there's anybody who really cares?"

She worried about it all the way to Waco; and didn't really stop then, I don't think. She just stopped talking about it.

W aco has a county courthouse that looks like a state capitol. I went in looking for a map, and they sent me across the street. I got one, chatted with the map guy for a few minutes, and he showed me a plat book. It took a while, but I eventually spotted Corbeil's ranch just outside a little town called Crawford, which was northwest of Waco proper. We stopped at a Barnes & Noble bookstore, LuEllen ran in and bought a couple of crumpets and some kind of health juice, and we headed for Corbeil's.

T here's a big lake at Waco, and a couple of rivers, which didn't fit with my mental picture of the place: but there they were. The November countryside was low and rolling, and as we got closer to Crawford, cut by gullies and a few creeks. There was some corn farming, and lots of hay around, but in general, the country was more ranch than farm. We crawled through Crawford, inadvertently ran a four-way stop that I thought was two-way, and almost got T-boned by a Chevy pickup. LuEllen was peering out the window and said, eventually, "Took me sixteen years to get out of a place like this."

"Really? A place like this?"

"Up in Minnesota," she said. I'd never known she was a small-town girl, though if I'd thought about it, I might've guessed. And I waited. No small-town kid has ever been through another small town without some kind of comment about the other town's inferiority. She said, "But the place I grew up, at least we had a Dairy Queen."

Yup.

Corbeil's place was set on a ridge above Texas Highway 185; the place was a sprawling yellow log-cabin-style house. Not new, but not antique, either: the kind of log place that city people buy. We couldn't see it all from the road, but a half-dozen outbuildings of one kind or another were scattered about the place: a steel pole barn stuffed with hay, what was probably a machine shed, a six-car garage, what might possibly have been a bunkhouse or an office building—two doors, and a row of windows with decorative shutters next to each window—a long, low stable with a training ring off one side, and what might have been a pump shed.

One pasture, surrounded with barbed wire and with a circular growth pattern in the grass that suggested a center-pivot watering system, contained a half-dozen Brahman cattle. The rest of the place was that kind of shaggy gray-green, ready for winter. A couple of hundred white-faced cows were clumped around what we could see of the rest of his pasture land, which continued to rise, in a series of steps, behind the ranch house.

According to the plat book, Corbeil owned 1,280 acres—two square miles, a mile wide and two miles deep. There were roads on two sides: Highway 185, which ran east-west along the front of the house, and Beulah Drive, which ran north-south, along the west side of the ranch.

A mile north of Highway 185, as we drove up Beulah on the west side of Corbeil's property, an old ramshackle farmhouse squatted well back from the road in a clump of trees, with weeds growing up in the two-tire-track driveway. The place looked dead, but there was a newer pizza-dish-sized satellite TV antenna on the roof, and another, old-style dish on the lawn out back, so we figured somebody probably lived there.

We continued on the county road to what we figured was the end of Corbeil's property, and then went two miles on, where we found the remnants of what must have been another old farm: a grove of trees set back from the road with traces of a track going back into the trees. I turned around on the track, and in the silence and emptiness of the place, got out and trotted back to the trees, and found an old crumbling chimney, and a parking spot littered with corroding beer cans. Maybe the local lover's lane.

On the way back out, as we approached the north end of Corbeil's land again, I pointed to the fence line that marked the edge of Corbeil's property.

"Up ahead—see those trees? I want to hop out with the glasses. You take the truck back up the road about five or six miles, then come get me. Give me fifteen minutes," I said.

"Where're you going?"

"I'm going to walk along that fence row, see what I can see on the other side of that hill."

"Probably a rancher who doesn't like trespassers."

"I'll tell him I'm an artist," I said. "I'll take my bag with me."

At the trees, I hopped out with the bag and the binoculars, and as LuEllen rolled away, I cut through a copse of junky roadside trees, crossed a fence where it joined another fence line, and headed up the hill. As I said, the countryside was empty: roads and fences and fields and not a lot of people. I was walking through some kind of ground cover, springy underfoot—it looked grassy, and it looked as though it were regularly mowed, but it wasn't anything like the alfalfa or clover I was familiar with.

I followed the fence line four hundred yards up the hill, and finally reached a broad crest where I could look down on Corbeil's ranch. Lots more cows and a big stock tank with a watering station. What interested me more, though, was the satellite dish that sat next to the pump station. It was one of the big ones, the old-fashioned dishes, but it looked well-kept; and there was nobody there to look at a TV. Still, it was moving as I watched. I couldn't actually see the movement, but when I looked away, and then looked back, it seemed that the dish had moved. I squatted next to the fence, lined up a barb on the barbed-wire with one edge of the dish: and yes, it was moving. It moved for the best part of five or six minutes, and then stopped.

As best I could judge, from the direction of the road down the hill, the dish was pointing northeast when it stopped. I could see the backside of the old abandoned-looking farmhouse a mile south, and with the binoculars, could make out the satellite dish behind it: that dish was also pointing northeast.

Huh.

Were the dishes coordinated? Were they talking to satellites? And if they were, so what? There are uplinks all over the place: even sports bars had them. But bars didn't have coordinated dishes scattered over a couple of square miles. If the dishes were linked, they would have, in effect, a huge baseline, which would be the same as having a much bigger and more sensitive dish. And with those photos . . .

We were onto something. A secret operation of some kind? But who were they hiding it from? If they were working with the feds, they'd just go ahead and stick the dishes up anywhere; they wouldn't be hidden away on a ranch in Waco.

I was waiting in the trees when LuEllen came back.

"Anything?"

"Yeah. I think we're getting a handle on something. Did you see a satellite dish at Corbeil's? One of those big babies?"

"I didn't notice . . . I don't think so."

We cruised the place again, running down Highway 185, but no dish was visible from the highway. "Could be down out of sight," she said.

"Or maybe there are only two . . . or maybe there are more, tucked away like that stock tank."

"What are you thinking?" she asked.

"A little fantasy," I said. "They were willing to kill for those pictures, and we have what might be code. We got that list of names for all those Middle Eastern countries . . . I wonder if somehow they aren't hijacking photos from the recon satellites and selling them."

"For what?"

"Sell surveillance of Pakistan to India, and surveillance of India to Pakistan. Sell surveillance of Iraq to Iran, and Iran and Syria to Iraq; of Israel to Syria. Of Taiwan to China, and China to Taiwan."

"They'd get caught."

"I could tell you ten ways to do it, that they'd never get caught. That the buyers would never see the sellers. That's what the Inter-

net is for. Any buyer who's getting this stuff . . . it'd be the biggest secret they had."

"Okay. So what next?"

"Let's go back to Austin. I need to do some shopping," I said.

"Always shopping."

"We'll come back tonight."

"A scout?"

"A scout."

In Austin, we went to an outdoor-sports store and bought a good
compass; a GPS receiver with a map function; topographic maps
of the East Waco area, including Corbeil's ranch; and a cheap black
daypack. At a building-supply place, picked up a builders' protractor,
a bubble level, and some duct tape. And in a sewing store, a card with
five yards of elastic banding. I spent an hour in the parking lot with
the GPS receiver, figuring out how to work it; especially interesting
were the time and distance functions, and the backtrack function.

Then there was the matter of the gun.

"We need a better one," LuEllen said. "Look what they did to
Lane, and what they did to Jack. Those were executions, so they just
don't give a fuck. If we go on a scout, and they catch us, and they've
got guns—this *is* Texas, Kidd—they're going to shoot us down like
dogs."

"Anytime you buy a gun . . ."

"Ought to be easy in Texas," she said. "Let me call Weenie."

It *was* easy in Texas. All we had to do was drive to Houston,
which was a little better than two hours away, meet a guy in a parking lot near George Bush Intercontinental Airport, and give him
$600 for a cheap Chinese-made AK with two magazines, fifty rounds
of 7.65 × 39, and a nylon sling.

"That's about a two-hundred dollar gun in a store," I told
LuEllen, as we left the parking lot.

"That wasn't a store," she said.

"Hope it works," I said. "Looks like it was made by a high school
kid in a shop class."

At five o'clock we were back in Austin. In the motel room, I
pumped some shells through the AK, bruised the tip of my middle
finger with the firing pin, and eventually decided that the thing
might work. We ate, and by seven o'clock, we were on the road again.

The land around Waco is fairly lush. Waco is just about south of
Dallas, and the really dry, sere land—serious prickly-pear country—
starts an hour or two to the west.

But the land just west of Waco, like lots of backcountry in this
day of Interstate highways, was lonely. All the land was used, in one
way or another, but when we'd gone out in the morning, we'd seen
only one person along the road, a woman walking out to her mailbox. In that kind of country, without the light pollution of the city,
it gets dark.

We'd picked a good night for it, windless, starlit, quiet. The
moon was already slanting down in the sky when we drove past
Corbeil's. There were lights in the house, in the building that might
have been an office or bunkhouse, and in the yard. A couple of cars
were parked outside the garage, but we didn't see anyone moving
around. We made the turn on Beulah Avenue, west of the ranch, and
headed north, until we found the track that headed back to the aban-
doned homesite that we'd discovered in the morning. Once there, we
shut down the truck, spent a couple of minutes looking around, and
mostly, listening.

We heard nothing but insects, and the gravel underfoot. Ten
minutes after we arrived, LuEllen broke out the taped flashlights,
and we started back down the road toward Corbeil's place.

The walk took forty minutes, moving slowly, and stopping to listen and scan ahead with the night glasses. During that time, we neither heard nor saw another vehicle. At the corner of Corbeil's property, where I'd followed the fence line in that morning, we stepped into the trees and with the flashlights, established our position on the GPS.

"Ready?"

"Go," she said.

We were both dressed from head to foot in black. In the city, we'd worn dark red jackets. They were nearly as invisible as black, when you were out of the light, and looked a lot more innocent to cops. Out here, if we were caught in the middle of Corbeil's pasture with the AK, there'd be no point in arguing that we were there by mistake.

We crossed the fence, with me in the lead, LuEllen following behind; the stars and fragmentary moon were just bright enough that we could see each other as shadows, and hear our feet swishing through the grass. When we'd walked a good distance up the hill, I moved over to the fence line, illuminating it with a spiderweb of light from one of the flashlights.

With the night glasses, I could clearly make out the dish next to the water tank. Nobody around, though down the hill, I could see cattle, lying down, grouped together like pea pods on a table.

"Anything?" The word was a breath next to my ear.

"No. Let's cross. Use the light and watch the barbs."

We crossed the fence and headed down the hill. The dish was two hundred yards away, and we took it easy, stopping often to listen. When we got close, we could hear trickling water, and then, even closer, a tiny electronic hum; the equipment wasn't moving, but was turned on.

I handed the AK and the night glasses to LuEllen; by agreement, she moved on down the hill about thirty yards, as a listening post. I took off the backpack and got the equipment out, marked our spot with the GPS, switched the GPS receiver to the time function, then started making measurements.

The dish was in what appeared to be its "rest" position. With the compass, I measured, to within a degree or to, the direction it was aimed in—about 290 degrees, or a little north of west, and not at all the direction it had been aimed earlier in the day. When I was sure I had it right, I got out the duct tape, taped one end of the elastic band to the top rim of the dish, stretched it across the face of the dish, so I had a tight, straight line with no sag, and taped it to the bottom. Using the level to establish my earth-line, I measured the angle of the elastic, which essentially gave me the current azimuth of the dish. I wrote it down, and then sat down to wait.

We'd agreed, earlier, that we'd wait for up to three hours for the dish to move. If it hadn't moved by then, we'd bail. We'd be getting tired, and our edge would be gone. With the elastic stretched out, I laid back on the ground and got comfortable. Watched the moon going down, the stars popping out. The lights from Waco, to the east, were bright enough that you didn't get the full clout of the Milky Way as you do up in the North Woods, but then, that might be northern jingoism; the stars were pretty good . . .

I'd been there for twenty-five minutes when the dish motor burped—an electronic burp, a change in the hum, and I sat up, listening, to be sure, then quickly checked the GPS and jotted down the time. With the level and protractor in hand, I moved around to the front of the dish and quickly checked the azimuth. It hadn't changed. But something was happening: the deeper note from the motor was unmistakable.

I was worrying about that when I felt a vibration in the disk, and slowly, surely, it began to move, tilting back. I looked at where it was pointing, at the horizon line, but could see nothing but stars. Sometimes, on dark nights, you could see them, the satellites, like tiny sparks scratching themselves on heaven . . .

I checked the azimuth, wrote down the GPS time signal. Checked the azimuth, wrote down the time. Checked it again, and again. Then hurried around behind it, got the compass, checked to make sure the direction hadn't changed: it hadn't. I went back to the dish and checked the azimuth as many times as I could until the dish was pointing at the local horizon, up the hill, and suddenly stopped. After taking the last azimuth, I ran around and checked direction again. Still the same. When I give the numbers to Bobby, I should have a straight line running through the sky from just north of west to just south of east, and even with the crude measurements of the protractor, should be able to give him a reasonable close approximation of times and azimuths.

At the top of its arc, the dish stopped moving for thirty seconds, then slowly began turning, more to the north this time, as the dish began to come down in its arc. At the end of the movement sequence, it was pointing at the horizon at about 320 degrees, or about 30 degrees further north than before. I noted that, packed up my stuff, took the elastic off the dish, and walked south about fifteen feet, and whispered, "LuEllen?"

A moment later, she was next to me: "Get it?"

"Yeah."

"I heard you clunking around."

"Not too much, I hope."

"Not too bad . . . are we good?"

"Unless you'd like to take a little walk."

"You're the boss."

Moving slowly, stopping often to use the night glasses, and staying as far away from the groups of cows as we could, we walked toward Corbeil's farmhouse. We sat on one hillside for fifteen minutes, taking the whole country in, then crossed a wash and climbed the other side; and from there, we could see Corbeil's clearly.

"No dish," I muttered to LuEllen.

"So let's go. We've been here too long."

"Let's head over that way for a couple of hundred yards first, and then head back," I said.

"That way" was east, toward the eastern edge of Corbeil's land. We first crossed back to the hill behind us, to get a little more distance between us and the house, and followed the backside of the ridge for four or five hundred yards. When the GPS put us three-fourths of the way across, we turned back up the hill. When we got to the crest, we looked down, and there, in a little hollow, was another dish.

"That's three," I whispered.

We crossed down to it, and I marked it on the GPS, and did a quick measurement: 320, just like the last one. Waiting. I considered waiting until it started to move, but we were running down. "Let's go."

We took better than an hour to get back to the truck. We approached it slowly, listening, loaded up as quietly as we could, backed out, and headed south toward the highway. Once on the road, LuEllen said, "Nice night for a picnic."

"I'm a little kicked," I said. She was driving, and I added, "When we get down to that old farmhouse, off on the side, if there aren't any lights, stop at the end of the driveway; just for a second."

There were no lights, and she stopped. I stuck the GPS out the window, got a quick read, noted it, and said, "Let's go home."

We took the county road south, then Highway 185 east, past Corbeil's ranch. As we passed the ranch, we saw two men walking out to a car in the driveway. One of them glanced at us as we went by.

"That guy . . ." LuEllen said. "The one on the right."

"Yeah. He's limping." We continued down the highway, and looking back, I saw the car pull out of the driveway, following. A few miles on, we stopped at an intersection before turning south toward Waco. The car followed, again.

"Still behind us?"

"Yeah, but they would be. There's no place else to go." They didn't seem to be coming after us with any urgency. "Slow down a little; bring it down to about fifty-even or fifty-eight," I told her.

She lightened up on the gas, and the car, a Buick, slowly crept up on us. When they were off our back bumper, they hung there for a while, then, at a flat spot, kicked out around us and accelerated away. I had the glasses ready, and picked out the tag number on the Buick.

"Guy didn't look at me," LuEllen said.

"Why should he? We're just another truck on the open highway. Even paranoia has its limits."

"For amateurs," LuEllen said. "Not for me. We wipe this truck, and take it back first thing tomorrow morning. Before the DMV opens, in case he can check the plate."

"Of course," I said.

W e went back to Bobby that night, and I summarized everything
we'd figured out. From the GPS receiver, I'd worked out precise locations of the three satellite dishes we'd seen, and the distances
between them, and also gave him the directions, azimuths, and times
I'd taken from the dish.

UNAUTHORIZED SATELLITE CONTACTS?

POSSIBLE. CUSTOMERS COULD GET HIGH-RES PHOTOS VIA THE
NET WITH PAYMENTS SENT TO FRONT ACCOUNTS. NAMES IN
JACK'S FILE WERE ALL WEST AND SOUTH ASIA, ISLAMIC, AND
INDIAN.

MUST BE SOME KIND OF ACCOUNTING ON TASKS. HOW COULD
THEY TASK THE SATELLITE WITHOUT NRO KNOWING?

DON'T KNOW.

I will show dish data to two friends if ok with you.

Must be *good* friends.

Both *excellent* friends. Both know some things about satellites.

Good. Any news on Green?

Yes. Attorney sez cops probably done with Green.

Is room monitored?

Will check.

Also check license plate . . .

I gave him the plate number and he said he'd get back. The next morning, we returned the truck, carefully wiped of fingerprints. The gun and other equipment we stowed in the back of the rental car.

"I'd hate to have a cop look at that collection: night glasses, compasses, GPS, the rifle . . . he'd figure we were assassins," LuEllen said as I put it all in the trunk.

"Maybe we are," I said. As the words came out of my mouth, I tried at the last minute to make them into a joke, but LuEllen looked at me with curious eyes. I had to be careful, now, around her.

More waiting. We spent the day stooging around, checking with Bobby every couple of hours. LuEllen was tired of hitting golf balls with bad equipment.

"Why don't you learn how to play golf? We're always waiting on these things, we're always trying to figure out what to do, and you always want to draw or some shit. Why don't you learn something social?"

"Golf is for morons," I said.

"How would you know? You've never played."

"If you don't shut up, I'm going to have to turn you over my knee."

"Ooo. That could soak up a couple of hours," she said.

The only thing we got from Bobby in the morning was the ID on the car driven by the two men from Corbeil's ranch. A William Hart, with an address.

"Back at the beginning of all this, I got a letter from Jack that mentioned this guy. He said to be careful around him, because he's an evil fuck, or something to that effect."

"So let's be careful around him," LuEllen said.

Late in the day, Bobby had something:

CAN YOU GO LITTLE ROCK?

YES? WHEN, WHY?

TOMORROW. PICK UP EQUIPMENT. NEED TO BUG DISH.

OK.

EXCELLENT. TALKED ATTORNEY. GREEN ROOM [348] PROBABLY
NOT FORMALLY MONITORED. MAN IN NEXT ROOM [350] NAMED
MORRIS KENDALL, HEAVY DRUGS FROM CANCER, PROBABLY DIE IN A
DAY OR TWO, IF YOU NEED TO ASK FOR PATIENT.

THANKS.

We checked out of the Austin motel and headed back to Dallas, found another room in another anonymous motel, called the hospital for visiting hours, and were told we could visit until nine o'clock.

"Tell me again what we can get from Green," LuEllen said.

"We can point out the benefits of stonewalling," I said.

"I'm sure he's figured those out," she said, putting her hands on her hips. "You've got something else working through your dirty little mind."

I nodded, reluctantly. "Yeah, I do; but I'm not going to tell you about it yet, because it'd probably piss you off, and then you'd piss me off, and I don't have the energy for all that. Anyway, tonight, I'm going into the hospital alone. I'll want you on the street, ready to roll, in case there's trouble."

"Kidd, if you think there's gonna be trouble . . ."

"I don't think there will be, but I'm more paranoid than our two friends at Corbeil's . . . Okay? Now, shut up for a while: I'm trying to think."

Something else *was* working through my dirty little mind, and I didn't want LuEllen to know about it. Not yet, anyway. I'd figured out how to drag AmMath and Corbeil and his goons right into the shit, but I didn't want LuEllen around when I did it. Texas was a bad state for all this . . .

I went into Mount of Olives hospital at eight-thirty that night, with LuEllen waiting in a parking spot on a street behind the doctors' parking lot. If I had to run for it, I probably wouldn't get out of the building; but if I did, and I could make it across the doctors' parking lot, we could be lost in traffic in fifteen seconds. A gift shop was open just inside the hospital's front doors, and I bought a bouquet of bright yellow flowers that looked something like daisies, but with a plastic sheen and a harsh odor. They came in a green glass vase; the whole thing looked cheap, but somehow right. I asked at the information desk for Morris Kendall's room, got the number, and went up.

The door to Green's room was open, and a grim, heavyset woman was sitting in a chair looking into a bed at the far end of the room. There were two beds in the room. I could see only the end of the bed closest to the door, where I presumed Green must be. Nobody told me that his room was only semiprivate. Goddamnit. I went on to 350 and found Morris Kendall in what appeared to be a coma, dying all by himself, a drip running into an arm that was pockmarked with needle sticks. I put the flowers on a sidetable and tried not to look at him.

After a couple of minutes, I went back out to the hallway and paced for a while. The woman was still sitting there, unspeaking, clutching a purse on her lap. She looked like she disapproved of this whole hospital thing. I went and sat with Morris for a couple of more minutes, and in those two minutes, decided that when I got old, I'd lay in a lethal supply of sleeping pills, just in case. I didn't want to end like this . . .

P eople were coming and going in the hall, and I kept looking for the heavyset woman; fifteen minutes after I got there, I was rewarded: she went by the door, walking with purpose, clutching her purse with both hands. I checked the hallway—a little cluster of a man and two kids, all, from their looks, from the same family, were gathered by a doorway fifty feet down—and stepped around the corner into Green's room.

Green was in the first bed, separated from the other by a pull curtain. A television was bolted into the far corner of the room, tuned to the romance channel. Green rolled his head toward me when I walked in. I turned my hands palm-up in a question, and raised my eyebrows; he shrugged, but put a finger to his lips. I stepped over next to his bed and put my head close to his. He whispered, "What are you doing here?"

"Needed to talk. Are you okay?"

"I will be. Gonna be in physical therapy for a few weeks."

"Sorry."

"Not as sorry as I am. I was supposed to cover Lane. She's dead." He looked ineffably sad when he said it.

"I need to know about the two guys. Were they both shooting?"

"Yeah, big time. Didn't bother with silencers or any of that shit. I think it might have been a pickup, but when they saw me, it was just *boom-boom-boom.* You got the computer?"

"Yes. I need to know what the guys looked like. You hit one of them."

"Not bad, I don't think. Maybe even ricocheted him. The short guy knocked me down first thing through the door, right on my ass into the bathtub . . . Not a goddamned thing I could do but keep pulling the trigger."

"Good thing for you that the tub was there."

"You got that right. I don't think—" but he thought anyway, for a second, for probably the ten-thousandth time— "I don't think I could have saved her."

"Not a chance," I said. "These guys: What'd they look like?"

"They were two mean white boys; nylons over their heads so you couldn't see them very well. But in good shape, thin and hard. I think, real short hair; I couldn't tell for sure, but that was the impression I got. One was maybe six-two or three, the other was maybe three inches shorter than that, but a little thicker. You'd notice if you saw them together. I shot the short one."

"All right. Are you headed back to Oakland?"

"I guess. I'd be happy to stay, but I don't know what good I'd do you."

"No, no. What we need the most is for you to go back to Oakland and do absolutely what you'd do if everything was just like you said it was. You're a bodyguard who doesn't know anything about anything. Go back, do therapy, go for walks, get laid. If the feds are still interested, you gotta bore them."

He nodded: "That's what I'll do."

From the other side of the curtain, a man's voice croaked, "Hey, Leth, you mind if I switch this over to Cinemax? I think they got one of them car-wash movies on."

"Go ahead," said Green. "I could use a car-wash movie."

I stuck a hand out, shook Green's, and went out the door. Down the elevators, across the doctors' parking lot, and into the car.

"How'd it go?" LuEllen asked.

"Fine. Green's cool, and we're good."

"Why do you look so bummed out?" She swung the car in a U-turn and we headed back toward the Interstate.

I told her about Morris Kendall, next door to Green. "There wasn't a single personal belonging in the room, that I could see. He's up there dying with nothing to keep him company but a cheap bouquet of yellow flowers from a stranger."

"Country song," she said.

That was the easy part of the day. We checked with Bobby, to see if he had anything new. He had a time and a place in Little Rock: three-thirty the next day, at a restaurant by Little Rock National Airport.

With that all fixed, I jumped LuEllen. Nothing slow and playful, the way her taste runs in sex, but straight ahead, pinning her on the bed, taking her down. When we were done, she said, "All right, Kidd. What was that all about?"

"I'm shipping your ass out," I said. "I figured you'd be pissed for a while, and I wanted some sex to remember you by."

She sat up: "You fucker."

"LuEllen . . . you're always reserving the right to take off when life gets too cranky, right? Well, it's going to get crankier, and there's no reason for you to be around. I'd just have to think about taking care of you, and I don't want to do that. I'm gonna have enough to do taking care of myself."

"You've never had to take care of me," she said. She said it in her dangerous voice.

"I don't mean *take care of you*, like a baby; I mean, watch out for you, too."

"What're you going to do?"

"I have an idea. I don't want to tell you about it, because it wouldn't be good for you to know yet. Maybe later. But what you've got to do is get somewhere public. You have your passport, right?"

"Kidd, what the fuck . . ."

"You've got your passport?"

"Yeah, I've got . . ."

"Tomorrow morning, early, I put your ass on a plane to somewhere—New York would be good, with the San Francisco ID. Then you shuttle back to Minneapolis, with the first ID you had—that's still good?—and then fly out to the British Virgins or the Bahamas under your own name. It's a lot of flying, but I want you checked through customs somewhere, and I want you in public for the next few days. Where people will remember you."

Now she was curious. Still pissed, but curious: "What are you going to blow up?"

"I'm not going to blow up anything. But this is all coming to a head, and you can never tell what these alphabet security agencies are capable of. If they put us together, you could be in trouble, and Bobby says they're peeling back the names."

"I'll never get all the flights . . ."

"I booked you this morning," I said. "You're all confirmed."

"This morning," she said. She turned that over for a second, then said, "Asshole. This morning? You . . ."

We argued about it, off and on, for the rest of the evening. Tried to get some sleep; she was throwing clothes around the next morning, but at eight o'clock, her little round butt was in line at DFW, for the New York flight. She's absolutely capable of turning her back on me and walking away, I think. But this time, she didn't. After several hours of chill, she gave me a serious kiss good-bye, whispered, *"Take care,"* and got on the plane.

I was on my own, and on my way to Little Rock.

24

The drive to Little Rock took six hours, with time out for a cheeseburger and a couple of bathroom breaks. I was in the part of the country where, instead of getting french fries, you get home fries. Home fries are actually pure grease, soaked into grasslike strips of potato so you can get it to your mouth. A waitress in a uniform the exact color of two-day-old pumpkin pie dropped off the burger and fries, did a searching scan of my tabletop and said, "My goodness; somebody forgot to put out your catsup." She was back in a minute with a bottle of Heinz, and said, "Home fries just ain't right without catsup."

She was, and is, correct. They just ain't right.

I 'd only been to Little Rock once before in my life. If you live in
St. Paul, Little Rock isn't on the way to anywhere except itself. I
didn't get to see much of the place, either. The guy I was meeting was
waiting at a Shoney's. I picked him out as soon as I walked in.

"How are you, John?" I asked, sliding into the booth. He reached
across the tabletop and we shook hands.

"Not too bad. I heard about Green and that lady: you're in some
shit." He looked at me sideways, his dark wraparound sunglasses
glittering in the fluorescent light.

"I'm sorry about Green," I said.

"I'm sorry about your friend," he said.

John Smith was a black man, originally from Memphis, but now
going back and forth between Memphis and a small town in the
Delta, where his wife lived. He was both hard and intelligent; a political operator, a friend of Bobby's, and an artist, a sculptor. "I just got
in," he said. "I'm having the open-face turkey sandwich, home fries,
coconut cream pie, and Diet Coke."

"Then you check in somewhere for a heart scan," I said.

I got a Coke and a salad; when the waitress came to take our or-
ders, I said, "Don't forget the catsup, for his home fries."

"How could I do that?" she asked, a look of puzzlement crossing her face.

J ohn said the package was in his car, and we could get it on the
way out. "Bobby says that you should get some duct tape, and tape
the box onto the receiver at the focus of the dish. That should be
good enough. Then, there are some tapes coiled around the box.
Those are pickups, like antenna. You should wrap those around the
support lines on the receiver. That gives the receiver a little extra
sensitivity. Okay?"

He was drawing a hasty diagram on a napkin, and it was all clear enough. "As soon as the dish begins to move, turn our receiver on," he said. "There's only one switch, a toggle on the side. While the dish is moving, make the same kinds of notations you did the other night—direction, times, and azimuths. The receiver will pick up both incoming and outgoing, and record them, and Bobby built in a timer function, but he didn't have time to do a level or compass function."

"All right."

"LuEllen with you?"

"I sent her away," I said.

"You guys ought to have a couple of babies," he said. "You're gonna wind up old, with nobody to care for you."

"Thanks for the thought," I said, and flashed to Morris Kendall, dying in room 350. "Has Bobby heard any more about Firewall?"

"I'm not all together on this; this is not my line," John said. "Bobby says Firewall is definitely phony—he says you think so, too."

"I'm leaning that way."

"But he says the feds, the NSA, are blowing it up into a major danger to justify their budget. He says that they don't have anything to do—they're completely obsolete—and this whole Firewall thing has been like a gift from heaven. A reprieve."

"What about the IRS attack?"

"Bobby says ten kids in Germany and Switzerland. He's sent four names, specific names, to the feds, but they're not paying much attention. Bobby says they don't *want* to catch Firewall. Not yet."

The salad came, along with John's food, and we spent twenty minutes talking about his wife, Marvel, and kids; and the political situation in Longstreet, where Marvel lived with the kids. He hadn't quite finished eating when he finished with the political situation, and I looked at my watch and said, "There's a phone booth out in the lobby. I'm gonna get online with Bobby; see if anything's happening."

"Be my guest," he said.

The phone had little business, and I got right on and dialed. I never got to dial the ten digits after the 800 number, because after seven, the phone rang once, and a woman picked up and said, "Montana Genetics, can I help you?"

"Uh . . . I'm sorry, I think I have the wrong number."

"Well, have a good day then," she said cheerfully, and hung up. I dialed again, "Montana . . ." and hung up.

Got a problem," I told John, when I got back to the booth. "Bobby's not online."

He looked at me, a wrinkle between his eyes. Bobby was always online. His life was online. "He's not . . ."

"When I dial the 800 number, I get something called Montana Genetics."

He sat back, hands on the table: "Ah, shit. He's pulled the plug."

"I need him, man," I said.

"So do we," John said. I never did know who *we* were, although I'd known for years that there was a *we*. He looked at his watch and added, "I gotta get back. I've got to be near a telephone . . ."

The waitress came over, carrying the check. She looked at John and asked, "Are you Mr. Smith?"

"What?"

"Are you Mr. . . ."

"Smith. Yes."

"You've, uh, got a phone call. Normally we don't allow customers, but the gentleman said it was an emergency . . ."

John was out of the booth, trailing her; she took him into the back. Two minutes later, he was back out. "Gotta go."

"Bobby?"

"Yeah. He knew we were gonna be here." He tossed five dollars at the tabletop and headed for the cashier. Outside, in the open, he said, "He says to tell you that Ladyfingers was busted and she gave them the 800 number and that the feds, the NSA, traced him all the way to the banana stand. He said there were only three more links between him and the feds before he was toast. He's shut down everything. He says you should recover the number just like you did before—he didn't tell me what it was, he's crazy paranoid—and said you will cut directly into him. It's the only link he's going to take coming in, until he reworks all his numbers."

"Bad time for this," I said. "Bad time."

At the car, John handed me a gym bag with the receiver in it. "As soon as you've recorded a full movement, mail it back to me, express mail, at the house in Memphis."

"All right."

"Good luck," he said. "Keep your ass down."

A t Texarkana, I found a gas station phone booth and hooked up with the laptop. I went out to my two mailboxes, and found, just as Bobby had promised, two pieces of a phone number. I called, keyed a "k," and Bobby came up.

VERY CLOSE. NEVER CLOSER. SCARED THE S OUT OF ME. I'M CLOSED FOR BUSINESS, EXCEPT FOR YOU. DID YOU GET PACKAGE?

Yes.

Can you mount tonight?

Yes.

What else can we do?

I told him, and got back a long silence. Then,

Take care. Take care. Take care.

The Interstate crosses some sparsely inhabited landscape between Texarkana and Dallas. After checking the map, I got off at
one of the larger white spots, and picked out a long piece of quiet
road. I parked on one side, got out my sketchbook, checked
around, then paced off 200 yards down the road, and stood a plastic Coke bottle on the shoulder. I was willing to bet I wasn't more
than a yard or two off—one of the things you learn in the burglary
business is how to estimate distances. My normal stride was thirty-
four inches long, and I'd learned how to swing a leg just a split-
second longer than I usually did, to come down right on thirty-six
inches.

Back at the car, I looked around again, then got the AK out of
the trunk, loaded it, rolled down the passenger-side window. When
I was sure nothing was coming from either direction, I ripped up
a couple of pieces of newspaper, made them into spitwads, put
them in my ears, and aimed the gun out the window at the Coke
bottle.

The scope was decent; I leaned back against the driver's-side
door, my left hand cradling the fore-end, and braced against the inside of my knee, held on the bottle, squeezed . . .

The rifle jumped, and I lost sight of the bottle; and when I got back on it—where it would have been—it was gone. I got the car straightened out, repacked the rifle, found the ejected shell and threw it into the roadside weeds.

Rolled slowly down the road until I spotted the bottle. There was a neat .30-caliber hole an inch off center to the right, maybe two inches below the shoulders of the bottle. Good enough; more than good enough.

At Dallas, I stopped at the motel to clean up, change clothes, look at the package—a plastic box with a toggle switch and a couple of pieces of tape antenna sticking out of the top, the whole thing the size of a VHS videotape cassette, but heavier—and get the rest of the gear.

Moving right along, it was still well past nine o'clock before I made it through Waco, and headed out to Corbeil's. The ranch house showed only one light, and I saw no cars in the yard; I continued up to the ruins of the old home place, took the car back into the trees, then got out, and sat down on the incoming track.

And listened.

Listening will always tell you more than your eyes, if you're in the dark and somebody might be hunting you. People get tense, try to see, don't know how to move, breathe too hard, and they stumble. If you're relaxed, breathing as quietly as you can, eyes closed . . . you can hear. Everything but owls. You hear birds moving at night, but never the owls; they're like ghosts.

After a half-hour, I was satisfied that I was alone. I stood up and scanned the area with the night glasses, then picked up the equipment, including the AK, and headed down the road. Halfway down, a truck came banging up the gravel. I stepped well off the road to let it pass, and watched until it had passed the car's hiding place. When it was out of sight, I listened again, then moved on.

Moving this slowly, it was nearly midnight before I crossed the fence line and started down toward the dish. When I was directly above it, I scanned it with the glasses for ten minutes, then moved down. I could hear the electric hum; and waited again, but only a minute or two this time, before taping up the package and extending the little antennas. Then I taped up the plastic bands, so I'd be able to measure the azimuth. That done, I moved ten yards off, into the pasture, laid down, and alternately listened and scanned the fields.

An hour passed, and then another. Halfway into the third hour, the electric hum changed pitch. At first I thought I might be hallucinating the change, because I'd been waiting so long. I scrambled over, listened again: no doubt about it.

I put my hand on the dish and at the first vibration, flipped the switch on our package. The dish was moving, and I began taking measurements; a half-hour later, I was crossing the fence with the package in my pack.

What Bobby could do with it, I wasn't sure. Bobby would take care of that. I'd put it in the mail as soon as I got back to Dallas—there must be an all-night post office out by DFW, I thought—and then I'd make my own run.

The killing of Lane Ward had put the idea in my mind: the anger and frustration growing as these people hit at us, for reasons we didn't know about, and—aside from Jack's death—barely cared about. The cynicism of the people who were supposed to help—the FBI and other agencies—was nearly as bad.

That night, on the way back to Dallas, I saw a Wal-Mart, and stopped to buy a box. I finally found one large enough: it contained the side boards and shelves for a do-it-yourself book case. I bought it, and threw it in the car.

At the same time, I called and got directions to the all-night post office, and mailed the package to John in Memphis. That done, I cruised the North Dallas house belonging to William Hart. There was the faintest glow of light behind a window, as though he had a night light; but never a sign of life. It was not a street where you could loiter. I made a few passes, checking out the neighborhood, and called it a night.

B ut I was back the next morning, at six-thirty, eyes grainy after only four hours of sleep. There were only a couple of logical, quick routes from Hart's house to the downtown offices. I couldn't hang out on his street, but I could sit in a McDonald's parking lot, eat an egg-and-sausage McMuffin and watch the street he'd probably come out of. I sat for a little more than an hour, and saw the Buick turn out of his street.

I fell in, but kept six or seven cars between us. He headed for an Interstate ramp, and I followed him up and toward town. Halfway down, he got off the highway, and began threading through local streets. I stayed with him, pulled off once, then got in behind before he disappeared. He stopped in front of an apartment house, waited. A moment later, a man hobbled out. Short hair, six feet, barrel-chested. Benson, I thought. The one we'd ID'd in San Jose. He got in the car, carefully. I waited until they were gone, and started scouting the neighborhood.

This neighborhood was different than Hart's. Lots of apartments, lots of older houses, commercial lots elbowing in on the residences: corner stores and hair-dressing salons, video-rental places, like that. After half an hour of careful scouting, I found a spot. There were drawbacks. Too many windows looking down on it, but I'd have to risk it, if it turned out to be the best I could do. After scouting it, I headed down to the historic district, hoping to find a better setup.

A mMath was a block from the end of the historic district. The district ended with a parking lot, and beyond that a jumble of freeway ramps. I intended to cruise the district for a while, hoping to spot their car. I cruised for about two minutes, and spotted it in a slot on the side of the building: if the guy with the limp was hurt badly, they'd probably kept looking for a space until they got one close to the building entrance.

All right: I had the car. When I rolled past it, I could see, straight ahead, a truck in the parking lot. The cars were actually parked in diagonals, from the perspective of the AmMath building anyway. I drove down to the parking lot, got a ticket, and went to the end of the parking area, next to the truck. From there, I could see the Buick's passenger side, and most of the driver's side, and some of the sidewalk beyond it.

I settled down to wait.

I n the movies, when the detective settles down to wait, the bad guys show in a reasonable time. These bad guys didn't do that. I waited for two hours, couldn't stand it any longer, and got out and walked around. Got a sandwich at a bar that gave me a view of the front of the AmMath building; plenty of people came and went, but not Hart.

I was back in the car, the rifle just behind the seat, at eleven-forty. They'd be going out for lunch, I thought. Lunchtime came and went, with no sign of them. I got out and walked around some more, always where I could see either the car or the building door. Got out the sketchpad and drew for a while: but I wasn't in the mood, and I don't like to draw concrete.

Several times during the day, I decided I'd had enough: but I never quite left. I was sure that if I left, they'd head for the car one minute later. So I stuck around: watched Texans come and go, big hair on the women, cowboy boots on the men; not universally so, but enough that you noticed.

At five o'clock, I knew the wait had to be short. At five-thirty, it was nearly over, I figured, and wondered if I should move the gun to the front seat. Didn't do it. And at five-forty-five, Hart walked out to the car, got in, and drove away. The wrong guy.

I went after him, and got close just in time to see Benson limp around the back end of the car and get in.

I followed them out to the Interstate, and up the ramp. They were headed for Benson's apartment, I thought. All I had to do was get him out of the car for a minute . . . I passed them on the highway, drove way too fast through Benson's neighborhood, and left the car in the parking lot of a dry cleaners that was closed for the night.

The rifle was in the bookcase box, the box I'd acquired at Wal-Mart the night before. I'd wanted a big box, one that would carry the rifle but not shout "possible gun." Something that looked awkward; the bookcase box did it. The bookcase itself was in a dumpster behind my hotel.

I got the box out of the back, and walked around the corner of the dry cleaners and set up between a garage and a hedge of a house down the street from Benson's apartment. I could see the door, the parking lot, and just the edge of the street, some two hundred yards away. I waited in the growing darkness, hoping I could see well enough under the streetlights to get a good look at him.

They arrived five or six minutes after I had. As the car pulled up, I slipped the rifle out of the box, braced myself against a corner of the garage, and looked at the car through the scope. Still enough light. Benson got out of the car, wobbled on his bad leg, then leaned back into the car to say something. For a moment, he was unmoving.

I took the moment, and shot him.

LuEllen always claims that you can get away with one or two loud noises: one or two shots, one large mechanical clunk, whatever. The first loud noise will cause people to wonder what it is; if it's not repeated, they'll stop wondering. That's the theory.

I didn't look down toward Benson after I fired. I simply eased back down, slipped the gun in the bookcase box, and backed away from the shooting scene, keeping the garage between myself and whatever was happening in front of Benson's apartment.

At the dry cleaner's, I put the box in the trunk, backed out of the parking lot, and drove away. As I passed the end of Benson's street, I looked down toward his house and saw two people on his lawn, looking down at what was apparently Benson's body, and a third person, a woman, running across the street with a big yellow dog in front of her, on a leash, I thought.

I kept going. Out to the Interstate, back to the motel. I carried the box inside, got the gun out, wiped it down, put it back in the box, carried it back out to the car. As long as I had the gun, I could be in trouble. I drove slowly, carefully, out of Dallas, north, until I was well into the countryside, stopping only once, to buy a cheap shovel. A half-hour north of the city, I turned off on a country road, drove until I found a nice patch of trees, got out of the car, and buried the AK a couple of feet down, kicking some dead leaves over the raw soil. Back on the highway, two or three miles from the gun's grave, I wiped the shovel and tossed it out the window into the roadside ditch.

Shooting somebody from ambush is not exactly the all-American way of doing things, but I was more intent on survival than etiquette. When I got back toward Dallas, I called the Denton Police Department non-emergency line. A woman answered—"Denton Police, can I help you?"—and I said, "Hi, this is Jack Hersh from the *Morning News.* Can you tell me who's handling that shooting a couple of days ago at the Eighty-Eight Motel?"

"I, uh, think that's Sergeant Frederick. He's out right now . . ."

"I'll check back," I said. "What's Sergeant Frederick's first name?"

"Hal."

"Thank you."

Got back to Bobby.

STILL TROUBLE?

YES. BUSTED CURTIS MEANY. SAY HE WILL CHAIN TO MANY MORE HACKERS. NEVER HEARD OF HIM. YOU?

NO. HAVE THEY BUSTED ANYBODY WE KNOW?

NOT SINCE LADYFINGERS.

NEED HOME PHONE NUMBER FOR SERGEANT HAL FREDERICK
OF DENTON POLICE DEPARTMENT.
WAIT ONE.

A moment later, he was back with the unlisted number. Bobby
is very deep in the telephone system.

WHAT HAPPENS?
WORKING. ANY MORE ON SATELLITES?
YES. BUT MAY MISS NECESSARY INFO. POSSIBLY CAN
RECONSTRUCT. DO YOU HAVE ACCESS TO AMMATH DOCS?
NO.
WILL TRY TO CRACK COMPUTERS FROM HERE.
TAKE CARE. THEY'RE WATCHING.
AND YOU TAKE CARE.

I stopped once more before heading back to the motel. From an
outside phone, I called Hal Frederick's number. He answered on the
fourth ring, sounding cranky. "Yeah?"

"Sergeant Frederick? I have a tip for you."

"Who is this?" Even crankier.

"A benefactor. You're investigating the shooting at the Eighty-
Eight Motel. About two hours ago, there was a shooting in Dallas, a
man named Lester Benson. He's been taken to the hospital with a
wound in the thigh. If you check, you will find that he has another
recent bullet wound in one leg. He was the man who was shot running out of the Eighty-Eight after the murder. If you check his blood
DNA against the blood you found in the parking lot, you will find
a match."

"Who *is* this?"

"Remember the name. Lester Benson. He was admitted to the

hospital a couple of hours ago. The Dallas police should have the details," I said, and dropped the phone back on the hook.

If *that* didn't create some serious heat, I'd just pack up and head home.

I had no more ideas.

25

ST. JOHN CORBEIL

Corbeil smeared his face and his hands, pulled the black hat on his head, and shuffled across the parking lot to the Emergency Room at Health North. Inside, a nurse behind the reception station glanced at him, an old man, maybe black—certainly black, with the X baseball hat on his head—as he looked uncertainly around and then shuffled down toward the patient rooms.

"Excuse me?" she asked. "Are you looking for somebody?"

"Bafroom," Corbeil said. "Men's room."

"Do you have a family member here?"

"My wife. Upstairs. Kicked m' ass out 'fore I could pee." Corbeil had to keep it short: he didn't sound that much like an old black man.

The nurse bought it. "All right, then. Just straight down the hall. On your right." She went back to her paperwork, and Corbeil shuffled down the hall.

Took the elevator, up four floors, turned out in the hallway, and walked down to the right. Room 411. The door was shut, but not locked. He stepped inside. Hart had said there was only one bed . . .

One bed with a man sleeping. In the ambient light from the window, he could see Benson lying on his back, one leg suspended in a trapeze, a saline drip hooked into his arm. Corbeil reached into his pocket, took out the cigar tube, slipped out the needle inside, jabbed it into the saline bag, and emptied it. Enough sedative to kill an elephant.

Well, he thought, looking down at Benson, he *was* supposed to be sleeping . . .

He couldn't hang around. He had a long way to go this night. Down the elevator, out through the Emergency Room entrance, driving back home. Scrubbing his face with clean-up packs from a barbecue joint, in case he met somebody in his apartment stairwell. But he met no one.

He glanced at his watch: A long way to go. In the bathroom, he washed his face and hands, scrubbed away the last of the Cover Mark. After drying his hands, he got the pistol from the dresser—detoured around the living room on the way out, unwilling to look at the wrecked wall—and headed for Hart's place. Hart was expecting him. Had to talk about the next move . . .

Hart was worried. "I don't know if it'll hold," he said. "I don't know if *Benson* will hold."

"Take it easy," Corbeil said. They were in Hart's study, a converted family room. In some ways, it aped Corbeil's study: a leather chair, but not quite as sleek. Books, but not as many, and with a narrow range: karate, guns, camping, travel.

Corbeil found it irritating. "If he's caught, he knows that we're his only chance. Giving us away won't help him: he'll wind up with a public defender instead of the best defense money can buy."

"I'm not sure he's that smart," Hart said. He dropped into the leather chair, brooding. Corbeil paced in a lazy circle. As he passed Hart, he took the pistol out of his pocket, paused, and, moving unhurriedly so the motion wouldn't catch Hart's eye, put the muzzle next to the other man's temple and pulled the trigger.

Crack!

Hart slumped. Corbeil waited a moment, listening—realized that if there were anything to hear, he probably wouldn't, being deafened by the shot—then reached for Hart's throat, pressed his fingers just under his jawbone. No pulse. He hadn't expected any. William Hart was thoroughly dead.

All right. Now: one more shot, with Hart's finger in the trigger . . . the *Webster's* should do as a backstop. He fired again, into the heavy hardback dictionary. The little .380 slug penetrated to page 480, and stopped. Corbeil picked up one of the two ejected shells, carefully added one loaded shell to the top of the gun's magazine, pressed the shell against Hart's thumb, replaced the magazine, and dropped the gun on the floor next to the chair.

He looked at his watch. Still a long way to go.

He picked up the dictionary and left.

H e drove through the night to Waco, his mind crowded with possibilities. Stay and fight. Run and hide.

The simple fact was this: if nobody knew about the satellite intercepts, none of the killing made sense. Even if somebody knew, it could be blamed on Tom Woods, and then he would kick free. The conspiracy never required his involvement, he thought. Woods could have set it up with the other two. He had the technical background—background that Corbeil didn't have.

As of now, the danger to himself had narrowed to a single point . . .

A car was parked in the driveway at the ranch, and there were lights in the main house. Corbeil parked, got out, felt the second gun nestled next to his leg. Took a moment to stand in the driveway, to look up at the stars.

Woods came out on the porch: "Hey, John. What's going on?"

"Hey, Tom. Need to talk about next week. I've got an order from Azerbaijan."

"Jeez, those guys . . ."

Corbeil was looking up. "Look at the stars. You can really see the stars out here."

Woods walked down the three steps of the porch and stood beside his friend to look at the sky.

"Glorious," he said. Then he said something that prolonged his life for a few seconds. "By the way, I'm not sure about this, but there might be something going on out here."

"What do you mean?"

"Somebody may be messing with the dish controls. I don't know where it happened—inside the house or out—but we got an odd signal the other night. I just noticed it."

"Odd?"

"Attenuated, as if the signal were being blocked somehow. Not interfered with, but physically blocked."

"What would do that, Tom?"

"Somebody standing in front of the dish. Something placed near the amplifier loops . . . that would do it. Could be nothing. Could have been a bird building a nest. Or, if it was inside, it could have been somebody messing with the gain controls, although they're all right now."

"Did you look at the dishes?" Corbeil asked.

"Yeah. Everything looks all right. Might have been nothing at all."

"Probably. We're all a little jumpy with this Firewall thing, that shooting."

"That fuckin' Hart. The guy's a killer, John. He probably enjoyed it."

"Look at the stars," Corbeil said.

"Glorious," Woods said again. The muzzle of Corbeil's gun was an inch from the back of his head.

26

I spent the next day intermittently monitoring the Net, watching news programs, and checking the newspapers' online editions, looking for something—anything—that would tell me what was going on with AmMath, Firewall, or with Benson or Hart.

When I wasn't doing that, I was playing with the tarot, or drawing. The landscape north of Dallas is interesting, in its own Southern Plains way, though not as interesting as the area around Tulsa, some parts of Kansas, or the Dakota grasslands.

Still: interesting. The relative flatness of the landscape, only sparsely inflected by humans and weather phenomena, gives the land and atmosphere a natural abstraction that you don't see in landscape paintings, but that you often see in nonobjective art. By working with the land and sky, without adding human inflection, you wind up with something that looks like abstraction, but has a kind of organic quality that pulls the eye in. Under the best conditions, the viewer falls *into* the picture, rather than colliding with the painted surface of the abstraction . . .

Either that, or I'm completely full of shit. In any case, the first real break came that evening, and left me astonished. I'd been clicking around the cable channels with the remote, and heard Corbeil's name mentioned. Channel 3: the newsreader had more hair than the average werewolf, and teeth just as shiny; he liked this stuff, and this story.

Benson had been found dead in his hospital bed, a victim of what police said was a deliberate barbituate overdose. He'd been murdered.

Benson had been with a man named William Hart when he was shot, and had given Hart's name as an alibi for the time that Lane Ward had been shot. After Benson had been found dead, police went to talk with Hart. They found him dead in an easy chair, a pistol on the floor beside him, an apparent suicide. The newsreader added that police had interviewed Corbeil in the case, but that he had not been charged with anything, nor was he being held.

"Corbeil says that his company, AmMath, a high-tech concern that creates top-secret coding software for the federal government, has been under attack for several days by the hacker group that calls itself Firewall, apparently because AmMath is one of the lead contractors on the Clipper II chip. The Clipper II, if you recall, is the chip that the government would like to see incorporated as a standard in communications hardware, including that used on the Internet. Firewall is the group that has taken credit for the continuing denial-of-service attack on the IRS.

"Corbeil said that he did not understand Benson's involvement with Lane Ward or her brother, Jack Morrison, who was slain last month after an alleged break-in at AmMath's secure computer facility. He said that he had asked Hart to monitor Benson's activities after the Morrison shooting, but hadn't known of Ward's presence in Dallas or his security officers' shootout with them," the newsreader intoned, his eyebrows signaling a moderate level of skepticism.

B enson and Hart were dead. Who'd done that? Corbeil himself? Or were there more security goons in the background somewhere? Corbeil's story was actually pretty good, from a legal standpoint: he took no position; he was confused. If it all got mixed in with national security and codes and spies and Firewall, and if the guy held out, he might walk . . .

I spent fifteen minutes pacing around the motel, then went out, found a phone, and dropped a message with Bobby. He batted it away: he was no longer interested in AmMath or revenge for Jack or Lane. He thought he might have found a way out for those of us still alive.

NEED MORE RECORDINGS OF RANCH TRANSMISSIONS. SENDING MAN TO YOU WITH PACKAGE, ARRIVES TONIGHT. NEED TRANSMISSIONS MOST QUICKLY.

OK. PROBLEM?

WE NEED SATELLITE PROTOCOLS, CAN'T GET INTO AMMATH. COMPUTERS SEALED OFF. CAN YOU COME MEMPHIS WEDNESDAY?

YES.

GOOD. WILL SEND ADDRESS LATER.

The idea of going back to Corbeil's ranch was not appealing, especially since I'd dumped the rifle. I still had the pistol that LuEllen had picked up in Lane's room, but I had little faith in pistols. With the very best of them, like a .45 Colt ACP, I could probably ding a guy up at twenty-five yards, if neither of us were moving. Otherwise, I might as well be throwing apples.

Still: Bobby had a plan. Crack the satellites, he said, then talk to the government. Demonstrate that we were *not* a danger. Build a case for ourselves . . .

Maybe.

At eight-thirty that night, a guy with one of those uneven Southern faces, the kind that looked like they got a little crunched in a vise or a wine press or something, knocked on my door, and when I opened it, handed me a box. "From Bobby," he said.

He did not look like the kind of guy who'd be hanging with Bobby: if you were going to cast a movie and needed a guy with hair like straw and pink lips and big freckles, to stand with his foot on a pickup truck's running board and talk about the Imperial Wizards of the Ku Klux Klan, this guy would be a candidate.

"How is he? Bobby?" I asked.

"Same as ever." He raised a hand in what used to be a black-power salute. "Off the pigs," he said. Then he laughed and I laughed with him, feeling ridiculous, and he headed down the hall in his beat-up cowboy boots, ragged stepped-on back cuffs, and jean jacket.

Gone.

So was I, five minutes later, headed south in the night.

T hird time's the charm.

That's what I kept thinking all the way back to the dish in the gully. I took it slow, like still hunting for deer. I started down the road at eleven o'clock, deep in the darkness, watching, listening. I didn't make it to the fence-crossing until midnight. Twelve cars passed along the road as I moved parallel to it, hunkered down in the weeds as they passed.

At midnight, I crossed the fence into the eastern pasture, and began moving parallel to Corbeil's fence line. At twelve-thirty, having taken a half-hour to move four hundred yards, I crossed Corbeil's fence and began working my way toward the nearest dish. As I got close, I spent some time watching the ranch house.

The yard lights illuminated the area around the house and showed a single pickup truck parked in front of the garage. The house itself was absolutely dark. The bunkhouse, if that's what it was, had one lit window. A shadow fell on the window once, and then went away. Whoever it was, was up late.

Nervous, but satisfied that nothing much was happening at the house, I crossed carefully into the gully, using the needle-beam flashlight now, and hooked the detection package into the dish. Then I climbed the far side of the gully and lay down, looking down at the farmhouse while I waited for the dish to start moving.

At one o'clock, or a few minutes later, the light in the bunkhouse went out, and a man stepped into the lighted driveway, walked over to the house, unlocked the door, went inside. A light flashed on, then, twenty seconds later, went out. The man stepped outside, closed the door behind himself, rattled it—locked—and walked over to the pickup truck. He got in and bumped slowly down the driveway to the highway, paused, turned left, and drove away.

Huh.

For the next three hours, I perched on top of the ridge waiting for the dish to move. Eventually, I realized that it wasn't going to. Lying in the dark, with nothing much to do, I began to work out my own version of Corbeil's caper.

He'd built a company that once must have been on the cutting edge of cyberintelligence, creating code products that could be used by anyone who needed absolutely secure communication. Other companies could do the same thing, but the AmMath people had an advantage: their product would be the software component of the Clipper II, and they would essentially have a government-sponsored monopoly on encoded transmissions.

Then, just as Corbeil stepped on the road to billionairedom, the catch jumped up and bit him on the ass.

Outside the intelligence community, nobody wanted the Clipper. The Clipper was an obsolete idea when it was floated the first time. By the time Clipper II came along, even the Congress recognized its stupidity. So they said the hell with it, and instead of the road to billions, Corbeil found himself in the alley to Chapter Eleven.

Corbeil had to find something else to sell—this was all part of my fantasy—and found it, circling the earth every few hours. Perhaps AmMath had developed the code that the National Reconnaissance Office used for its satellite transmissions. However they did it, AmMath was pulling down the recon stuff and retailing it. Jack Morrison had been killed for knowing about it, and his sister was murdered because they *thought* she might know about it; and Firewall had been invented to cover it up, or at least to confuse any trail that might lead to it.

Could it be some sort of official dark operation? I doubted it. There are plenty of people working around the U.S. intelligence community who would be willing to kill if ordered to—I'd known some of them—but the fact is, nobody will give the order. American intelligence, in my experience, doesn't kill people.

So Corbeil was almost certainly out in the dark by himself, and if he was, then it was impossible that many people knew about it. Not more than three or four, I'd bet. The danger of what they were doing, and the penalties, were just too great to let too many people in on the secret.

———

At four o'clock in the morning, the dish hadn't moved. Bobby wouldn't have sent me back unless he really needed the information from the transmissions; and down below, the house that probably acted as the control center for the dish array was sitting dark and apparently empty.

LuEllen would have given me a ton of shit for even thinking about it, but a few minutes after four o'clock in the morning, I began scouting the house. First, I stripped the recording package off the dish and stuffed it in the backpack; then, using the needle-beam, I changed batteries in the night-vision glasses and checked to make sure they were still working.

I followed the gully as far to the north as I could, duckwalking the last fifty yards, staying below the horizon so I wouldn't be seen from the house. I listened and, for a while, worried. And then, working from the northeast corner of the house, I began closing in. Watched the windows for movement, for light, for anything. Stopped often, and long, to listen, but heard nothing but my heart and the occasional passing car.

At five o'clock, I was fifty yards from the house and facing the decision. Go in, or stay put. We needed any docs that might be inside: we needed anything we could find. Nothing moved. Nothing even breathed.

I crossed the last fifty yards quickly: now I was so close, with enough ambient light from the yard lights, that if anyone were looking right at me, they'd see me, even without night-vision glasses. The base of the house was landscaped with a variety of broad-leafed cactus—Spanish bayonet, I thought, so named for good reason— and I pushed through them with care. Overhead, a balcony. Too far overhead. But the house was a log cabin, and I could put one foot on a window frame, then step up two feet or more on a log, and then, doing a quick step-up, catch the edge of the balcony.

And it went like that: I made the step, I did the pull up, and boosted myself over the edge of the balcony. There were four rustic chairs on the balcony, and a sliding glass door that led into the house. I waited, listened; tried to feel vibration, but felt nothing. Got the flash out of the backpack, and looked at the door. As far as I could see, it wasn't alarmed, but I would have to assume that the house was. So: inside, five minutes max. If the call went out instantly, it would be purely bad luck to have security arrive in five minutes . . . unless there was another man in the bunkhouse.

I sat thinking about it.

I looked through the window with the needle-beam again. Took a deep breath, used the butt of the flashlight to crush the glass near the door handle, flipped the lock, and went in.

There was no time. I turned on the needle flash and followed it through the top floor: bedroom, bathroom, bedroom, bathroom, bedroom, moving as quickly and quietly as I could. I suspected an intrusion alarm was already dialing out.

With three bedrooms and two bathrooms already down, I almost didn't push the fourth door. But I did, and behind the fourth door I found the control room, such as it was: a computer, what looked like a ham radio setup—is there still such a thing as ham radio?—and a couple of notebooks, all stuffed into a windowless cubicle that was more like a closet than a room.

I turned the computer on, looked at my watch. Almost a minute gone since I entered. I *would* be out in five. The computer was a standard IBM-compatible running the last generation Windows, but it was probably running nothing more complicated than a time-of-day and switch program, which would orient the receivers and turn them on and off. So Windows was a logical program; what drove me crazy was the time it took to load. As I shifted from foot to foot, waiting, I pulled the notebooks off the shelf and flipped them open.

They were empty. Well, not empty—they were filled with blank paper.

Oh, shit.

I'd been suckered. Pulled into a small room with exactly one exit. Forget the computer. *Move.*

I stuck the flashlight in my jacket pocket and pulled the revolver. The hallway was still dark, and I went into it hard and low, on my knees and elbows, the pistol in one hand, already pointed down the hall.

I saw movement and then the overwhelming, bone-shaking blast and brilliant muzzle flash of a fully automatic weapon. A long burst burned past two feet overhead. I was in an ocean of noise and light, without being much aware of it: aware only that I wasn't yet dead. I fired once, lurched forward to the bedroom door, and rolled through it.

A half-second later, another burst chewed up the carpet where I'd just been. I did a quick peek, then stuck my head around the corner and fired again.

Bedroom. I looked around, panicked. I didn't have a chance against the automatic weapon, if it came to a straight shootout. The bedroom had a glass door and a short balcony, but if I went over the side, I'd have to run across fifty yards of lighted, bald-as-a-pool-table lawn before there was any cover. I'd be cut in half before I made ten of them.

What to do? Who was that out there? Had to be Corbeil.

"Corbeil! Why are you killing us?"

"Who the fuck are you?"

"We're just some guys, trying to stay away from the feds," I shouted back. "Why are you killing us?"

He said nothing for a moment, then: "Because I like it. I'm gonna cut you to pieces, dickhead."

No way for a CEO to talk, but he was right about one thing: if I moved, he'd cut me to pieces. I did an inventory. I had the flashlight, the revolver, the night glasses, LuEllen's usual break-in kit . . .

Ten seconds later, I had the quilt off the bed behind me. A fat one, a nice traditional quilt filled with cotton batting. I balled it up, watching the door, snapped LuEllen's lighter under the blanket, and got it burning. When the fire was going hard, I threw it over across the hallway and over the railing onto the main floor.

"What the fuck are you doing?" Corbeil screamed, "What are you doing?"

"You burned Jack's house down," I shouted back. I pulled the pack back on. "You burned it down: so suck on this."

Another row of gunfire and the edge of the door splintered. I risked a quick peek the instant it stopped, and saw—felt—another movement, on the stairs, going down. Had to risk it: crossed to the railing in the near dark, saw the blanket burning on a couch below. And in the glow of the small fire, movement.

I took a quick, unsteady shot, and missed. Corbeil turned and fired a burst along the railing, but by that time, I was further up the hall, crawling toward the bedroom where I came in. At the stairs, I paused.

Corbeil was screaming something unintelligible, and then a cloud exploded across the room below. He'd gotten a fire extinguisher from somewhere, CO_2, and I fired another shot at what seemed to be the source of the cloud. He screamed again and the cloud suddenly went sideways. Had I hit him? I moved, fast and low as I could, scrambling, and nearly lost the gun.

He opened fire again, this time shooting at the railing further along the balcony, but not as far as I had gotten. The light was growing: the couch was now fully on fire.

Run, or wait? I could run fifty yards in maybe six or seven seconds, dressed as I was and carrying the pack. But now, caught in the break-in without a chance to clean up behind myself, I really wouldn't mind seeing more of a fire. So I waited.

Corbeil, whether he was hit or not, was soon back with another extinguisher, this one firing some kind of spray. But the couch was burning too hard, the fire now running along what looked like a big Oriental carpet under a grand piano. He began shouting again, but I was concentrating on the gun. I had no wish to lose any shells, but I couldn't for the life of me remember how many times I'd pulled the trigger. Four? Five? Was it empty?

I flipped the cylinder out, pulled the flashlight out of my jacket, looked at the primers. Four of them had firing-pin dents. Two shots left. I clicked the cylinder back into place, so a shell would come under the hammer with the next trigger pull.

Move or wait? The fire was growing and Corbeil had shouted something unintelligible again.

I shouted back: "Satellites."

One loud word. One word to get him thinking about what I was saying, get him looking up at the balcony. I was out the window, over the edge, and running. Waiting for the impact at my back. Across the lighted lawn, running, running, thirty more steps, twenty, five, and down on the ground. Laying still. Then up and moving again, fast, running hard for fifty yards, dropping to the ground again. Listening.

I could hear Corbeil, still in the house, screaming: and I could see firelight in all the windows now.

A minute later, Corbeil ran out into the yard, running as I had, but at an opposite angle. He dropped to the ground, and I realized that from his angle, he could see most of the lighted yard around the house—that the only part that he couldn't see was the driveway. He must have thought that I was still inside, but if the fire was building, he knew I'd have to run for it. And I probably wouldn't run down the driveway. He waited, patiently, as the fire spread through his log palace, and began eating it alive.

Moving as slowly as I could, I shrugged off the pack and got out the night glasses. The yard lights were still burning, and the fire glowed from the windows of the house: I turned down the gain on the glasses, and looked toward the last place I'd seen Corbeil. He was still there, looking toward the house, then away, then back toward the house.

I studied him for another minute, then flattened into the ground cover. He had night glasses, just like mine, and was scanning the fields around him. I didn't dare move, except snakelike, pushing backward on my belly, watching him. Every time his face turned toward me, I flattened, frozen in place. I would wait fifteen seconds, then look: each time I expected a quick slap on the forehead and the final darkness.

I made progress. At the beginning, we were fifty yards apart. Ten minutes later, I had another fifty. I was there, a hundred yards out, studying Corbeil's position with the glasses, when a car swerved off the highway, drove up the driveway, and a man got out and ran up to the front door of the house and began pounding on it, shouting. Then he ran back to his car, took what must have been a cell phone from the front seat, and staring up at the house, made a call.

Two or three minutes later, I heard the sirens, and far down the road, the flashing lights of the first fire trucks. The man who called them was running around the house, looking in the windows. I could see Corbeil watching him with the glasses, and I backed further away.

When I was two hundred yards out, I stopped to watch the fire: the house was now fully involved, flames leaping from the rooftop. One of the fire trucks sprayed foam on the bunkhouse and garage.

They didn't bother with the house: they had no good water source, and the house was burning so hard it probably wouldn't have helped if they did have water. The best they could hope for was to keep the flames from spreading to the outbuildings.

I switched back to Corbeil. He was standing now, just outside the circle of light cast by the flames. He was turning, his hands to his face, scanning the fields.

And I thought: how odd.

He'd been questioned about a murder. He must've worried that the cops—or the FBI, if we'd made any impression with the NSA— were going to break down his door at any moment. Anything in his apartment would be up for grabs.

It stood to reason that he'd move anything incriminating out of his apartment, out of his office, out of any place that the police or the feds could get at by looking at records, like safe deposit boxes. He couldn't actually destroy it: the docs and software used for controlling a satellite system would not be something you commit to memory.

My eyes drifted back to the burning house. I'd gone in because the last guy who left took the only vehicle. There were no other cars visible. It seemed unlikely that Corbeil would take the chance of being stranded on foot, so he probably had a car somewhere.

Like in the garage.

I looked back at him, still scanning. I was due east of the garage, if I moved out, and around to the south, I could come up behind it. As long as I could see him . . .

I started moving . . .

27

Fifteen minutes later, I'd crawled and pulled myself through the ground cover to a spot fifty feet behind the garage, in the deep shadow cast by the fire. For the moment, I was safe. But you win a little, and you lose a little. Halfway through the crawl, I lost Corbeil. He'd been looking up the hill, toward the satellite dish in the gully, when I'd last checked.

I checked again from the shadow, and he was gone. Had he seen me? But if he'd seen me crawling, why couldn't I see him stalking me? He couldn't have seen me using the night glasses, so he wouldn't have known that he needed concealment. If he were walking anywhere, up to four or five hundred yards or so, I should have been able to see him.

Unless he'd moved opposite of the fire. When I turned so that my line of sight crossed too close to the fire, the glasses whited out. But if he were on the opposite side of the house, I was good for a few minutes, anyway.

Staying in the shadow cast by the fire, I edged closer to the garage. Fifteen feet out, I had to commit. I took one last look around, stood up, and trotted to a back window and looked in. A car squatted inside. I punched the glass out with the butt of the pistol, unlocked the window, lifted it, and crawled through into the utter darkness inside.

Waited, listened. Corbeil couldn't be inside, I thought: I'd have seen him coming. If I moved quickly, I'd be okay. Went to the car: Mercedes-Benz S430. Looked in the front seat with the needle-beam flash, saw nothing. And in the backseat, behind the passenger seat, a briefcase. The car doors were looked. I looked around the garage, which also served to hold yard gear, and found an axe.

I was going to make some noise, here. A car this expensive had an alarm, for sure. I put the flashlight back in the pack, put the gun in my pants pocket, where I could feel it if it began to slip out—I'd seen one too many of those TV shows where the good guy loses his gun at a critical moment—took a breath, and swung the ax. It went through the window like a spoon through whipped cream. The alarm went and I used the ax handle to smash the rest of the glass out, grabbed the briefcase, and went out the window.

Nothing subtle about this: I ran as hard as I could, fifty yards, a hundred. Out of the deepest shadow, out into the dark, and then flat on the ground.

Listening. The garage was suddenly full of firelight: somebody on the fire side had gone into the garage and pushed the door up. I took the moment to run another fifty yards; and dropped.

A human head appeared in the garage window, silhouetted by the firelight. Another head appeared in a moment, then a third. Looking out the window, toward me. Dressed as I was, I was almost certainly invisible. But the car alarm was going, and Corbeil, wherever he was, would be hunting me in the dark.

I scanned the hillside, saw nothing. Thought about it for a moment. Corbeil was between me and my car. I might be able to slip around him—that would certainly be the most direct route—but if I headed south instead, crossed the highway, and stayed to the roadside ditch, or on the other side of the fence on the far side of the highway, I could make a circle away from him and get back to the car.

If I could only see him . . .

But sooner or later, it would occur to the cops who were with the firemen that anyone who broke into the garage would have to be somewhere in these surrounding fields. If they started crawling through the fields in their squads, with searchlights, I'd be cooked.

I started crawling toward the highway, moving slowly, stopping to scan, then moving on. At the fence line along the highway I paused, scanning. And saw him coming. He was jogging straight down toward me, carrying a gun across his chest. He stopped and scanned for me. He was too far away for a quick shot, so I crawled to a fence post, tossed the briefcase over, stood up, put my hand on the post, and vaulted over into the ditch.

In the ditch, I recovered the briefcase after a moment of panic—it wasn't exactly where I thought I'd thrown it—pivoted, turned, looked up the hill. He was coming, running as hard as he could.

I went left, running hard for five seconds, paused, scanned, saw him still coming, put a hand on another fence post and vaulted back over and got the glasses out again, scanning. He ran to the fence, stopped, scanned. Waited. He *knew* I was on the other side. When he hadn't seen me in fifteen seconds, he stood up and clambered over the fence, knelt, and scanned up and down the ditch. Then he went left, as I had: passed me not fifteen feet away.

He was moving slowly, but not as slowly as he should have, and a hundred feet down the highway, suddenly crossed the two-lane strip of blacktop into the opposite ditch. I started moving away, crawling again, dragging the briefcase, trying to keep track of him. When he got far enough down the highway, and I got far enough up the hill, I was covered by a line of brush. I turned and started jogging up the hill, breathing hard. Running through the tall, clinging pasturage, whatever it was, was tough.

I reached the ridge without knowing it, really, and dropped. I must've been silhouetted against the sky, for anyone using glasses. But now I was so far ahead of him . . .

I stopped and looked back: the house fire had passed its peak, but the house was still burning fiercely. There were now forty or fifty people gathered around the place, firemen, cops, and probably neighbors. I sat catching my breath for a moment or two, then started back toward the car. Taking it slow, now, stopping to listen and scan.

I crossed his eastern fence line, into his neighbor's pasture, then moved slowly down the fence to the north road. Once on the gravel, I could jog back to the car in a hurry.

At the fence, I threw the briefcase over, then stepped to the left and knelt, scanning back up the hill. Caught a spark of light straight up the hill, maybe a hundred yards away; and then the fence post shattered, and a split second later, the sound of a shot banged down the hill.

I rolled left and kept rolling, into a little depression, and froze. He was out there, and he'd seen me, but he didn't have an exact fix. He probably couldn't fire accurately and scan at the same time.

He couldn't afford a whole burst of gunfire, I thought. One or two shots probably wouldn't be a problem, but a burst of full-auto would be a definite cop magnet.

If they knew where the gunfire was coming from. There were a couple of hills between us and the house. With all the racket of the fire and the fire equipment, the sound of gunfire might not be all that easy to pick out: not a single shot, anyway.

When the first shot was not repeated, I slowly, a quarter-inch at a time, lifted my head with the glasses to my eyes. Corbeil was fifty yards away, standing in the dark, looking through his glasses. Then he took them away from his face and groped forward, and I eased further left. When he stopped again, to scan, I ducked, but still watched him.

He scanned for a moment, then moved forward again, in what to him must have seemed like absolute silence. When he was twenty yards out, he stopped, looked through his glasses. I reached back, got a good grip on the fence, and when he was looking to my right, about where the fence post should have been, I gave it a hard tug.

He dropped the glasses and the gun came up. And then he said, speaking softly, "If you give yourself up, I'll just take you in. There's no point in dying."

Like Br'er Rabbit, I said nothing, but just laid low.

"I can see in the dark," he said. "I've got starlights, and there's plenty of light. I'm looking right at you."

Like Br'er Rabbit . . .

He moved forward, still scanning; I was pressed against the fence, with no way to make a major move. He had the glasses in one hand, and the rifle in the other. The rifle had a pistol grip, like an AK. The barrel tracked along the fence, then back, then my way.

Had he seen me? The muzzle tracked past me, then swung back. I flinched.

"I can see you," he said, confidently. "Lift up your hands. If you don't, I'm gonna have to shoot you; I can't get any closer without giving you a chance with that pistol of yours. C'mon, man, I don't want to hurt you . . ."

Then he did see me. I don't know what it was—maybe I rolled my foot, or he caught a starlight reflection off the glasses, whatever, he dropped his glasses and the muzzle snapped round and was aimed right at my head.

I hadn't wanted to shoot him. He was twenty feet away and I was rolling, the muzzle of my pistol aimed more or less at the extra-dark piece of sky that was Corbeil, and his rifle popped and in the muzzle flash I saw him, pointed the pistol and . . .

Click.

The *click* was inaudible, but I knew nothing had happened; I could now see Corbeil only as a blinding afterimage that moved when my eyes moved. I pointed the gun at where I thought he might be and pulled the trigger again. This time it bucked in my hand; I heard a grunt, saw him in the muzzle flash, the barrel of his rifle pointed more or less at my head, fired again, and rolled.

And that was it; I had no more shells.

I didn't need any. The next sound from Corbeil was a rapid thrashing, followed by a low, everlasting moan, as the breath flowed out of his now dead body.

28

Memphis is a crappy place to spend November. The sky gets cloudy and stays that way, and the days get cold, but instead of *really* cold, the kind of cold you can enjoy, the kind of cold that spreads snow over the landscape, Memphis gets that English bone-chilling wet cold. Instead of snow, there's icy drizzle. You go around with your shoulders hunched and your hands in your pockets, feeling like you're being pissed on.

Six of us were living in three different motels around town. We'd sleep half the day and work most of the night, rotating any necessary meetings among the three motels. Bobby attended by conference line, and in the last three weeks of November, with a break for Thanksgiving when two of the guys had to go home, we got the software package together.

We also hacked out the implications of what we were doing.

That, in most ways, was the hardest part. Three of the guys wanted to write the software and turn it over to the NSA as an example of what could be done. The rest of us wanted to go ahead and do it. Bobby and I were the hardest of the hard-liners: we'd had experience with these government assholes.

"If we don't break it off in them, they're gonna break it off in us," Bobby said. "In fact, they're doing it right now."

And they were. There was something of a reign of terror running through the hack community, with the bully-boys from the FBI kicking down doors and seizing equipment. Evidence of wrongdoing no longer seemed to matter. If you were an independent computer hack operating above a certain level, you were a target. The general line seemed to be the same one that the government used against gun owners, with whom I began to sympathize for the first time.

The argument ran like this: nobody *needs* these big powerful computers unless he or she intends to do something wrong. Sure, stockbrokers, accountants, and suits from Microsoft and Sun might have some reason to own them, but a kid from Wyoming? That kid has no reason to own anything more powerful than a Gameboy . . . Powerful computers are prima-facie evidence that they're doing something wrong and un-American.

It was only a matter of time before we had Mothers Against Computer Hackers marching in Washington to make sure we wouldn't be rolling any software while we're not drinking, smoking, eating cheeseburgers, getting high, shooting guns, or having unprotected sex.

Of the five other guys in Memphis, I knew two, Dick Enroy from Lansing, Michigan, and Larry Cole from Raleigh, North Carolina, and had vaguely heard of the other three. Bobby said they were all good guys, and Enroy and Cole were, so I took his word for it on the others. Nobody asked exactly what anybody else was doing in their computer lives, but everybody wrote good code. A guy named Chick from Columbus, Ohio, wrote a piece of switching code that was so tight and cool and elegant that I was almost embarrassed for the stuff I was writing.

As it happened, Corbeil's briefcase contained mostly financial papers: he had money stashed all over the place. One nonfinancial item was a simple 3M 1.4 megabyte floppy that he carried around in a fluorescent blue Zip-disk case. The disk explained the whole OMS code thing. OMS *did* stand for Old Man of the Sea, the Sinbad story. The OMS code was a piece of code that sat on top of a highly intricate encryption engine inside the computers running each of the National Reconnaissance Office's array of Keyhole 15 satellites.

The OMS code sat on the satellite controls just like the Old Man of the Sea sat on Sinbad's back. Whenever they needed to, Corbeil's group could go into a satellite, order a photo scan, get it transmitted to their ground station, and then erase any sign of what had been done. Even the satellite's internal photo-shot counter had been reset.

The problem from our point of view was that if the NRO found out about the OMS code, they could block it. The NRO still controlled the satellites and could send up software patches and workarounds that would effectively take the OMS out of it . . .

The code we were writing would prevent that. The code that we were writing would give *us* the control of the satellites . . .

In the arguments about whether we should write the code and give it to the NSA as a demonstration, or actually take control of the satellites, one of the guys I didn't know, who said his name was Loomis, said that we were about to become the Old Man of the Sea.

"From the way Sinbad looked at it, he couldn't get the Old Man of the Sea off his back. From the Old Man of the Sea's point of view, he couldn't get off Sinbad's back, or Sinbad would kill him. If we get on the NRO's back, or the NSA's, we can never let go, or they will hunt us down like rats. If they just say fuck it, and put up a new Keyhole system, and we're locked out of it, we're cooked."

"But there's a time element," Bobby said, his voice rattling down the phone connection and then out a couple of cheap computer speakers. "If we can keep the government off for three, four, five years, it'll be too late to really do anything about us. The control of the world is slipping away from those people; in five years, it'll be gone."

"Still . . ."

"There's another thing. We'll let it be known that this whole thing was pulled off by Bobby, the phamous phone phreak. I've got maybe five years left on earth. I'll be on a voice synthesizer by this time next year. If I'm their target, and they catch me two or three years from now . . . they ain't gonna catch much."

"Goddamn," I said. "That's harsh."

"Life sucks and then you die," Bobby said.

We took control on December third.

Bobby transmitted the changes over a four-hour period from a dish normally used for satellite telephone communications. The way it worked, essentially, was this: we took the NRO's spot, giving us control of the system. The NRO got the OMS controls, plus some enhancements we added—this would not be a secret for very long, so we didn't have to go to all of AmMath's trouble to hide what we'd done.

If we hadn't told them about it, the NRO might have taken a while to discover what we'd done. They still talked to the satellites with the same encrypted commands; they could still take pictures and maneuver the satellites; in fact, before we told them about it, the only change that would have given us away was a difference in the number of computer bytes in the satellite's memory. But that changes often enough that we expected that they wouldn't notice. Not right away . . .

On December third and fourth, we ran checks, and tried to find ways to break our control. We made a couple of small patches, and the other five guys headed home. I went to Washington.

Rosalind Welsh, the NSA security executive, left her home at six-thirty in the morning, driving a metallic blue Toyota Camry. I noted the license plate; Bobby'd gotten the number the day before from the DMV, but he we wanted to make sure. I couldn't follow her all the way to the NSA building, but we'd done a time projection, and I called Bobby on a cell phone and said, "She's crossing the line now. Four or five minutes to the parking lot."

"Did you get the plate?"

"Yeah. Your numbers were right."

"Are you nervous?"

"Yeah."

"So you've still got your sanity." He chuckled. "One way or another, this is gonna be interesting . . ."

The next day, I was in eastern Ohio, on my way home. I pulled into a truck stop on I-80, got out the cell phone, and called Rosalind Welsh at her desk. Her secretary answered and I said, "This is

Bill Clinton. You've got fifteen seconds to put Welsh on the phone. This may be the most important call she'll get this year, so I'd suggest you find her."

Welsh came on five seconds later. "What?"

"I need a phone number where I can dump a computer file."

"Why should . . ."

"Don't argue with me. You'll want to see these photos. Give me a number or I'm gone."

She gave me the number.

I called Bobby from a truck-stop phone, gave him the number, and headed back east. I didn't doubt that the NSA could spot the cell that my call had gone through, and would be able to spot the next one. From that, they would be able to tell that I was headed east . . .

I called again twenty minutes later. "This is Bill Clinton," I told the secretary.

"Just a minute . . ."

Welsh picked up, but the phone sounded funny. "What are you doing with the phone?" I asked.

"We've got some people here who want to listen in," she said. "You're on a conference call."

"Did you look at the pictures?"

"Yes."

"Do you know what they are?"

"Well, we have an idea. They look like our parking lot."

"They are. If you check the arrangement of cars—that's your car up in the northeast, and that's you getting out of it—you'll find out that the pictures were taken yesterday, with a Keyhole satellite. That's what AmMath was doing. They'd written a code sequence—which you approved, by the way—that sat on top of the satellite encryption engine, and allowed them to use the satellites. They've been retailing satellite recon photos all over the Middle East and South Asia since the Keyholes went up. From what we've figured out, they were supplying recon for both India and Pakistan."

"Who have you told about this?" A man's voice, deep, harsh, angry.

"Nobody," I said. "But we've got a PR package ready to go to a dozen congressmen and senators, as well at *The New York Times, The Washington Post,* the *L.A. Times, The Dallas Morning News,* the *Chicago Tribune,* and a few other places you wouldn't want to see it. I mean, maybe we're going to do that."

"Maybe?"

"If you don't get off our backs. You fuckin' fascists are running innocent people all over the place, this so-called Firewall crackdown. AmMath invented Firewall and the IRS attack was just a bunch of punks from Europe. You know it, we know it, and most of the press knows it, but they're riding along with you for the amusement value. We want you to knock it off, or we'll ship our PR package, and the NSA becomes a greasy spot on the road. A few of you, I wouldn't doubt, will be looking at the inside of Leavenworth."

"We know who you are: we're tracking you right now, we're breaking down the walls," the male voice said.

"Bullshit. You've only found a couple of serious people so far and you only got them because they got careless," I said. "The rest of us are going to fuck you up if you don't back off."

"You're talking to the U.S. Government here, asshole . . ."

"No, I'm not. I'm talking to a scared bureaucrat. But not as scared as you will be when we start sending recon photos to the press."

"You're gone; you no longer have any access to the Keyholes."

"Sorry, pal, it doesn't work that way," I said. "We own Keyhole.

The only access you have is entirely walled off by our software. We built a firewall around your access port. Go ask your guys who are trying to get inside; go ask them . . . They can take pictures—if we let them. They can even retask the satellites, if we let them. But if we get pissed, we'll eliminate your access and then we're gonna start taking pictures of nude beaches and the Royal Families and the president's vacation, and start flogging them off to *The Star* and *People* and whoever else wants them . . . With a nice little Keyhole credit line on them."

There was a long silence; then Rosalind Welsh said, "Don't do that."

"It's up to you," I said. "You'll be able to tell when we're pissed, because we'll cut off your Keyhole access. I mean, you could go ask Congress for another twenty billion to put up another Keyhole system, but I suspect that they'll be pretty pissed when they find out you lost the one you had."

The male voice: "You fucker . . . you fuckin' traitor."

"This is Bill Clinton you're talking to," I said. "We don't want to overthrow anything. We just want you off our backs."

"We can't promise anything in detail . . ." Welsh said tentatively.

"Look, we're not bargaining with you," I said. "Don't get that idea. This is a straightforward extortion. If you get off our backs, you can run Keyhole like you always have. Nobody'll ever hear about how AmMath was selling American recon photos to Pakistan, or how AmMath invented Firewall to cover up a couple of murders and that you knew about it, or about how Keyhole now belongs to a bunch of hackers. All you have to do is stop. If you don't, well, you better grab on to something solid and bend over, because something ugly is about to happen . . ."

I hung up, got off at the next exit, wiped the cell phone and threw it into a ditch, and headed back to St. Paul.

A nd they quit.
  The IRS announced that Interpol, in coordination with U.S. authorities, had issued warrants for the arrest of a half-dozen European hackers for their attack on the tax-return site, and said that the IRS site was now fully protected. The FBI declared victory over Firewall, said that we were seeing the fine results of eternal vigilance. Other hacker organizations, the FBI spokesman said, had better take warning, and not mess with the bulldog of federal law enforcement.

I was lying on the couch, reading the St. Paul paper, the Cat sitting next to my head, when somebody knocked at the door. I opened it, and LuEllen was standing there. She was wearing jeans and cowboy boots under a waist-length coat that looked suspiciously like mink.

"We cool?" she asked.

"We cool," I said. "Come in."

She came in, and we had a cup of coffee, sitting at my kitchen window looking out over the Mississippi. The river was locked in ice, and down on the streets, we could see people in heavy parkas puffing up and down the hill. Twelve below zero, the weather service said: a splendid day to stay inside and paint.

We had a lot to talk about. About the relative quality of our safety, about Jack and Lane. About whether the government might come creeping around. About the collapse of AmMath, and the disappearance of Corbeil.

"The government's out of it," I said. "At least for a good long while."

I told her how the Net would occasionally be saturated with the cryptic message, "Bobby, call your Uncle."

"Does he?"

"I don't know. I leave that to him," I said.

"You think he's going to die?"

"That's what he says. But not for a while."

We were silent for a moment, then she said, "The devil card—it was like the tarot said."

"In hindsight, I suppose."

"Don't be skeptical with me, Kidd. You're getting messages from somewhere, and I think maybe you oughta stop it."

"Right. Messages," I said. She was so serious about it, I had to laugh. Superstitious claptrap.

The Texas newspapers reported that a man carrying Corbeil's passport had crossed into Mexico shortly after his Waco ranch house burned down—a ranch purchased under a phony name, the papers said, and which was now cordoned off by the FBI. Corbeil hadn't been found yet, but there were hints that he might be in Southeast Asia.

LuEllen was worried that he might somehow come back on us.

"Not to worry," I said.

She didn't ask.

LuEllen stayed over. Clancy, the computer lady who had been de-signing the America's Cup boat, had found somebody else to design it with, and my feet, had, in fact, been cold all winter. So LuEllen was welcome.

But as I lay beside her that night, awake, listening to her easy breathing, I felt the finger of darkness pressing on me again. It had come any number of times in the past two months, usually just before sleep: the ghost of St. John Corbeil.

I was the only one who'd ever know, but the passport that crossed into Mexico was the same one that Green, Lane, LuEllen, and I had passed around a diner table after the raid on Corbeil's apartment. The man who'd carried it was a friend of Bobby's, reliable, and who, for a price, was willing to check the passport through Mexican passport control, without asking why. He'd burned it in a bathroom of the California Royal Motel in Matamoros; and that is the last, I hope, that we'd hear of St. John Corbeil.

Corbeil himself was buried under a foot of sandy Texas soil, in a hastily scratched-out grave, a few miles northwest of Waco, Texas.

At night, lying in bed, I sometimes felt his loneliness out there.

Maybe, I thought, as I turned over and touched the woman's back, LuEllen could make him go away . . .

Maybe.

F
SAN

9/9/11